AFTER YOU VANISHED

AFTER YOU VANISHED

E.A. NEEVES

HYPERION

LOS ANGELES   NEW YORK

First Edition, August 2023
10 9 8 7 6 5 4 3 2 1
FAC-004510-23167

Printed in the United States of America

This book is set in ITC Slimbach Std.
Designed by Phil T. Buchanan

Library of Congress Cataloging-in-Publication Data
Names: Neeves, E. A. (Emily Angela), 1987- author.
Title: After you vanished / E.A. Neeves.
Description: New York : Hyperion, 2023. • Audience: Ages 12–18. • Audience: Grades 10–12. • Summary: Nearly a year after her twin sister went missing during a midnight race across Bottomrock Lake, eighteen-year-old Teddy Ware sifts through Izzy's secrets, hoping to find evidence that Izzy is still alive.
Identifiers: LCCN 2022027003 (print) • LCCN 2022027004 (ebook) • ISBN 9781368092708 (hardcover) • ISBN 9781368095990 (ebook)
Subjects: CYAC: Missing persons—Fiction. • Dating—Fiction. • Secrets—Fiction. • Twins—Fiction. • Sisters—Fiction. • Massachusetts—Fiction. • Mystery and detective stories. • LCGFT: Detective and mystery fiction. • Novels.
Classification: LCC PZ7.1.N3915 Af 2023 (print) • LCC PZ7.1.N3915 (ebook) • DDC [Fic]—dc23
LC record available at https://lccn.loc.gov/2022027003
LC ebook record available at https://lccn.loc.gov/2022027004

Reinforced binding
Visit www.HyperionTeens.com

SUSTAINABLE FORESTRY INITIATIVE Certified Sourcing

www.forests.org
SFI-01681

Logo Applies to Text Stock Only

for Dave & Luke

PROLOGUE

Your Big Reveal

THERE'S SOMETHING I HAVE TO TELL YOU, YOU TEXTED. MOM AND I WERE already westbound. We'd just stopped at a café, and a steaming chai was balanced in my lap.

How ominous, I'd texted back, expecting a mundane reply. Like, *So I bought those racing goggles,* or perhaps, *We should've signed up for the scuba-diving course instead.*

Remind me, okay? you said. Which was odd, because no one ever had to remind you of anything. Your brain was a Google calendar and spreadsheet combined.

Okay, I said. And that was it, for a while.

That night, as Mom and I settled into the hotel, my curiosity swelled to the point of bursting and I'd texted, *What's the thing?*

You hadn't texted back.

But you had swim practice in the morning, so you'd probably gone to bed early. I figured I'd get your response while Mom and I ate mini muffins from the hotel's continental breakfast.

By the time the campus tour started, you still hadn't replied. I was curious, not worried. The storyteller in me wanted there to be drama in your withholding. A statement like yours builds tension before a big reveal. But while dramatic wordplay was something I might do, it wasn't your style. You were too straightforward for narrative games. Whatever it was you had to say, I knew it wouldn't live up to your lead-in.

I was still waiting for the telltale quiver of my phone in my pocket when Mom's rang instead. She silenced it. Her cheeks flushed. During the interruption, the kid who was giving our tour never stopped speaking.

We were directed to the university's gym, and I thought about texting you a picture of the pool. It was maybe the dingiest college pool I'd ever seen. Only four lanes. Nothing along the bottom to mark the center lane. The over-chlorinated water was slightly green. I snapped the picture, but my phone vibrated in my hand before I could hit SEND. Dad.

Our guide was scowling at me, so I hit IGNORE and shoved the phone back into my jeans. The tour returned to the quad as we meandered our way toward the campus garden. Mom leaned over and whispered, "Did Dad just call you?"

"Yeah."

She dug her phone out and called him back. The tour guide was gesturing at a flowering tree with low, thick branches and an iron bench beside it.

"What?" Mom's voice was somewhere halfway between disbelief and panic. "What?" she asked again.

"If you're going to take a personal call," said the tour guide, "would you mind stepping away from the group?"

"Mom?" In the space of a moment, her face had paled. Her lips were pressed together in what you'd dubbed her thinking face. I hypothesized the worst-case scenarios for whatever news she was receiving. Nana had died. The house had burned down. Dad had lost his job. I could have hypothesized a thousand more theories, and I still never would have landed on the truth: that the night before, you'd met your friend Tobias Smith at Bottomrock Lake and then you disappeared.

ONE

The Boy Who Watched You Disappear

BEFORE I'D EVER SPOKEN TO HIM, I HATED TOBIAS SMITH. I HATED his skinny tie with its cartoon swimmers angled all up and down the fabric. I hated the way his hair always looked like one of his comic book characters, standing unnaturally on end. But most of all, I hated who he was: the boy who'd watched you disappear.

Six months after you melted into the night, our parents organized a memorial at Bottomrock Park. Note that *memorial* wasn't the word I would have chosen. Memorials are for dead people. People with bodies to bury. Ashes to sprinkle. But Mom and Dad felt they needed to do something, and no one could think up a better word for the service that was held in your memory.

People wore all sorts of stuff to your memorial-that-wasn't-a-real-memorial. Some wore black, which bothered me, like they were giving up on you. This was Mom. Some people dressed really nicely but in muted colors, a kind of compromise between what you wear when someone's died and what you wear for the living. This was Dad: gray suit, navy shirt, no tie. He looked stupidly young without one. And then there were the people who wore their regular, everyday clothes. Jeans. Sweaters. This was me. In the end we were all clad in our best winter puff wear, anyway, because it was February in Massachusetts and the air had a bite.

Toby wore a navy suit and skinny tie, patterned with little people doing all four strokes in repetition. I recognized him from your swim meets, but even if I hadn't, I think I would have known anyway. He was wandering around, fidgety and reticent and alone. Mom asked me if I saw *him*, hissing the pronoun like she was referring to the devil himself.

He circled the fringes for most of the service. I say *service*, but that's another word that doesn't really fit. There was no religious officiant reading passages from a holy text. There was no music or schedule of events. Just people going up to a microphone and remembering you. I mostly stuck to this picnic table behind the guardhouse, in the woods. Toward the end of the event, Toby approached me. He said, "You look like her."

No shit, Sherlock, I thought.

"Can I sit?" He was already sitting anyway. "Hankie?" He whipped out a handkerchief from somewhere inside his suit coat and waved it at me. I wasn't actually crying, but there were tears welling. I gave him my best eyebrow sneer.

"Toby." He offered his hand. The other still held the handkerchief, its bright blue silk visible through the clutch of his fingers. "I swam with—"

"I know who you are." I like to think there was a sharpness to my voice, but if I'm honest, it was probably more of a quiver.

"I'm glad you didn't use it." He nodded to the handkerchief. "I just kind of think it goes with a fancy suit? Handkerchiefs as tissues are gross." His mouth teased into a smile, but I knew if I held out my hand at that moment, he'd have given the handkerchief to me.

"Anyway." He went back to fiddling with the handkerchief, weaving it through his fingers like a loom.

I had a million questions I wanted to ask Toby. Of course, I'd imagined that night a thousand times over. You, wading into a lake dusted in moonlight. Him, waiting on the beach under the spindly bough of a pine tree. He watched you start to swim until your perfect strokes melded into the shadows and you were gone.

All of my million questions swirled, and like a rush of water striking a dam, not a single one managed to make it to my mouth. I think I was scared of what his answers would be.

"If you ever want to . . ." He stopped there, unable even to bring himself to look at me. "Well, you know how to find me." He left then, and I wondered why he had bothered sitting down. You hadn't told me a lot about him. I'd figured your friendship was a swimming-only thing, until that night everything changed.

Over time, thoughts of you became tidal. There and then not. Strong and then faint. A predictable force, lapping at my toes as the ground, like wet sand, settled beneath my feet, waiting for the next wave.

Life resumed. I went to school. I started hiking with Petra. And when summer rolled around, I signed up to return to work again at Bottomrock Park. I could give you a long list of reasons why. Good pay. A preference for sunshine and lake breezes over the mildew-and-bleach-filled air of an indoor pool. I actually liked the crop of lifeguards who came back to Bottomrock summer after summer. But the truth is, Bottomrock always felt like my place. The lake was where I spent my time while you were training and racing. It didn't seem fair that of all the places in the world you could have picked to disappear from, you picked mine.

You never did like the open water. The earthy smell, the murky color, the silted texture. You liked your water crisp, clean, clear. Bromine-spiked. You liked seeing stark lines on the tiles of your internationally standardized swimming pool as you sliced through the water. You'd always overlooked the charm of Bottomrock Lake. How it curls around the forest like a kitten in a bed. How the sunfish swim in their little saucer nests and lily pads creep along the water's edge, their pink-and-white blossoms bringing bursts of color to the earth tones. How at dawn, light glints off the water in golden hues that mingle with the shadows created by overhanging branches, and the place really does look like it popped out of a Monet.

So, yeah. You vanished from the shores of Bottomrock Lake, and I decided I would keep working there anyway.

Every Bottomrock summer starts in earnest in the spring. There's a lot of work to do to get the park ready for opening weekend, and before all of that, there's the first preseason staff meeting. A formality where we schedule recertification classes and review safety protocols. I got to the community center early. And at the front of the room, standing next to the director of Greening Parks and Recreation, was none other than Tobias Smith. I hadn't seen him since your memorial. His long swimmer's arms dangled at his sides and his eyes shifted everywhere but my face. I swear my whole body slackened.

"Teddy." Bill Quimby waved me over. "Let me introduce you to our new hire, Toby!"

I should have smiled, or offered my hand, or done something remotely professional for the sake of my summer job, but instead I simply stared. *It has to mean something, right?* That's the thought that swam through my head. That the boy who'd watched you disappear on the shores of Bottomrock Lake would come there to work. That was significant.

"Hi, Teddy." Toby gave a little half smile that I found infuriating.

Somehow I found the strength to mumble a greeting as I folded into a plastic chair and swallowed my nerves. I took out my phone and thumbed absently through apps, feigning busyness so I didn't have to look at him. I already knew he was going to cloud everything. I could feel myself slipping back to the place I'd been in the weeks immediately following your disappearance. My heart started pumping hard, one thousand rapid-succession dolphin-kicks. My mind started positing theories again, resurrecting the what-ifs I had taught myself to bury: What if he'd helped you leave, what if he knew why you'd gone . . . ?

I barely noticed when Nadia sat down beside me. "Teddy?" she whispered, and from the tenor of her voice I knew she'd seen Toby. She put her hand on my knee, and I whispered back that I was fine.

The great lie I'd been telling myself all year, so often and so hard it was starting to feel true.

In my best friend's presence I began slowly to relax. Toby had sat down several seats apart from the rest of the returning staff. Quimby jabbered about the new guard station rotation and how Derek Danvers was coming back as head guard. Derek was still at college, participating in postseason training for his wrestling team, but he would be our day-to-day manager. And even this news—my old crush Derek Danvers! Back at Bottomrock!—was not enough to take my mind, or my eyes, off Toby Smith.

Then the doors opened and in walked Petra. Quimby excitedly beckoned her to the front. Despite his outward bubbliness, he took his job as parks director way too seriously, which is probably why you once said he was like a porcupine with his dander up, thinking himself menacing. He looked a little like a porcupine, too: rotund body, bushy beard, and a coat of coiling brown body hair that peeked out from under the edges of his clothing. "And now Petra Schaffer has a development to share with us."

Curling a pane of blond hair behind her ear, she gave me a finger wave as she walked past.

"So, umm. Hi. I'm Petra." Her hands braced against the podium, she laughed a little because we all knew who she was. Our high school wasn't that big. "And, well . . ." She looked at me briefly before her gaze darted away. "I want to plant a tree for Izzy."

Quimby leaned into the microphone, and Petra shambled to the side. "We'll have a ceremony in August, on the first anniversary. We'll get a plaque made. It'll be very official and special. And for *you all*"—Quimby gestured at us—"this means we'll have to work extra hard this summer to clean the park up, make it presentable."

As Quimby moved on, Petra awkwardly shuffled down the aisle. A tree for Izzy? Shouldn't she have talked to Izzy's family about that first? I'd seen her earlier, in the cafeteria at school. She'd said nothing.

The rest of the meeting was a blur. I caught Toby looking at me a few times as Quimby read the employee handbook aloud. What did he have to stare at? He can't have been caught by surprise that I was here. We were in *my* hometown. At the orientation for the summer job I'd held for three years running. Working at the place where you'd disappeared was going to be hard enough without an interloper.

I know you would have wanted me to like Toby. He was your friend, after all. A friend you trusted more than the sister who shares your face, apparently. But every time I caught him staring, I grew more incensed. What was he thinking? Given what he said had happened there, and given the fact that you're still gone, Bottomrock should have been the last place on earth he'd want to take a summer job. Hypocritical of me, I know, but I figured I had a claim to Bottomrock that Toby didn't.

The meeting ended and I ghosted out of there, telling Nadia I would text her later. I ducked into the bathroom. With my back against the door, I did a few of Dr. Joshi's breathing exercises, inhaling long and deep. Toby's reemergence in my life didn't mean you were coming back.

I left the bathroom and nearly walked face-first into Toby's sprawling chest.

He retreated. Cleared his throat.

"Were you waiting for me?"

"No," he said, too fast. Lying. Then, "So, a tree planting, huh?"

"Yeah, it's . . . whatever. Can you move?" The hall was narrow. If I tried to squeeze by, I'd brush against him. He was like a tree himself, sturdy from so much swimming and tall enough that I had to tilt my head to look him in the eye.

Toby grabbed hold of my wrist before I could move again. "Can I talk to you?"

"Nope." I yanked free and pivoted around him. I knew I'd have to speak to him eventually, but I wanted to delay that awkward moment where he said something and I said something because I knew that moment would not be about whatever it was we were saying—it would be about what we were not saying, and I wasn't ready to so pointedly not talk about you.

TWO

Stories of You Vanishing

THE FIRST TIME YOU TOLD ME ABOUT TOBY, YOU SAID HE WAS A JERK. *Gorgeous jerk*, I believe was the exact phrase. It was in passing, just a detail in a conversation about your training regimen and how Coach had stopped helicoptering you now that this gorgeous jerk had moved into town and joined the Wahoo swim team. And you were doing your motormouth thing where you talked a mile a minute, you were so excited about how you were one year away from being invited to the Olympic trials. I didn't even get to ask why the gorgeous person was a jerk.

I pieced together later on that the gorgeous jerk was Tobias Smith, a midrange distance swimmer specializing in butterfly, who'd moved to the Boston area from Hartford.

And so Toby Smith became just a guy you were friends with because he was on your swim team and was the only person who could even come close to beating you in your favorite event, the two-hundred-meter butterfly. Together, the two of you were going to take the Wahoos to Nationals. Until the day you brought him to Bottomrock in the middle of the night and you vanished like a sunfish, darting from light into the shadows.

I DIDN'T BELIEVE Toby's story. Not entirely. The bones of it, sure. That you'd asked him to meet you at Bottomrock. That you'd been upset. That you were gone. But the details, the midnight challenge: It felt crafted. Maybe it happened that way. But maybe it didn't. Maybe he'd tweaked the fine points. I had no reason then to question him, to think him untrustworthy, but I did.

Here's what he said happened: You were upset. You were in a reckless mood. You told him you were going to swim across the lake in the moonlight and that you were so fast you could beat him running to the other side. And he said he agreed because what was the harm? Though trials may have confirmed you weren't an Olympic-level swimmer, you were an almost-Olympic-level swimmer. A one-mile swim should have been no big deal. So he watched you wade into the dusky water until it swallowed your shoulders, and you turned around and said, "Don't do me any favors. Get running," and so he turned around and got running. But when he got to the other side, you weren't there yet. And he waited for you and waited for you, longer than it should have taken to swim across, longer than he should have waited, but you were already gone.

I've come up with a lot of stories about where you went. A brain aneurysm and a body swept through the dam and downriver. A deranged swim fan stalking you to the lake, waiting for Toby to leave you alone before striking. A hulking creeper in a boat who happened upon you swimming alone and hauled you away. A struggle with Toby, your body buried in the woods.

As much as I don't believe any of these sorts of stories, I can't help but write them. You'd probably tell me that's good practice, but

I'd rather not practice my storytelling craft by imagining all the ways you might have died.

But these stories are just that: stories. They're me trying to puzzle together that night in a way that fits, and so far, I've failed. None of these stories have any evidence, except for one: You ran away to Australia.

You and I were supposed to go together, after graduation. We were going to take a gap year before college and do a walkabout.

Two months post-you, I marched into the Greening Police Department looking for the chief. She'd called my parents not an hour earlier and told them she was pausing the department's investigation into your disappearance.

Boy, did I have a bone to pick. Rarely did I act with such conviction. But now with you gone, I had to start advocating for myself. You would have been so proud.

"You can't stop," I blurted.

Chief Anderson was at her desk. She pressed her forehead into her palm and sighed. "Teddy, as I told your parents—"

"You haven't found a body. So you can't stop. You can't just close the case."

"I'm not closing the case. I'm reallocating resources."

"What about Australia?"

"I haven't found anything that suggests she went there."

"What about what *I* found?"

"Teddy—"

"What else do you have to investigate anyway? This town isn't exactly flush with crime."

"Teddy—"

If there was a warning in her voice, I blew past it. The words were flying out of my mouth almost faster than I could think them. "How does an Olympic-level swimmer drown in a pond? You know Toby wasn't on anything. You know Izzy never got high or drunk or—"

"Teddy—"

"You know she was healthy, she wasn't injured, bodies don't just disappear—"

"Enough!" The chief rose out of her seat. "I don't need you to recite the case file to me. I'm sorry about what happened to your sister. Really, I am. But we—*you*—have to stop this."

"Officer Kelly—"

"Has been told to move on. Please." Her voice softened as she came around the desk and put a hand on my shoulder. "You need to do the same." She nodded to someone behind me, who called our parents.

While I was waiting for them in an empty office, Officer Kelly brought me a vanilla chai latte. As our family liaison with the department, he'd been my favorite of the police officers who'd looked into your disappearance. Maybe it was because of his boyish face, or because his cousin had swum with you on the Wahoos, but he felt trustworthy. He was the one who kept us abreast of your investigation. When the volunteer rescue divers stopped searching the lake, he'd told us that it was so they could focus their efforts on the forest. There, in a wooded campsite across the lake from the beach where you'd last been seen, they found one of your favorite earrings: a lone gold-and-blue peacock feather from the pair you'd been wearing so often that summer. *Coincidence, not evidence*, Chief Anderson eventually said. You must have lost the earring at some other point.

But Officer Kelly hadn't waved the earring off. He'd come to our house and searched it top to bottom, trying to find the other piece of the pair. It was gone, just like you, and I had to think that's because you had it with you.

"You'll keep looking?" I asked him now, tapping the lid of the drink he'd brought.

"I can't, I'm sorry, Teddy." So many *sorry*s for people who didn't have to give up.

I liked Officer Kelly because he didn't bother to try to convince me you drowned by listing off all the evidence his department lacked. He didn't excuse away how you hadn't been found by spouting off stats about the size and depth of Bottomrock Lake. He didn't talk about the silt in New England kettle ponds, deep enough to devour a body. He didn't bring up the weeds that are so thick and tangled they block the light, making a safe but thorough search impossible. He didn't explain away his department's failure. He simply sat with me as I didn't drink the chai and waited for our parents.

The police department gave up on you, but I didn't. I followed every lead I could think of. I tried to track down your mode of transportation. Had you taken a ride share? Hopped on a stowed away bicycle? Had someone given you a lift? I'd looked for evidence of ticket purchases in your email or the caches on your laptop. I'd pored through your social media, even spent considerable time walking the trails of the park. None of it had panned out. But even as my own investigation hit dead end after dead end, I knew the evidence I'd uncovered was not *irrelevant*. It meant something.

You had left town of your own free will.

Runaway seems like such a disco term, but that's what I think you are. A runaway. That something more was going on and you used our gap-year plan to escape. It's the only theory that explains your cryptic text. If something had been going on, maybe you were planning to tell me more or ask for help. But then you'd backed out. Gone off to Australia alone. You'd threatened to do it once that summer. Fresh off the devastation of trials, you'd lashed out. Then, I thought you hadn't meant it. But after you left? I think you could be hiking in the Mossman Gorge or camping in the outback. I think this not just because you're gone without a word, not just because we talked about doing these things and they haven't found your body. You see, I searched your room not long after you went. Folded into your wallet was a cash receipt for the sort of supplies you'd need in the outback: a new sleeping bag and pad, a camp stove, a water-purifying wand. But the gear you'd bought about a week before you disappeared? That I didn't find anywhere.

There was something else missing, too, even more curious than misplaced camping supplies and the lost earring. Your passport is missing, and so are you, and the one thing I wish I knew is why you didn't take me with you.

THREE

Row, Row, Row Your Dock

AFTER THE POLICE ENDED THEIR INVESTIGATION INTO YOU, I SPENT weeks walking the Bottomrock trails. Hoping to stumble across something, anything, that would confirm what I already knew: You'd climbed out of the lake that night alive. Even after I, too, stopped my search, I came back to the lake a few times throughout the winter and spring, to sit on the shore and watch the water. So it wasn't strange or nerve-racking for me to head to the park for the first day of preseason setup. It felt normal. Like something I would have been doing regardless of whatever had happened to you.

A cool mist descended over the lake. It spiderwebbed through the trees in gossamer wisps and crept across the water, shrouding the other side. Our job was to move the docks off the beach and settle them some hundred feet or so from the shore.

"Do you remember how we did this last year, Teddy?" asked Pat. You might remember Patrick Murphy, the little redheaded boy who could never sit still. Well, he grew up into a gangly goofball who looks uncannily like Shaggy of the Scooby gang. I'd probably said all of four sentences to him throughout the school year, but we'd worked together every summer at Bottomrock since we were both fifteen, and at the park, we had a certain rapport.

"Fondly." Last year the weather had been almost as bad as it was today, and we'd developed a very efficient system for stringing the lane lines up and getting the docks into the water. "We rowed them out in teams."

My eyes shifted to Toby. A part of me had hoped he'd have quit in the days since the staff meeting. Was this his first time being back at Bottomrock? Was he thinking about you?

"Boys versus girls?" Pat suggested.

I bristled. Neither Nadia nor I was strong enough to lift the cement weights that would anchor the docks. And as the two most senior staff members, Pat and I shouldn't pair up. So Toby and I were going to have to work together. Which meant we were going to finally have that talk-that-wasn't-a-talk about you.

Nadia hugged her chest to stave off the chill as she angled her head at me. She'd figured out the same thing I had, and her big brown eyes said sorry. Nadia Almonte has a very expressive face, and she's sensitive to people. She and I have gotten a lot closer, post-you. "Uh, Pat, not to be reverse feminist or anything, but that's not going to work."

"Why not? Teddy's been working out, right? You can lift this?" He gestured at the weight.

And it's true: I was in better shape than I'd been in my entire life. Every day, as my muscles toned, I looked more and more like you. Not that I would ever be as fit as you'd been. I mean, *I* hadn't switched from public school to a private tutor so I could devote myself to training for the world's most elite athletics competition. I'd merely been hiking a lot. "Toby and I will take the right."

Our feet sunk in the sand, the floats scraping deep enough to dig up the pebbly soil below. Beads of mist caught in my eyelashes, and I blinked them away. When our dock grew suddenly weightless, my grip slipped. My sandy arm grazed Toby's. He caught me at the elbow. Our eyes locked for a moment and I saw something in them. A question or a regret. Some thought unsaid that vanished as he placed my hand back on top of the dock and looked quickly away.

The morning's fog had yet to dissipate, and the lake stretched before us a still mirror of the woods. The farther we pushed the docks into the lake, the hazier the world around us became. By the time the water reached midchest, I could no longer see the shore. The lake was cold from a winter that had lasted into April, and I told myself that *that* was why I shivered. It had nothing to do with my place beside the last person to see you alive, in the lake where you'd vanished.

The silky paste of the lake bottom wove through my toes as I sought stable ground. Toby braced his hands on the surface of the dock and gazed out into the mist. I felt too much, all at once. He shouldn't be here. I wanted to know why he was here. He'd known you, supposedly cared for you, and maybe even missed you. In a way, that made him my ally, and it certainly made me curious about him. But I thought he was hiding something, and that made him suspect.

I held his gaze a little too long. His lips peaked at the corner as he looked down at the dock. A drop of water glided off the edge of his shoulder. *He has butterfly shoulders*, I thought, and I could see that wide chest leaping out of the water in tune with the pumping of his hips. Your racing buddy. Your swimming friend. You had not been exaggerating when you called him gorgeous.

I stopped staring and jumped like a loaded spring onto the dock. Toby quietly followed suit. I handed him an oar.

Pat and Nadia had been lost to the fog, but I heard them, a hundred yards to our left, splashing water as they began to row. The ropes that tethered our docks together pulled taut.

A loose plank on the dock creaked as Toby shifted. I turned to him.

And there it was. The not talking. All the questions I'd had back at your memorial when he'd given me a window and I'd let it slip by. To ask why you'd invited him to Bottomrock that night. If he knew what you'd wanted to tell me. Why he let you go. If there was another story, one he'd been afraid to tell our parents and police officers and news reporters.

I'd never believed that Toby had killed you. I didn't even believe that you were dead. But as he leaned against a canoe paddle and tendrils of fog obscured everything beyond us, my questions fell away.

"All right, go over there." I gestured with my oar to the far corner of the dock. "We want to paddle kind of diagonally."

"So east."

"Yeah, sure, twenty-two degrees northeast if you want to be precise about it," I said with as much snark as I could muster.

"I love precision."

I couldn't help myself: I smiled. But as quick as it came, I reined it back. I did not want to be smiling at Toby Smith.

As we paddled, Nadia's laughter carried through the mist. She and Pat were having fun, at least. From Toby, I hoped for silence. Either that, or spontaneous and total confession. When he asked me what I liked to write about, the whole dock swayed under the shuffle of his feet.

"How do you know I like to write?" I asked, suspicious. I didn't think it possible that Toby might simply want to know me.

"Izzy told me."

And Iz, that was probably the best, bravest, smartest thing he could have done in that moment. Say your name. Mom and Dad hardly did anymore. I hardly did. And suddenly, you'd been acknowledged, and not for what had happened to you. He'd tossed you into the conversation like he was bringing up the weather, and that was such a relief.

"I'm kind of just cataloging at the moment," I said.

"Cataloging?"

"Writing down things that happen. Trying to make sense of them." I didn't tell him that I was cataloging for you.

By the time we stopped paddling, the fog had thinned. Nadia and Pat dropped their weights, one for each corner, into the lake. With a *thunk*, the weights flung up a spray of water and sank to the bottom.

Toby picked up our first weight easily and dropped it overboard, the chain unraveling as the weight sank. But as the line tightened, the dock swayed, too much. Our weight hadn't hit the bottom.

I told Toby to stay put as I dove in.

The water out here was chillier than the shallows. It clung to my body, raising goose bumps. The weight had shaken muck loose from the weeds as it went down, making the water murkier than usual. To reach the chain, I had to swim under the dock. Its shadow blocked what little sunlight crept through the clouds, so even though I was only about five feet underwater, it was dark enough that I couldn't see my hands in front of me. I closed my eyes and felt for the chain. There was a kink somewhere. I just had to jigger it loose.

I'd done this before. We were trained to swim under the docks. To confront the darkness, the murkiness, the coolness of the sunless water. We'd learned how to swim in the shadows. How to use our sense of touch to feel our way along the lake bottom. In theory, this would help us find a drowning child. In actuality, none of us had ever had to search for one.

I played with the loops in the chain until it straightened. The weight dropped its last few inches, and a cloud of silky silt rose up to kiss my feet. I didn't want to be down there anymore in the dark and the cold, and I shot up too quickly, bopping my head against the underside of one of the floats.

The knock startled me. I suddenly needed very badly to see, and I opened my eyes, but that made everything worse. The guck stung. I'd been under too long now, just a little, maybe twenty seconds total, but I knew I needed air, I just didn't know which way was up. It was too dark and I was disoriented. Suddenly a hand was on my wrist, pulling me. I fought against it, panicked, but the hand was strong, and with one firm tug I surfaced and was gazing at Toby, who treaded water beside me. He was still holding my wrist.

"You okay?" he said so softly his words were almost eaten up by the fog. His dark hair had a piece of lake weed in it.

"Just give me a sec." My breath was coming back, but I was still shaking. I'd dredged up thoughts of you, in the weeds and the dark, alone.

We treaded for a few moments more, his thumb and index finger lightly pressed on either side of my wrist, like he was afraid to let go all the way. When I said, "I'm good now," his fingers dropped. He placed his hands on the dock and did an impressive upward thrust of his body to launch out of the water, then offered me a hand.

We put the rest of the weights in without issue and swam back to shore.

FOUR

In Which I Run with Petra

MY CENTER OF GRAVITY HAD SHIFTED, AND AT ANY MOMENT I COULD have toppled over. Tobias Smith at Bottomrock brought back all the questions I'd worked hard in therapy to let go of. Dr. Joshi and I had run through the possibilities. If you hadn't drowned, but run away, then why? And why stay away? Why make no contact? And the longer you went without making contact, the more likely it was that you never would, either because you couldn't, or didn't want to. I was supposed to accept that I might never know exactly what happened to you and try to move on. And I had. Mostly.

But now Toby was working at the lake where you'd last been seen and I had no idea why.

The park opened for the summer on Memorial Day weekend, and that Saturday I asked Petra to run to the park with me before my first shift started. I guess I thought we were still close enough that her company might make me somehow a little less nervous, a little more prepared, for the day ahead.

"Hey." Petra sighed.

"Thanks for doing this." I had been hiking and running with Petra regularly for months, ever since I confessed that I still wanted to go to Australia after graduation, but that I didn't know if I was capable of getting ready for a trip like that by myself. Cross-country star that she was, Petra offered to train me.

She sat on the wooden steps of her porch, lacing up her sneakers. "I wanted to say I was sorry for how you found out about Izzy's tree."

"Yeah, you should have told me."

"You mean asked for permission."

"No." The accusation stung. There was a time when I'd known all of Petra's secrets. But we've been falling away from each other in slow motion ever since you'd gone, and this was merely another reminder. "Do my parents know?"

"They think it's a nice idea. Do you hate it?" she asked as an afterthought.

"No." What else could I say? It didn't matter how I felt about her tree planting. I couldn't stop her now, not with Quimby on board and making plans. He'd probably already invited the mayor to your ceremony.

"Do you want to help me plan it?"

I shrugged.

We jogged toward the park. I had no idea what to say to Petra anymore, and not just about your memorial tree. You might think all the time we had spent together in the last nine months would have brought us closer. But honestly, the training trips were the only reason she and I had managed to hold on to our friendship at all.

It's not like you disappeared and we stopped being friends. I can't pinpoint when the shift happened. She and I ran and hiked and went through the routine of school, but we didn't really talk. I began eating lunch with Nadia and her friends, while Petra started eating with her new girlfriend, Karen.

Was our drifting apart natural, or a by-product of your absence? Outside of your swimming life, the three of us had formed a triad, and without you, the math was off.

As we weaved our way through the neighborhood, I relaxed into the rhythm of the run, which I always imagined must be like the way you relaxed into the rhythm of swimming. I liked the feel of gravity. The smoothness of the asphalt, the ragged bumps of gravel, the soft give of dirt, the sink of sand.

"So I've been reading about the best kinds of trees for this area, and I have a few candidates," Petra said as we entered the park. I thought about you, on the beach in the dark with Toby, daring him to race on foot as you swam across the lake.

I shifted the clip that cinched my pack at the waist. "I don't know a lot about trees."

"I don't, either, but I found this site and you can put in all this information about where the tree will be planted and what kind of light it will get and all that sort of stuff and then get a list of trees that will grow well there."

You knew better than to swim alone. It was a cardinal rule of water safety. I thought, not for the first time, how Toby's story made no sense. "So can't you just pick one from the list?" I said to Petra.

She stopped to catch her breath on an incline. Her ponytail wagged. "Sure, I can."

A beat. Overhead, a bird hopped from one branch to the next. My gaze flicked to the trail. Though I no longer expected to solve your disappearance by spotting some clue mixed in with the moss and leaves, my heart still lurched, hoping. We kept running.

One good thing about having a running partner is there's no need to fill the silence. Maybe that's why Petra and I no longer knew how to talk to each other. All of our time was spent huffing and puffing, with no breath left for words.

We stopped for a water break at the summit. Bottomrock Lake shined below us, puffy clouds reflected on the surface. The beach with its twin guard chairs overlooked the swimming area. Picnic tables hugged the tree line and the guardhouse perched at the edge of the woods on stilts with boats stored underneath. On the other side of the lake, the muddy embankment rose up from water teeming with lily pads, their flowers already in bloom. It was a long way across.

I sipped my water and looked back at Petra, trying to think of a conversation starter. The three of us used to stay up so late talking in sleeping bags in Petra's basement that she and I would snooze through your early rising to head off for swim practice. We'd gorge on Twizzlers and popcorn as we hate-watched terrible movies just to make fun of them. She came out to me before anyone, even you.

Petra capped her water. Her sneakers crunched fallen leaves. "Is Derek working this summer?"

"Yeah." My crush for two straight summers was coming back after his freshman year at college in Boston. I hadn't seen him since last summer. After the search for you had been called off, Bottomrock Park reopened. I'd insisted I could work, and amazingly, no one stopped me. I wouldn't have been a safe guard, but that didn't matter. The news of your vanishing act was still fresh, and a lot of people thought you were out there in the deep of the lake somewhere, tangled in the muck and the weeds. The park was open for three days without a single patron before Quimby shut it down for the season.

Anyway, on the last of those days, I was taking my lunch out of the refrigerator when I freaked out. Just broke down into tears. Nadia was sitting at the picnic table in the guardhouse, and she rocketed to her feet and hugged me. Pat asked if there was anything he could do. And Derek looked at me from under the hood of his blond bangs that you had called perpetually windswept, with those cool gray eyes I'd been fawning over all summer, and told me to go home.

I hadn't thought about Derek much since then. He went off to college and I started investigating what had happened to you.

I tried to imagine what it would be like to see Derek again. If the heat would rise in my cheeks when he smiled. If I'd still stumble over my words when he tried to talk to me. But my obsession with him felt like the postscript to another lifetime, and he was not the person I wanted to talk to Petra about. "Toby's working there, too."

"No shit?" Anger flashed across Petra's face. She blamed Toby, like Mom and a lot of other people. As if he could have stopped you from swimming that night. She should have known better, though: When you set your mind to something, no one could stop you. "I can't believe he'd . . . Are you okay with that?"

"I don't really have a choice."

Petra narrowed her eyes. She thought it was strange that I still wanted to work at Bottomrock, and I knew what she wasn't saying. *So quit.* But instead of saying what she really wanted to say, Petra echoed one of my own arguments for keeping my job at Bottomrock. "Gotta get that Australia money."

A black-and-blue butterfly perched on a bush, precariously near a spider's web. I watched its wings beat, waiting for the moment when it would catch in the sticky strands.

"You tell your parents yet?" Petra asked.

"Technically I told them months ago." Mom and Dad were not on board with my plan to go traveling alone for a year. When I first started talking about taking our trip without you, I think they thought the planning was good for me, because I was focusing on something that wasn't finding you. They figured I'd grow out of it. When they realized I was serious, they tried to convince me not to go. *Won't you be lonely, what if you get into trouble, why don't you do this after graduating college instead, when you're older and more experienced and ready?* They went so far as to forbid it, which of course they couldn't do. By the time of the trip, I'd be eighteen, and I was using all my own money. So I let them believe I wasn't serious. It was an inside joke. Oh, that gap year, ha-ha-ha.

Mom and Dad knew about my hikes and runs with Petra, but not why I was doing them. Dad had wondered sometimes why I didn't just join the cross-country team. After I told him competitions reminded me of you, he stopped asking.

Sometimes I thought even Petra believed I wasn't going to go through with the trip. No one knew the true reason I still wanted to go. The sliver of hope I had that if I went on our walkabout, I'd somehow find you. I'd bought my plane ticket already. I was flying to Sydney in September.

"I have to get to work, so . . ." I wanted to start running again. But something had shifted between us, and rather than finish the run with me, Petra said she had to head home.

After Petra had disappeared down the trail, I gazed upon the lake, wondering if she might be right. If I really should quit. If the list of reasons why I loved Bottomrock was just a list of excuses to mask my hope that if I spent time there, I might stumble across some clue as to what happened that night. And maybe I kept coming back to Bottomrock because there was a small part of me that wanted to be there if your body ever surfaced, while every day that it didn't added more credence to my belief that it never would. And now, even though Toby made me nervous, he also made me very, very curious. The only ties Toby had to Bottomrock were the ones you gave him. One way or another, he was there because of you.

I finished the second half of the trail faster than the first. I wanted to be at the beach, eye level with the water, where I didn't have to see the whole expanse of the lake. Where I didn't have to think about the parts of it that some people thought had swallowed you whole.

FIVE

How to Catch a Turtle

QUIMBY PUT A LIST ON THE REFRIGERATOR IN THE GUARDHOUSE. Tasks he wanted us to complete throughout the summer in moments when the park wasn't busy, from the ongoing-and-simple "clean up trash" to the so-complex-he-really-should-hire-professionals "refinish the guardhouse floors." At the top of the list it read: "To do by August 28."

Anniversaries were supposed to mark happy things, weren't they?

Quimby stuck around for the rest of opening day. Supposedly he was there to make sure Derek was management material. But really, Quimby was nervous. I could tell by the way he was pacing the beach before we'd even opened to the public. He'd always been a worrywart, and I wondered if your incident was going to mean he'd been spending more time here than ever before.

Like a good soldier, Derek fell in line, barking Quimby's orders back at us. As Derek repeated commands to clean this and organize that, I remembered why, at the lifeguard barbecue I brought you to once, you'd dubbed him G.I. Ken: His looks were Barbie doll, but his sternness was all military.

"We have a situation here," Derek said over the walkie-talkie in his deepened I'm-in-charge voice. Some kids swimming by the dock had started shrieking and scrambling for the ladder.

"What's going on out there? Is someone hurt? Is someone drowning?" Quimby's words were almost pleas. I rolled my eyes at Derek's need to impress as I unclipped my walkie from my rescue tube strap. We didn't have a situation. We had a snapping turtle. "It's just Snappy."

Every summer, Snappy showed up now and again underneath the docks. "I knew he'd survive the winter." Pat jumped in on his own walkie from the beach chair.

"Well, he can't stay there!" Quimby paced the shore, one hand pulling at his beard.

"We could evacuate him," Derek offered. A few summers back, the former head guard, Kyle, had convinced Quimby to supply a pool net, ostensibly for cleaning leaves off the surface of the swimming area. (As if *that* really needed to be done.) Really, Kyle wanted to catch Snappy. And he had, three or four times, though Snappy always did a number on the threads. After catching Snappy, Kyle would plop the netted turtle in a canoe, row him across the lake, and deposit him on the other side.

Taking credit for what had been Kyle's lone venture, Derek explained to Quimby how we might rid the dock of its turtle menace. Quimby nodded, clearly pleased with this plan. I scowled at Derek across the lake.

Snappy wasn't a menace, really. He'd never bitten anybody. If anyone swam near him, he darted away. We didn't need to evacuate him. We just needed to leave him be.

Toby ambled up the beach. He didn't have a Bottomrock tee yet, so he wore a white shirt that said GUARD in big red letters. His hair was sticking straight up. He scaled the side of a guard chair and hung there to watch.

The few kids who'd been in the shallows had stopped playing and were just standing in the water, curiously eyeing the dock, where the older kids were still huddled. Quimby continued to pace. He flicked on the walkie. "Teddy, should I send out one of the boys?"

"No," I radioed back. "But you'll have to send Derek around with the canoe, so we can transport Snappy across the lake." I retrieved the net.

The dock kids oohed and ahhed and asked me what I was going to do. "Catch him," I told them simply. I peered over the edge of the dock. The big turtle floated about a foot under the water. I dipped the net in.

Snappy zipped away as soon as the net broke the surface. The kids shrieked. Quimby radioed to ask me what happened. I ignored him. Snappy resurfaced a couple more times and dashed below at the first sign of the net. It didn't help that the kids kept moving around, shaking the dock, but eventually I snagged him.

He snapped his beak and whipped his long, scaly tail, trying to sever the threads that surrounded him. They held.

"Need a lift?" Toby rowed a canoe alongside the dock.

"I told Quimby to send Derek," I snapped, and then felt guilty, like I could hear you chiding me for being mean to your friend.

"Well, you got me" was all he said, but he said it in a voice that was less chipper than before.

I placed Snappy in his net into the center of the canoe, then climbed into the front and Toby paddled us away.

Snappy calmed somewhat, now that he wasn't suspended in air.

He was no longer thrashing, though he was chewing the threads of the net.

"Are you all right?" Toby asked.

That's when I realized I was shaking.

"Yes." I didn't look at him. It was easier to stay angry with him—for being here, for taking my place as your confidant, for maybe helping you run away—when I couldn't see his face.

"Are you scared of the turtle?"

"Yes," I pretended, not wanting to admit to Toby the real reason for my unease. That I had realized only too late what this canoe ride would mean, doing something I hadn't done since you disappeared: crossing the lake.

Snappy's tail thwacked the bottom of the boat.

Toby's deep, powerful strokes had us gliding atop the water. His muscles contracted beneath his shirt. I looked back at Snappy instead. The turtle was practically prehistoric, all gray-green scales and sharp edges. His tail seemed jagged enough to slice.

"Teddy? Toby?" came Quimby's voice on our walkies. "How's it going?"

I answered the call. "Doing fine, Mr. Quimby."

"Try not to take too long. We need you back on the dock."

I rolled my eyes. I could have definitely stayed on the dock if he and Derek hadn't been so insistent on trying to catch the turtle that wasn't going to hurt anyone anyway. "Toby's paddling as fast as he can." I set the walkie down.

Toby paddled in steady strokes. His eyes were unfocused, like he wasn't really seeing what was right in front of him.

"Why are you here?" My brusqueness caught him off guard. He blinked. Brought his focus to me.

"Quimby told me to get a canoe and pick you up."

"That's not what I meant."

"Oh." He took another couple strokes with the oar.

"You have to admit, it's weird."

"You're here, too."

"I wasn't the last person to see her."

The playfulness vanished from his face. He let the oar rest across the canoe and looked at his lap. For the first time since we'd been in each other's orbit, I knew he was uncomfortable. Good. If I was, he should be, too. "I didn't hurt her." He spoke softly. I was reminded of the boy who'd nervously twined a handkerchief through his fingers as he tried to talk to me at your memorial. And there was your voice in my head again, telling me to be nicer to your friend, making me feel guilty for forcing him to relive that night. Until I remembered that just by being here, he was doing that exact same thing to me. "Are you really not going to tell me?" I said, fast and hard and with a bite worthy of our netted travel companion.

"What do you want me to say?"

"I want you to tell me whatever it is you're not telling me."

"We don't know each other very well. There are a million things I haven't told you." He tried to cut my anger with his grin, but not even that could simmer me down.

"Don't be smart."

"Okay." He looked down at the turtle, who had finally stopped chewing on the net. Though the turtle's pointy beak angled up at Toby, he kept a marbled, reptilian eye on each of us.

"Why are you here?" I asked again. I waited for him to say, *So I can tell you what really happened that night. How I helped her get away.* I waited for him to say, *Because she told me she was going to leave, and I let her say good-bye.* I watched him watch Snappy watch us and I waited.

Toby's expression grew serious again. "I just . . . that night . . ." His mouth parted, then paused, whatever words he'd planned to say stalled before they could take form. I waited, heartbeat spiking, until I could wait no longer. "Yeah?" There was a secret message on his face, if only I knew him well enough to decode it. But when he pressed his lips together and took a breath, I knew that whatever it was he'd been about to say, he'd abandoned the words before he could work up the nerve to voice them.

He cleared his throat and his voice went soft and playful once more. "I couldn't get this place out of my head, okay?" He grabbed the oar and thrust it back into the water. "I'm a firm believer in facing your fears, or whatever, head-on. So here I am." I glared at him. That wasn't the answer I wanted, but I could tell it was the only one I was going to get, for now.

But if Toby wouldn't talk to me, maybe I could glean something from the conversation you'd had with him that night. "I want to see your phone."

"My phone?"

"You're not one of those people who actually deletes their message history, are you?"

"No."

"You said Izzy texted you that night, asking you to come to Bottomrock? I want to see."

"You don't believe me?"

"I just want to see, okay?"

Toby rested the oar in the bottom of the canoe and dug into the pocket of his swim trunks. I hadn't actually meant *in this moment,* but I wasn't about to object. He had the phone in a waterproof pocket. He keyed in his passcode, pulled up his text history, and handed it to me.

You had said: **Hey, can you meet me somewhere?**

Toby: **Now? What's up?**

I need to talk.

Everything OK?

According to the text time stamps, five minutes elapsed before you replied.

No.

That one lonely word shouldn't have surprised me. Toby's story all along was that you'd been upset that night. But seeing the confirmation in your own words was like a riptide pulling me under. Before Toby had a chance to reply to your declaration, you'd texted a follow-up.

Take your mom's car. Come here. There was a pin for Bottomrock Park in Google Maps.

I can be there by 11.

You hadn't texted anything in response.

The canoe swayed, drifting slowly toward the dam. I reread the conversation twice. You needed to talk. Everything was *not* okay. Why hadn't you called me?

"What did she want to talk about?"

"She never said."

I arched my brow, skeptical. You're a straight shooter. Evasive maneuvers were not your style. I returned Toby's phone, feeling like all I'd gleaned were more questions.

"Why not just read that on Izzy's phone?" Toby asked as he put the phone back in his pocket.

"I can't."

"You don't have her phone?"

"My parents do." I *had* had your phone, for a brief period of time, after the police returned it and before Mom and Dad confiscated it. Sometime before you'd disappeared, you had changed your passcode, and I no longer knew what it was. "But it's locked."

"And the police couldn't get it unlocked with like a warrant or hacking or something?"

"Apparently that's something police can only do on TV." I'd tried to crack the code, too. Every conceivable six-digit variation of our birthday and our parents' birthdays. The numbers from your locker at school. Your record-setting butterfly times. The world-record times for your favorite events. Holidays. Names of the people in your life. None of it had worked. My obsession with getting into your phone was the reason our parents eventually took it away.

Toby looked away for a moment before he sighed and said, "Did you try five-two-five-four-five-two?"

"Are you trying to be funny?"

"That was her passcode last summer." He shrugged when I stared at him, undoubtedly slack-jawed like a cartoon character. Of all the answers I'd imagined Toby held, the passcode for your phone was not one of them. When had he become your secret-keeper instead of me? "I had to key it in every single practice when she wanted me to log her swim times."

You had an app that organized your athletic life: racing times, practice times, workout regimes, diet, even sleep, so his explanation rang true. I knew exactly where Mom and Dad had stashed your phone, and I was already reciting the six digits in my head, so I'd be ready to steal it back and try them the moment I got home.

"Teddy? Toby?" Quimby's voice came through the walkie. "You're not moving."

I picked it up. "Yes we are. We're just small, so it's hard to tell." I lifted my fingers off the receiver. "God, every winter I forget how annoying that man is."

"He's not so bad."

"You've had half a day of him. And you're a boy."

"What's that supposed to mean?"

"How many times have you cleaned the bathrooms today?" I waited, but he didn't have to say anything. "And you know what he asked me to do after I finish my dock shift?"

"Clean the bathrooms?"

"Teach Nadia how to clean them. Because apparently only women are capable of cleaning?"

"Oh, well, that's a given." Toby smirked.

"Keep paddling or I'll unleash Snappy on you."

"Yes, ma'am."

He kept paddling, and I stewed in my own annoyance, which, if I'm being honest here, was about a lot more than just a sexist but well-meaning boss who liked to micromanage. It was about how Snappy didn't deserve this transplant. How Toby had reverted to a person who smirked and laughed and seemed just like someone you could have been friends with, even though I knew there was something else he wanted to tell me, something crucial. How you'd shared with him things you hadn't shared with me. How you were not okay, and I had no idea why.

How I was on a boat in the middle of the lake I loved, and I hated it. How I hated that I hated it, because I used to love this lake.

A crackle on the walkie. "Teddy?" I didn't even listen to what Quimby had to say. I chucked the walkie into the water. The boat rocked, and the turtle stirred, swishing his tail left and right. The walkie slipped under the surface with a satisfying plop.

"Teddy?" I could hear Quimby's voice again on Toby's walkie. Toby held it out to me. "Want to throw this one, too?"

"Not today." I decided we were far enough away to release Snappy. As soon as the net breached the surface, the great turtle shot to life, ducking under the reeds.

"I guess I should paddle us back?" Toby said.

"I can take a turn."

"Only if you'll let me take a turn with the bathrooms." He passed the oar to me across the canoe, and I thought about his earlier hesitation. He'd known you so much better than I'd realized, and I was more confident now than ever that he knew something more about that night. I just had to figure out how to get him to tell me what it was.

SIX

Our Only Real Fight

SOME THINGS MAKE A PERSON SEE THEIR OWN MEMORIES IN A NEW light.

You were not okay, you'd told Toby in your text.

July of last summer, I came home late from work covered in sand and sweat. You met me at the bathroom door.

"You're smiling," you said, and for a second I felt like I shouldn't be happy about something because your summer had been hard. I tried to rein in my grin, but it sprang back into place despite myself. "Yeah," I said. "We stayed late to play with the rescue board in the lake."

You looked at me, suddenly alert. "We? You and Derek?"

"I wish. It was everyone. We did have a moment, though." I sighed and pushed through the door. "In or out? I wanna shower."

You came in and closed the door. "You're too stuck on him."

"You don't even want to hear about it?"

"No," you said, fast. "I'm sick of it."

"Fine. I won't tell you about him anymore. I won't tell you if anything between us ever happens. I won't tell you when—"

"Just forget about him, okay? Please? You can't even bring yourself to speak to him. You hardly know him."

I narrowed my eyes. You usually didn't take digs at my timidity. "This isn't about Derek," I said. You were gazing into the mirror.

"You're always at that place."

"At my job?"

"You're never *here*."

An accusation or a plea? Then, I thought the former, and I resented you judging me for having my own life. With a voice full of snark, I said, "Well, I'm here right now."

"I need to . . . I have to . . . there's something . . ." You weren't the type to have trouble getting words out. Had you really stumbled this much? Or was my memory distorting your speech, adding the distress to make you not okay?

"Izzy, just spit it out." I know I said this, that I spit the words out of myself with venom. I don't remember exactly why I was so harsh. I was itchy from the sand and sweat, impatient for a shower. I was annoyed with you, for brushing off my desire to talk about my crush. And I thought you should get why I was working so much. Shouldn't it be obvious? You wanted to travel around a foreign country for a year, having grand adventures. We couldn't do that without money. In this, I'd taken over your role of being the practical one, while you were the one with imagination.

"I want to do a walkabout," you said.

"A walkabout?"

"It's this big trek. In the outback."

"Like where you go out into the desert with a knife and a canteen and you try to survive?"

"Basically."

"Izzy." I was panicking a little because I knew you were serious and my greatest fear had finally happened. You were finally suggesting something so adventurous that I couldn't follow you. "Be real."

"I *am* being real."

"What about scuba diving? Surf lessons? The shark-cage diving?"

"Now I want to do this."

"You don't even *like* camping."

"Sure I do." You shrugged, like my point shouldn't matter, like you hadn't spent at least a portion of every camping trip Dad took us on begging to sleep in a hut instead of on the ground.

"Well, I don't want to do a walkabout."

"Then don't come. I'd rather do it alone, anyway."

The panic snared my reason. I felt shaky and hoarse. "And what am I going to do? Twiddle my thumbs in Sydney?"

"Twiddle them here, for all I care!"

You slammed the door on your way out.

It took four days to get your apology note, the longest it ever had. I think it said something along the lines of *Sorry for snapping at you.* I remember feeling it was insufficient, and I crumpled it up as soon as I'd read it.

When I got home having seen your texts with Toby, armed now with your passcode, I wrote drafts of my apology to you.

Sorry for dismissing whatever you were about to say.

Sorry for not carefully considering your walkabout idea until after you were gone.

Sorry for letting my anger at you linger, even as we got back to normal, even after you left.

They were all insufficient, until at last I wrote:

Sorry for not realizing there was something going on with you last summer. It's probably too late, but I promise I'll find out now.

SEVEN

A Window to Your World

THAT NIGHT, I SNUCK INTO OUR PARENTS' CLOSET WHILE THEY WERE watching a movie in the living room and dug your phone out of a box marked ɪᴢᴢʏ. They kept it on the top shelf, stuffed back in a corner like a once-favored childhood toy. Though dust coated the flaps of the box, there were some smudges at the edges. One of my parents, at least, had been fingering the cardboard.

Most of your stuff was still in your room, so this box held my parents' mementos of you. The stopwatch Dad had used to time your races from the sidelines. The workbooks Mom followed while homeschooling you. I found the birdwatching journal Dad had given you. Sometimes post-you I'd seen him with it, rereading your observations, smiling lightly at your poor attempts to sketch your sightings.

And then there was your phone. I tucked it in my pocket and slid the box back.

Unsurprisingly, your phone had no battery, so I plugged it into my charger. Fifteen antsy minutes later, it had enough juice for me to power it on. I stared at the familiar screen: a touch keypad asking for a six-digit code. The numbers 525452 sang in my head.

I entered them.

The screen flickered to life, and I blinked as if looking at a mirage. But I wasn't. All your apps, meticulously organized in alphabetized folders, were now accessible with a few swipes of my fingers. If Toby had been sitting next to me, I could have kissed him.

The first thing I did was pull up your text messages. I saw the conversation you'd had with him. Of course it didn't look any different from your end. I saw the cryptic text you'd sent me, too, and the unanswered texts I'd sent in response. You hadn't texted anyone else that day.

I put the phone down and leaned back in my desk chair. What evidence was I hoping to find? A detailed map, outlining your route in your travels abroad? A note you'd typed but decided not to send to anyone explaining why you were leaving and never coming back? I was an addict literally staring down her next fix. A voice in my head, maybe it was *your* voice, told me to put the thing back in our parents' closet and forget about it. I was moving on, right? Whatever had happened to you, wherever you'd gone, time had proved that you weren't coming back. Unless you couldn't. Or unless you wanted me to come find you.

Quickly I snatched your phone and shoved it in the pencil drawer of my desk. I could peruse your phone without reigniting my obsessive search for you. I told myself I'd look through your phone later. Look at your photos. Click through your swim app and see all the goals you'd set and beaten. For the memories. So I left it in the drawer, for now.

———

THE PHONE STAYED in my drawer overnight; then I began carrying it around in my bag. I didn't know what I might find on it, and I swore my days of hunting for your bread crumbs were behind me, but the very fact that I *could* get into your phone was a comfort. Occasionally, I took it out and flipped through your photographs during the slow periods at the park. There were plenty I hadn't seen in years, and some I'd never seen at all. These were mostly shots of your teammates, people I'd barely known. Toby was in many. They didn't tell me anything about what might have happened to you, but I liked seeing the water-clumped hair and dripping grins as you all goofed around poolside.

Sometimes I'd look at other apps, too. I listened to your workout playlists, with their odd mix-ups of pop and classical, as I worked the sign-in bench. During lunch I played that color-by-numbers game you had found so soothing on those long bus rides to your away meets. After I'd had your phone for about a week, I opened Evernote, thinking I might scroll through some of your signature to-do lists, always so ambitious. The most recent to-do list had been created the afternoon you'd disappeared.

Meet at Bottomrock. Midnight.

My chest tightened.

According to Toby, by midnight you were swimming across the lake, never to be seen again.

I was on my feet in two seconds and storming toward Toby in three.

The only thanks I'd given him for granting me access to your phone was slightly less of a cold shoulder and a somewhat creepy stalker gaze as my curiosity about your friend swelled. My eyes followed him when he stretched to grab an extra rescue tube from the highest rung. I'd listened as he assured a worried mother that the snake she'd seen gliding over the water wasn't poisonous, and I'd noticed he was starting to greet some of the regular patrons by name. I was accumulating all these little facts about your friend, like how he doodled in a notebook while we watched a training DVD, and when he read on breaks, it was almost always a comic book. But I didn't know what I could do or say to make him tell me why he was really working at Bottomrock. I didn't even have the nerve to start a regular conversation.

Now it seemed he'd been lying. To me, the police, everyone. Someone else had been at Bottomrock that night.

I burst through the open guardhouse door, where Toby sat at the picnic table, a thick grinder in one hand as he thumbed through a digital comic on his phone.

"Who else was there that night?" I offered no preamble. This was too important to beat around any bushes.

Toby took a moment to swallow. Then he said, brows skewed in confusion, "What?"

"Izzy had plans to meet someone at Bottomrock at midnight, *before* she texted asking you to come. You were with her at midnight. So you must know who she met."

"Teddy. There wasn't anyone else there."

"I don't believe you!"

"I wish there was!" He raised his voice, too, matching me in both volume and indignation. "If there had been anyone else with us, maybe the police wouldn't have spent *months* studying my laptop, dropping by with more 'questions,' and just generally acting like I murdered my best friend." These final words slapped. Your best friend? A part of me had guessed as much, but it still hurt to hear it. When had your best friend stopped being me? His declaration deflated my anger, but didn't erase my skepticism.

"She didn't say anything about meeting someone else there that night?" Surely you would have told him if someone else was expected.

"No," he huffed. "But . . . I wasn't actually with her at midnight."

Right. The race. That part always had sounded suspicious to me. Could it have been an excuse to send Toby away while you met with someone else? If so, why?

Another thought dawned: If you'd merely been sending Toby away with the ruse of a race, maybe you'd never swum across at all. I thought of the campsite where your earring had been found. It was a popular meeting spot for kids our age. To party. To hook up. None of that sounded like you.

I plopped down at the picnic table on the bench opposite Toby and picked at its peeling paint. He could still be lying. Covering for you, or someone else. But I didn't think he was.

"What makes you think she was meeting someone?" Toby asked.

I shifted my gaze up at him. "It was in her phone."

"So it worked?" he asked casually. Apparently his temper cooled a lot faster than mine.

"Yeah." A beat passed before I added, "Thanks."

"You're welcome." He picked up his lunch. I kept chipping loose paint. How would I figure out who you'd been planning to meet? If someone else had been there . . . I now had a whole slew of new stories that could fill in the gaps of that August night.

And possibly more answers preserved in your phone.

EIGHT

Parents Post-You

TRY AS I MIGHT TO RESUME MY LIFE, A NEW QUESTION PLAGUED ME:
Who might you have been planning to meet at midnight?

A midnight meeting might be romantic, but you didn't have a
romantic interest. You'd never so much as expressed any interest in
anyone specific beyond your revolving crushes on Olympic swimmers Katie Ledecky and Eamon Sullivan.

Certainly you'd have told me about any potential or actual
partners, especially your first, so I didn't think I was looking for
a romantic candidate. But a midnight meeting could also be for
some nefarious purpose. You hadn't put the midnight meeting in
your calendar as you did with pretty much everything, and since
the calendar was shared with me and our parents, I assumed you'd
wanted to keep it secret. Had you gotten into something dangerous
or shifty? Was that why you'd left?

I thought back to your exchange with Toby. You were not okay.
Because you were worried about whoever you were about to meet?
Maybe you'd called Toby there for support or backup. I wouldn't
know for sure until I tracked down the person you were supposed
to meet.

But there was another person besides Toby who might know something about your plans the night you went missing: our father.

He was the last of our family to see you. He didn't talk about that night, at least not with me. But then again, I had never been able to bring myself to ask him about it.

Post-you, Mom and Dad became a lot more restrictive, most notably in the form of a curfew. For the first several months after, I wasn't leaving the house much, but they came up with the curfew idea once I started venturing out again. I'd only broken the curfew once, and only by a few minutes. They were both up, watching a movie in the living room. (That's another thing they started doing: waiting up for me.) When I walked in—I'd been hanging out at Nadia's—Dad said, "You're late," in the flat voice he uses whenever he's upset, and I stared at him for a second before it clicked that he was calling me out for breaking the curfew. Something on his voice, though, told me he wasn't angry: He was scared.

Pre-you, of course, there was no curfew, so Dad had no reason to wait up for you that night. He trusted you to make it home okay. Pre-you, our parents were pretty laid-back when it came to things like making us tell them who we were hanging out with, what time we'd be coming home, and what we were planning to do, though usually we volunteered those details anyway. I figured there was at least a chance you had said something offhand about your plans before you left the house that night. Maybe Dad would remember. Maybe he'd even already told the police and they'd already investigated and the new lead I'd stumbled across in your phone wasn't a new lead at all, just new to me. But I had to know.

I shuffled into Mom and Dad's shared office after dinner. With the window open, the room was as muggy as it was outside after a surprise evening rainstorm had left a dampness in the air. Mom was finishing up grading the final projects in her AP Language class while Dad was listening to bird sounds on his iPad. There was this bird that had been caw-cawing from somewhere nearby the house for a couple of weeks, and he really wanted to figure out what it was.

"Quick: Name that bird!" he said as I walked into the room, the hooting coming out of his iPad paused.

"Some sort of owl." You might have known which, given how you'd taken to Dad's passion, but I had no idea.

"A Northern Saw-whet."

"Are you sure you haven't started to lose your hearing, Dad? Because I'm pretty sure the tweeting we've been hearing is not that." I flashed him a snarky grin, and he flashed one right back.

"A little diversion."

"Mom, how can you grade with him birding in here?"

"It's not birding unless you're outside actually looking for specific birds," Dad threw out as Mom said, "I don't even really hear it anymore."

"Uh-huh." I folded myself into Mom's reading chair, knees tucked to my chest. There are very few things I've ever felt hesitant to talk about to our parents. My trip to Australia was one. My still-pulsing belief that you hadn't drowned was another. And what it had been like for Dad here alone when Toby called him to say you were gone. I was pretty sure he'd talked about it with Mom. If they were close pre-you, they've been closer post-you. Some people pull apart when tragedy strikes. Others glom together. Our parents, you'll be pleased to hear, are the latter type.

Beside Mom's chair is a bookshelf, and curled as I was, I sat eye level with that picture of the four of us from San Francisco, where the wind was blowing my hair into your face as we posed in front of the Golden Gate. Your gaze was caught halfway between me and the camera. You had said, *Your spaghetti hair is strangling me*, and it was so random and silly and that's why the two of us have the dorkiest grins we'd ever worn in a family photo taken from Dad's neon-green selfie stick.

"So you're graduating in a couple weeks." Mom swiveled her desk chair to the side, angling it toward me.

"I'm graduating in a couple of weeks," I echoed, but the sentence got caught in my throat and cheeped out. I'd gotten pretty good about ignoring all the things that should have been *we*, but this one got to me.

Mom leaned forward to toy with my hair. "Sometimes I can hardly believe it. I was thinking, maybe this summer, before you go off to college"—I looked away at her mention of college; I wasn't ready to peel *that* Band-Aid—"we can reboot our book club?"

"I don't know, Mom." I hadn't thought about our book club in a long, long time. For more than two years we'd alternated monthly suggestions, reading in sync with each other so we could spend a Sunday afternoon sequestered in the office together, discussing the story and characters and writing. We'd stopped because of you. Not because you vanished, but because you took Mom as your private tutor and travel chaperone in that last year before trials, when getting you to the Olympics was family priority number one. I hadn't minded that Mom and I had stopped our little club. It had happened so subtly, almost accidentally. By the time I'd realized we'd missed a couple months, I'd assumed we'd start it back up again after the Olympics. But then you hadn't made your times and then you'd evaporated, and neither Mom nor I brought it up again.

"It was just a thought. We don't have to. Have you written any stories lately?"

I shook my head. I knew Mom didn't want to hear that I was still writing to you. I glanced over at Dad, who'd put his earbuds in, apparently thinking I'd come in to talk to Mom.

"Do you and Petra have any fun plans?"

"Um . . . no. But Pat's throwing a party." I threaded my fingers together as I watched Dad smile at whatever he was listening to.

"Well, of course you can go as long as you're home by curfew."

"Riiight." The fact that I still had the curfew as an eighteen-year-old almost-high-school graduate struck me as a bit unreasonable—your being gone didn't suddenly make *me* less trustworthy—but I understood why Mom and Dad needed it.

Mom, however, interpreted my annoyance with the curfew as annoyance that I couldn't stay out late for Pat's graduation party. She did that lip thing she does when she's trying to be delicate with her words. You know the thing I'm talking about, where she bites the inside of her bottom lip and lets the top one overlap just a little. "Maybe we can make an exception . . ." She tapped Dad on the shoulder. "Henry?"

Dad snapped the earbuds out. "Yeah?"

"How late do you think Teddy can stay out at Pat's graduation party?"

"Why does she need to stay out late?" It wasn't a dismissal. He genuinely wanted to know. Nearly a year with a missing daughter, and Dad had managed somehow to hold on to all his grown-up innocence. He was still the same blasé birdwatching accountant who missed more than half of the social cues around him and rolled with the other half like they didn't affect him.

"Or maybe I don't need a curfew, you know, in general." Suddenly your voice was in my head saying *Maybes are for babies*. "It's almost summer. And I won't really be living here anymore in a few months." I tried to reason out my argument, the way you had done every time you wanted to buy some expensive training swimsuit or take trips to the ocean in January to swim against the waves or do some other intense thing that would lead you to athletic glory.

"Maybe we can make it case by case?" Mom said, without even pausing to think. I shot forward in the chair, ticked off. Maybe if I had come equipped with an actual outline, the way you had when you'd convinced Mom to take a leave of absence from teaching to homeschool you, down to a thesis and a bulleted list of points and counterpoints, Mom would have at least considered my proposal. "Forget it. Nadia said I could sleep over her house if I wanted to the night of Pat's party. Can I at least do that?"

"That seems fine to me," Dad said before Mom could get beyond her lip-pursing. If they had this much trouble with the idea of me staying out as late as I wanted, what were they going to say when I finally told them my plan to defer college and go on our gap-year trip alone?

I thought I might have to avoid telling them about Australia until I had one foot on the plane.

"Is there something else, Teddy?" Mom asked. Dad still hadn't put his earbuds back in.

"Yeah. I wanted to talk to Dad." Mom sat back sharply, while Dad's brows perked. I didn't wait for Mom to leave or for my temper to settle, though maybe I should have on both counts. "Can I ask you something?"

"You just did." Dad smiled.

I resisted rolling my eyes at Dad's favorite overplayed joke because I needed to set a different tone. "Dad."

"Oh. Okay. You mean a serious thing." He closed the case of the iPad and set it on his desk. Mom sat quietly at hers, watching us.

"It's about the night Izzy went to Bottomrock."

"Oh." Dad looked down at his knees. Mom made a sound, but whatever objection she started to raise was stopped by a slight wave of Dad's hand. "Sure, honey. Ask whatever you want," he said softly, all the pep from his birdwatching mood zapped.

"Did you know she was going there?"

"She got dressed up and left sometime after dinner, said she was meeting a friend. I didn't ask where."

"What do you mean . . . she was dressed up?" You'd gone night swimming, and according to Toby, you'd worn a bathing suit under your clothes. Had you gone somewhere else *before* Bottomrock?

"Not very dressed up," Dad clarified. "I just mean . . . makeup. Jewelry. She didn't do those things very often. I actually thought she might have been going on a date."

"And you didn't say anything? Find out who she was meeting?"

I didn't mean to be accusatory. How many times pre-you had our parents failed to ask that question because the answers were always the same: Petra, if it was me or us, or a swimming teammate, if it was just you? But Dad didn't take my question as just me trying to be thorough. He reddened. One hand squeezed his kneecap while the other ran through his thinning brown hair. "No," he said, his eyes bloodshot and damp. A few feet away Mom watched him, such love and understanding and acceptance in her eyes. He'd had this conversation with himself, probably multiple times, and she'd comforted him through it.

And then there was me. Bumbling abruptly and inconsiderately around the worst memories of his life. Nearly a year and I had never once considered Dad's guilt.

"Dad, I didn't mean—"

"It's okay, Teddy. It's not like if she had said she was meeting Toby at Bottomrock, I would have said no."

You had met Toby at Bottomrock, but I knew from the texts you'd sent that night that your meeting with him was arranged *after* you'd already left the house. So who had you been dressing up for? Did you meet someone *before* going to Bottomrock? What about the note in your calendar to meet at midnight?

That night sighed romance.

One thing was certain: Toby had never once mentioned you being dressed in an atypical fashion. Dad was right: You didn't wear jewelry often, and you wore makeup even less. I thought of your earring again, found in a popular spot for a teenage hookup. You would have told me if you'd been dating someone, surely. But Dad said you'd been wearing jewelry when you left the house, and the police had found your earring in the woods.

Dad's story didn't mesh with Toby's. I knew Dad wouldn't lie to me.

Which meant Toby was lying for you.

NINE

A Refund for Rain

MAKING TOBY FEEL COMFORTABLE AROUND ME WAS MY NEW GOAL. It was the only way I could think to get him to tell me the truth. Since he'd told me what your passcode was, I'd been talking to him in snippets, trying my best to be amiable. In an odd way, the idea of being friends with Toby made me feel closer to you.

In the meantime I continued to scour your phone, trying to find evidence of who you'd planned to meet that night, be it Toby or someone else, but I was quickly discovering the true meaning behind the saying *like a needle in a haystack*. Take your photos, for instance. You had 15,342 in your iCloud account. It could take me the entire summer, and then some, to carefully look through them all.

Only a fraction of those made it to your Instagram, the best of the best. I was more familiar with your personal Instagram, but you also had what you called your professional account, which was entirely swimming focused. Not that you'd never posted swimming-related pics to your personal account. But IzzyWareSwims was created about a year before trials, to document your progress toward making Team USA. I was one of your followers, naturally, but I honestly hadn't paid much attention to your posts in this account.

Now I made it my mission to view every single one. I didn't know what I was looking for. A comment about Bottomrock? A person cropping up more often than any others? Some veiled reference to something shifty or secret?

I flipped through the posts while I manned the sign-in bench at work, stopping to take people's cash and write their names on the sign-in log. In this age of wireless everything, at Bottomrock Park we were old school with our record keeping, and the log was a binder we maintained by hand.

Toby slipped onto the bench beside me.

"It's my shift now. You're on first aid." Being "on first aid" was the same as being on break. Maybe three times a summer someone had to treat a bee sting or apply a bandage to a skinned knee, but that's the worst it got. I flicked to the next picture. One you had posted the morning of trials. You were bent over the starting block, back arched as you prepared to dive. Mom had probably taken it, or maybe your coach.

"Those are Izzy's." He clicked the sign-in pen once, then again.

"Yup." The diving picture had a lot of likes and comments, but they were all along the lines of *Good luck!* and *Swim fast!*

"Are you looking for something?"

"Just looking." I made a point of smiling. Toby would never lower his guard if I didn't at least pretend to lower mine. "Thanks for taking over." I looked back at your phone and froze. My thumb hovered above a comment from WhisperingWahoo.

Nice ass, Miss Pompous. Going to screw your way on to Team USA?

I swiveled in the sand. "Who's WhisperingWahoo?"

"On Instagram?" Toby put his comic book down. "It's this gossipy account that posts pics from our meets and parties. They comment a lot on other people's stuff, too."

"And you don't know who runs it?"

"No. Why?"

I hesitated before handing over your phone.

"Ugh. The day of trials?" Toby shook his head. "I'm sorry."

"Excuse me." A man stomped up the beach with a sunburned belly, camouflage swim trunks, and two little kids trailing behind him. "I'm leaving and I'd like a refund."

Toby slid your phone back to me as he said, "A refund? Why?"

"It's going to rain," said the man.

"But it hasn't rained. Not yet," Toby replied slowly with a look on his face like the guy had just asked him to try to keep the sand off the beach.

"I said it's going to rain. Look at that cloud."

Toby looked up. I did, too. There was a cloud. It was big and grayish and currently blocking part of the sun. It was maybe a rain cloud. It was hard to tell.

"Just to be clear, sir, you want a refund for the entire day because it might rain later?" Toby said, each word evenly measured.

The man turned to me. "Can you get off your phone and help me?"

I put your phone away and mustered up my best patron-placating voice. "What's your name, sir?"

"Dawson."

I scanned the sign-in sheet. I had to go back a page in the binder because it had been a hot, busy day, and he'd arrived that morning. More than four hours ago. If he'd been at the park for only a few minutes, I might have given him his money back just to get him to go away.

"Well, we're not in the habit of giving refunds. . . ."

Mr. Dawson's forehead creased.

"But I'll tell you what. You spent twenty-four dollars here today. So I'm going to give you a special voucher for that amount that's good toward the purchase of a season family pass." I slipped a check-shaped piece of paper from our money box, wrote out the voucher, and handed it to him.

Mr. Dawson took it with a look of triumph on his face.

I handed Toby the pen and walked over to the tetherball court, WhisperingWahoo's taunt still ringing in my head. With one lazy tap of my fist, I hit the ball. The cord twined around the pole until it could no longer, then momentum carried the ball backward and the cord unraveled. Toby followed me. "Wow. That guy. *Thank* you for dealing with him."

I shifted my gaze from the unwinding ball to Toby. Even with the maybe–rain cloud covering the sun, it was still bright enough that I had to squint. "Yeah. No problem."

He tapped the ball back to me. "You okay?"

"Why would someone say that to Izzy?"

"Because some people are gross jerks."

I laughed a little.

"It was one comment out of hundreds. *Hundreds.* Izzy probably didn't see it until after her races, anyway. If at all."

"Yeah." Toby actually was making me feel a bit better. I gave the ball a spin before sending it back around. "Thanks."

"You're welcome." We batted the ball back and forth in a lazy manner for a few moments while I tried to put WhisperingWahoo out of mind.

"So what's this voucher thing you gave him?" The ball glanced off Toby's fingertips and circled around again.

"It's just a receipt. We give them to anyone who asks."

"Well, thanks for jumping in. I'm terrible with annoying patrons. This one time—"

"Toby, what are you doing?"

His toes skimmed the sand. He said softly, "I'm not doing anything."

He was right, of course. I was the one in a sour mood, and he was only trying to lift it. I had to remind myself again that I wanted him to trust me. So I made myself soften. "What're you reading?" I'd noticed the covers of his comics. The characters were colorful, vivacious creatures that I could only assume were aliens, given the tech they sometimes possessed and the spacescapes in the background.

"It's a comic book about this couple trying to raise their kid in the middle of a never-ending intergalactic war." Toby batted the tetherball in my direction. "It's a science fiction–fantasy comedy epic."

I tapped it back. "That sounds like too many genres."

"Then you have obviously never read *The Hitchhiker's Guide to the Galaxy*, which is precisely a science fiction–fantasy comedy epic."

"That book is too tiny to be an epic."

"Not the Ultimate edition. And anyway, epics aren't about word count. They're about scope."

"Scope requires a certain word count."

"What about high stakes? An expansive universe? A feeling that the characters are embarking on a mission of great importance? You should read *Hitchhiker's*."

"Maybe I will." I caught the ball and swung it around. For a moment there, I'd forgotten how we were tethered by you. This guy sitting next to me spouting theories about epic literature—he had been your friend. Your good friend. Maybe even—I have to admit this now, don't I? Because you told him things you didn't tell me?—your best friend. Was this the way you and Toby had chatted, or had your closeness evolved purely around swimming? Sharing in the burden of double-day practices and the pressure to always be better. Despite the tragedy of that night, he was so nice. He seemed to roll with everything. I'd known him only a few weeks, but I couldn't believe he'd done anything to make you call him a jerk.

When I offered nothing further, Toby changed topics, swinging the ball back around to me. "So what would you have done if the refund guy didn't accept the receipt?"

"Probably banned him from the park for life."

"We can do that?"

I twisted the ball in my hand. "Of course not. Though we *can* ban kids from the docks."

A mischievous smirk spread across his face. "Noted. Any other penalties for annoyingness we can enforce?"

"There are none in the handbook. Unfortunately. Why don't you come up with some?" I launched the tetherball back at Toby, thinking about suggesting he voluntarily commit himself to whatever his next idea was.

The ball soared over his head, but he caught it with one hand and let it drop to waist level. "What about a time-out in a changing stall?"

I laughed.

"What's so funny about the stalls?"

My face flushed. "Nothing."

"No, there's a story. I see it in your eyes."

"They have . . . a reputation." Among Bottomrock lifeguards, the changing stalls were considered the place to go if you wanted to hook up during a slow day. During my first summer as a guard, I'd stumbled across Derek and a girl who used to work at Bottomrock coming out from one, disheveled and quiet.

"As what? Are they dangerous? Or a bad influence, perhaps?" He said this with all seriousness. I smirked at him. I was beginning to think he was the type of guy who was easy to smirk at. Now what was *I* doing? Being nice to Toby was one thing. A means to an end. And probably what you would have wanted. But we were teetering close to goofing around together, and any friendship I started with Toby risked inviting more thoughts of you. The many imagined scenarios of how you'd houdinied out of my life. That awful day when the college tour guide asked our mom to please hang back if she was going to talk on the phone and she just kept repeating *What?* like the word was foreign, like her tongue was heavy from a bee sting.

We continued to tap the ball back and forth. Some kids dashed past us in a game of keep away. Soon a family walked up the beach, heading home for the day with towels draped over their shoulders. The walkie we'd left at the sign-in table crackled with chatter from Nadia, who was on the lifeguard stand, to Derek in the guardhouse— something about the dark clouds gathering overhead. Pat, from his own walkie on the other chair, intoned his wish for thunder.

Across from me on the tetherball court, Toby said, "I was wrong, you know."

I caught the tetherball, suddenly nervous.

He went on. "When I said you looked like her."

"So I don't look like her?"

He shook his head. "I mean, you have the same face."

"So I do look like her."

"Wait a sec. Let me finish. It looks like the same face. But it's not actually. Your hair, for one."

I fingered the end of my ponytail. My hair was long. It'd gotten a bit longer since you'd last seen it. An image popped into my head of you tucked away in the wilderness somewhere, your hair grown out from your favored pixie cut. You would hardly need to fit it smoothly underneath your swim cap anymore, giving you that streamlined skull.

"I mean, yeah, your hair is longer but it's also lighter. More reddish, I guess. Probably because you spend more time in the sun."

"And less time in a pool."

Toby stopped batting the ball around and stepped closer. "You have freckles. On your nose and under your eyes. And your nose has a little hiccup." He mimed running his finger over the bump, but did not come close enough to touch me. Wearing only a bright red one piece that stretched over my torso, rode high on my hips, and compressed my still-inconsequential breasts, I felt suddenly self-conscious about my lack of clothing, as if the exposure of my body were flirtation on my part, and not the standard uniform of a lifeguard.

"Izzy kicked me in the face when we were five."

"Did she really?" Toby laughed.

"Swimming accident. She was practicing her butterfly." I wasn't sure why he was giving me a litany of all the ways I did not look like you. I didn't think they were meant as pickup lines, though they definitely had that effect: I gooed up inside, the way I used to when Derek spoke to me. Part of that was probably because we were alone and I was wearing hardly anything and that I couldn't help but feel drawn to him. I took a purposeful step back and said, "Are you going to hog the ball now?"

He stepped back, too, and fisted the ball in my direction. "God,

Izzy would have hated this game." He laughed as some memory of you danced across his face.

"You do realize we haven't *actually* been playing tetherball?"

"We haven't?"

I shook my head. "Not at all. Though you're right. Izzy wouldn't have been able to stand this lazy back-and-forth tapping."

"True. I meant because of the ball, though. *Every game has a ball*." He heightened the pitch of his voice to mimic your confident cadence. *"It's so uncreative and boring."*

I smiled, his impression spot-on. That sounded just like something you could have said. And I realized Toby didn't just bring on memories of the loss of you. He was the key to you. To the life you'd had that I hadn't paid enough attention to. The international swimmer. The late-night swims you'd probably taken with your teammates in hotel pools. Jokes shared in countless locker rooms. Toby, there to lend a shoulder when Coach pushed you too hard, when you were droopy-eyed at those four a.m. practices, when you didn't get the times you'd wanted at trials.

A light rain started to fall, and we shared a knowing smile. I needed to do more than just chat with Toby at work if I ever wanted him to open up to me. I thought of Pat's party. Which Toby hadn't been invited to. Because of me. Not because I'd told Pat not to invite him, explicitly. But Pat took his cues from Nadia these days, who I'm pretty sure he had a crush on, and Nadia was standoffish around Toby on my behalf.

Of course, if I was trying to befriend Toby, the natural thing to do would be to invite him to Pat's party. Maybe I could get him drunk enough to tell me all his secrets. The thought made me smile as Toby batted the ball back around.

A familiar weight of nerves sat in my center as I turned the ball around in my hands and thought about asking him. I remembered telling you and Petra a couple summers ago about how skittish I would get before talking to Derek. Funny how I had no trouble with words when I wanted to put pen to paper, but when it came to speaking them, they often clogged in my throat. Your advice had been to power through. Petra's was softer, telling me to wait until I had a natural opening. Relationships shouldn't be forced.

But I had to force this one with Toby, and so I took your path. "Pat's having a graduation party this weekend." I took a breath and made myself slow down. "You should come."

He blushed. *Shit. Did he think I was asking him out?* Did *I just ask him out?*

"Thanks, but . . ." Toby pushed a hand through his hair.

"I just mean . . . Pat totally won't mind. He likes you." Pat liked everyone, but I didn't need to be *that* honest with Toby. "And most of the other guards will be there."

"Ah." Was that disappointment on his voice? He toed a pebble in the sand. "Yeah. Okay. Maybe."

Maybe. Relief flowed through me. *Maybe* wasn't *yes*, but it wasn't *no*, either, so it felt like a victory.

TEN

To Kill a Theory

THE ALMONTES LIVED ABOUT A HALF MILE FROM THE MURPHYS, with Bottomrock almost directly in between. I met Nadia at her house before Pat's party so we could get ready together.

While Nadia collected supplies from her cosmetics drawer, I pulled out your phone. Looking at your photographs had become my pastime. I was on IzzyWareSwims, paused at a photo of you and your friend and teammate Bryce. He had his arms around you, and you were both huddled over and laughing, like he'd just tackled you from behind.

"That's a great photo," Nadia said as she dumped tubes of mascara and lip gloss on her dresser. "Can I?"

I handed her the phone.

"Her boyfriend?"

"Just friends." I knew, at least, that there was nothing romantic between you and Bryce. He was gay. I was impatient for the phone back—I didn't want Nadia to realize it was yours.

"You know, I used to think you two were impossible to tell apart. But it's not so hard, actually. She's really fierce-looking. In like a

68

pretty way. You're pretty in a quiet way." Nadia was still looking at the photo. I shifted. "Thanks."

"Ugh. I hate trolls. Who's WhisperingWahoo, anyway?" She finally handed the phone back.

"Just some anonymous gossip from her swim team." Whispering-Wahoo had commented on this photo: *Now the #WahooWhore thinks she can turn a queen. #UglyBitch #MissPompous.*

"I'm sure your sister told this person off."

"Yeah," I agreed, because it seemed like something you would have done, though really I had no idea. WhisperingWahoo hadn't commented on your personal account, and I hadn't paid enough attention to your professional one. You'd never mentioned the cyber-bullying. Because it hadn't bothered you? Or because it had, so much that you couldn't bear to bring it up? Guilt nagged at me for not knowing.

"So." Nadia tossed me a tube of mascara and another of lip gloss. "What's the deal with you and Derek? When Pat invited him, he asked if you'd be there."

Since Petra's comment about Derek, I'd been on the lookout for my former crush to exhume itself, but so far, nothing. Derek's fair hair had darkened from Barbie blond to dirty blond, and he was experimenting with some orangy scruff on his chin that played at being a beard. The roughness suited the sharp angles of his face, but it didn't make me swoon. Neither did the fact that he might be coming tonight, apparently just to hang out with me. Toby was coming, too, hopefully. "There's no deal."

"She says with ruby-red cheeks."

I leaned closer to Nadia's vanity mirror as I unscrewed the

mascara. "Anyway, I don't think Derek's into me." What I meant was I wasn't into Derek. Why couldn't he have liked me last summer? Had I changed that much since you'd gone?

"Oh, Derek is into you. But you don't seem super into him anymore."

"Anymore?" You and Petra were the only people I had told about my Derek crush. Nadia and I had barely been friends back then.

Nadia just shrugged.

I swapped the mascara tube for Nadia's blush. "I invited Toby."

"I thought Toby made you uncomfortable?"

"I'm getting over that."

I caught Nadia's reflection in the mirror as she set her makeup down and turned to watch me. I kept dabbing at the blush, waiting for her to say something or stop studying me. After a few moments she picked up the mascara tube again and resumed applying. "I guess you are," she said. Then she added, "He wasn't hooking up with her or anything, was he?"

"I think they were just friends." But I planned to find out for sure tonight.

"I guess I've been a bit rude to him, haven't I?" Nadia said.

"Don't worry, I have, too."

"You're totally justified."

"And you're not?" I said.

"Do you think this is too much?" She meant her blush. I told her no.

Nadia glanced at the clock.

It was time to go to a party.

———

PAT MURPHY LIVED in a large, chaotic, cluttered house on a wooded property in the same neighborhood as Nadia. Luckily for the Murphys, it was a warm, clear summer night, and the party was being held largely in their backyard. A folding table was set up for beer pong and another for flip cup.

Two dozen people were already milling about, playing at one of the tables or else bopping heads to the folk rock Pat had blasting. No one was stupid drunk yet, but a few were on their way.

This was not my crowd. Most of Pat's friends were the friendly and loud sort. I guess they were the clique defined by their lack of cliqueness. Nadia fit right in because she could talk to anybody, though tonight she seemed focused on talking to Pat. I had a few quick drinks as I glanced around for Toby. I think I'd convinced myself his *maybe* meant *yes*.

In another life, we would have spent the night of our graduation with Petra. I remembered the night of our eighth-grade graduation, how we'd had a sleepover and Petra and I had begged you to sneak out with us to go night swimming at Bottomrock. Man, I hadn't thought of that in years. You'd said no. That you didn't break rules and had been excellent at resisting peer pressure.

Petra's absence—your absence—hit me then like a vise around my gut. Our best friend for more than a decade, and I hadn't even thought to invite her to this party. Instead I'd thought to invite Toby, who still wasn't here.

The night dribbled on. More and more of our classmates trickled in, and Toby was not among them. I played quarters with Nadia and a couple girls she knew from debate club. I was roped in to judge as Pat and Nadia alternately critiqued and praised each other on their respective speeches (they'd both given one, Nadia as valedictorian, Pat as the class-elected speaker) while getting increasingly touchy.

There's a lot I should probably tell you about the graduation you missed. The missteps in the music, the messages people had chalked on their mortarboards. But any other details I might add would just boil down to this: Graduation should have been a day I shared with you. I was beginning to realize these sorts of days would crop up now and again, ad infinitum. Days with momentous would-be joyful moments tinged by your absence. Days like our birthday, sure. Graduations. One day, maybe, a wedding, or the birth of your future nieces or nephews. But also quieter days. When I spied a strange bird in the backyard. When I first kissed someone new.

Neither Toby nor Derek had shown up, but I wanted to give Nadia some alone time with Pat, so I left them to flirt and climbed up the porch steps, sitting down in the first chair I reached. It was a slanted wooden chair with wide, flat armrests, just like the one in our own backyard, where Dad liked to sit and watch birds. I had a memory then, a novelistic flashback of you and Dad setting up different kinds of bird feeders in the backyard and betting on which ones would attract the most birds. All night my head had swarmed with thoughts of you. You were not okay, you claimed, but where did *not okay* fall on the spectrum of *elated* to *despondent*? I told myself I was being selfish—I was trying to have fun while you might be out there somewhere, alone and distraught, otherwise you wouldn't have run away in the first place. You would have come home by now. In one sense, your not-okay-ness made sense with you running away. An okay person wouldn't abandon her family without a word. Sometimes I hated you for leaving. Mostly I just missed you.

Your phone was in its new usual place, tucked in my pocket. I slipped it out. Tonight I flicked through the shots you'd taken in July last summer.

There were hundreds—literally hundreds—from trials alone. I knew you used to hand your phone off to Mom so she could document your meets, but Mom really went overboard this day. She wasn't as good a photographer as you, and it was surprisingly easy to spot the difference. Shadowy lighting. Skewed composition. Off-center framing. I flicked past dozens of half-blurry pictures of you dashing through the water, turning against the wall, or launching off the blocks. I couldn't even tell if these were from warm-ups or one of your races. But there was one photograph that gave me pause. You were in the background of the shot. I doubt Mom was trying to take a picture of you. It looked like she'd meant to focus on a group of female swimmers, among them your celebrity crush Katie Ledecky. But several feet behind the chattering women, you sat alone and hunched on a bleacher. I zoomed in on your face. Your brows were pinched together and your eyes were tense. Your bottom lip hung as if you were taking a deep breath. I've seen your face a million times, expressing a million different emotions. Your expressions were mine, too. And yet I couldn't recall ever having seen you look so . . . unnerved.

Was this before your big race, I wondered, or after? Could you have known immediately that your dream of attending the Olympics was dead?

Below me, Nadia squealed as her beer-pong ball landed in her opponent's beer. Then she touched Pat's arm, jumping and continuing to squeal. Somewhere in my tangled, depressive thoughts and drunk brain, I was happy for them.

My thoughts cycled back to anger. I should be having fun, but I wasn't. Where was Toby? I had his number because we were coworkers, though I'd yet to use it.

Hey.

That's all I sent. I didn't know what else to say. *Tell me the truth* was not really something a person could demand via text and expect results. As I waited for his reply, I thought about how he'd said he was working at Bottomrock to *face his fears*. What was he afraid of? What was I afraid of?

I couldn't wait for him to maybe text me back. I made a decision: I was going to Bottomrock Lake, at night. Something I hadn't done in all the time post-you.

Once I'd left, I texted Nadia that I was going to bed. If I told her I was leaving, she'd have insisted that she come along, and I didn't want her to abandon Pat when things were going so well. More than that, I didn't want her with me. She'd probably try to stop me from going to Bottomrock—I was drunk and alone and it was the middle of the night. Sober me would have known that this was a dumb idea, but I was determined to see it through.

My sandals crunched the gravel, adding to the chorus of nighttime chirps from insects and frogs. I kicked some pebbles onto dried-up leaves that lined the roadside. There weren't any streetlights on Bottomrock Drive, and most of the houses were recessed from the road and obscured by trees, but the lane cut a wide enough chasm through the woodland that I could see the sky brimming with starlight. When I walked onto the driveway for Bottomrock Park, the road narrowed, and the tree canopy crafted shadows. I didn't begin to question what I was doing—the eeriness of being alone in the woods and the dark—until I reached the parking lot. There was one car in it.

Someone was here.

That in and of itself wasn't unusual. Families would sometimes camp on Bottomrock's shore, but I knew no one was scheduled for tonight. The car probably belonged to a couple who'd come to hook up. They could be on the beach, or in the woods, or even still in the car. As I neared, though, I could see it was empty. I stopped at the top of the walkway to the beach, and from the parking lot all I could see was a glint of moonlight on the sand fifty yards down the path. I couldn't make myself go any farther, so I stood there, glued, until an indistinct form began hiking up the path.

A few thoughts flashed through my mind.

That the people who thought you'd been murdered were right, and the person stalking toward me was a serial killer, lurking on the beach to await easy prey.

That it was Quimby, checking on the beach at night for no good reason, and I was about to be fired for trespassing.

That it was you.

The person who approached was tall, with wide shoulders and a lean body. It wasn't Quimby, and it wasn't you. I'd never believed the serial killer stories. Still, my heart hammered. I told myself it was the alcohol. I also told myself I should call out to this person, or run away, or *do* something. Then the shadows fell away and I knew who I was looking at.

"Teddy?" Toby's voice shook on the word, uncertain. He stopped walking for a moment.

"It's me." I backed up into the parking lot and the moonlight.

Even though not fifteen minutes ago I had texted him, I did not want to see him here, of all places.

He resumed walking and joined me in the lot before he said anything else. "I thought . . ." He bit his lip, then twisted his head to the side so he wasn't looking at me. He didn't have to finish his sentence for me to know what he'd been about to say. He'd thought I was you. "Never mind." He stuffed his fists into his pockets. Frogs filled our silence.

"Why are you here?" I demanded, more loudly and harshly than intended.

Toby's eyebrows cinched. "I was going to stop by the party but . . . I've been coming here sometimes, since." Another sentence he did not need to finish.

"Why?"

"To figure out what happened."

His answer was a douse of water to my rising dander. Everything fell flat. I managed to sputter, "Don't you know?" His reason for working at Bottomrock. I'd convinced myself it was because he had something to tell me, about what had happened to you.

"I've gone over it again, and again, and again." He kept his hands fisted in his pockets. "Everything she said, everything she did. I see her walk into the water and I . . . It doesn't change."

"What d'you mean"—my words were stringing together, and I'm not sure if it was the beer or my panic that tied the knots—"it doesn't change?"

"Like maybe going over it again, I'll remember something that she said, the way she said it. Maybe there'll be this gesture she made, or, like, a sound I heard when I was on the path. Maybe there'll be *some clue*. But there's nothing."

I stood very still, thoughts trilling. I heard the words he said but was slow to process them. I had to take each one and wring it out like one of your swimsuits after practice. I tried to convince myself he was lying, but I was already beginning to accept that he wasn't. He looked confused and sad and maybe even a little scared.

"You didn't help her?"

Running a hand through his hair, he said, "I didn't know she was in trouble."

"No." I shook my head. The question hadn't come out right. I tried again. "You didn't help her run away?"

He exhaled long and slow. "No."

"And you didn't see anyone else there that night?"

Another deep, languid breath, in and out. "No."

And on that sigh I believed him: He didn't know what had happened to you any more than I did.

My throat felt swollen. All this time I'd been holding out hope that Toby knew something, and that if I just buddied up to him enough, one day I would know it, too. But if he had been telling the truth all along, then I was faced with the prospect of never knowing what had happened to you, and that was too much. I dropped to my bottom. Jagged stones and dried leaves prickled my legs. I pressed a hand to either side of my heavy head.

"Teddy?" Toby's fingers grazed my shoulder. He was squatting beside me. "Are you okay?"

"I'm fine," I said. And then, "I'm drunk."

"Pat's party?"

I nodded. "I was wai—" I stumbled over the word. "Wai-waiting for you." He rolled from squatted to seated. We sat side by side, quiet. I calmed.

"Why did you want me there?" he asked after a time.

"I was going to ask what happened that night."

"Oh." A beat. The frogs still sung. "Do you still want to hear it?"

"No." Not if it meant I still wouldn't know what had happened to you.

"'Cause I can . . . I mean, I don't mind. . . ."

But he did mind, and I wasn't going to be that cruel. "D'you have any water?"

He brought me a bottle from his car. It was nearly full, and I drank about half of it before I pulled it away from my lips. "Thanks."

"You're welcome." He sat beside me again, his hands dangling uselessly over his lap. I had mine wrapped around the cool metal bottle.

"Happy graduation, by the way," he said.

"Thanks. You too."

"Mine's next week."

For some reason, I laughed at that.

"What'd I say?"

"I dunno." I twisted my hands over the bottle. Despite the gravel digging into my legs, it was peaceful, sitting in the parking lot beside him listening to the forest sounds. There was something about Toby—his quiet nature paired with his goofy attitude, perhaps—that I found calming. Had he calmed you? Is that why you'd called him, instead of me, that night? Had you asked him here to tell him whatever it was you'd planned to tell me? This is what I should have asked him, but as I thought about your liking Toby in a more-than-friendship way, the question morphed before I could get it out. "Were you together?"

"Huh?"

"Were you seeing Izzy?"

"Seeing?"

"Was she your girlfriend?"

"Oh. No. I mean, I see why you would think that, but no. We weren't together."

"But you came out to meet her in the woods. And she dressed up."

"Dressed up?"

"That's what my dad said."

"I don't know. Maybe. It was dark when I got here. But there wasn't anything romantic about it."

"For you. But what about for her?"

"You think she lured me here so we could cheat together?"

My head shot up, and the world spun for a moment as I stared at him. "What?" Maybe I was far drunker than I realized.

"I know you don't know me that well, but Izzy was too loyal to cheat on anyone," Toby said, totally serious and completely oblivious to my confusion.

"No." I shook my head. His assessment of you was right. You *were* loyal. But even in my inebriation I knew: to cheat with Toby, you had to have had someone to cheat on.

The earring at the campsite. How you'd dressed up before leaving the house that night. The midnight meeting. All these things could be connected by one person.

You'd been hooking up with someone.

Why hadn't you told me?

Ever since I'd confided my first crush to you, in elementary school, you hadn't once talked to me about someone you liked. You came out to our family as bi over the dinner table at twelve years old and since then had only ever talked about people as attractive in an offhand way. You talked about athletic celebrities, and especially guys and girls on the USA swim team, but you never mentioned anyone from real life. Your only kiss was with Jenna Parsons in the ninth grade, after Petra dared you both to do it.

Toby was reading me now and realizing that I hadn't known. He looked incredibly guilty at having spilled your big secret, if that means anything to you.

"Who?" I had to talk to this person. Maybe they could bear witness to the night you disappeared.

"Teddy, I'm sorry. I thought—"

"It's not your fault she didn't tell me. Who?"

"I don't know."

"Then how d'you know she was dating someone?"

"Maybe *dating* isn't the right word."

"What's the right word?"

"Come on, Teddy, I really didn't know she hadn't told you. I figured she was just keeping it a secret from other Wahoos."

"So it was a Wahoo?" I tried to remember you telling me about your swimming friends. There was a girl, our age, tall with long, dark hair. I'd seen her at a number of your meets. She was good-looking, but so were all of your swimming friends because they were all in top-notch swimming shape. I remembered this girl taught you how to shave some time off your finishes. But the way you talked about her, it was more of a professional admiration than a romantic one. That was the way you seemed to talk about everyone on your swim team.

"I thought so. Or someone she met at a Wahoo party, anyway."

"Well, what pronoun did she use? He? She? They?"

"I don't remember. Teddy, are you okay?"

"I'm fine."

"I'm really sorry she didn't tell you." Toby placed his hand on my knee. He had big hands, which were good for swimming. You'd always complained that your hands, which were just average-sized, were your weakness. Bigger hands could cup more water, serve as better paddles. He circled his thumb once before he pulled his away.

I drank some water and thought about your last text to me. Maybe you'd been planning to tell me about this secret relationship, but that didn't explain why you'd waited. What else had you lied about? And then it hit me: You'd been keeping secrets. If you had one, there could be others. You'd been lying to me and you were good at it, and that's why I hadn't been able to find you.

Toby plucked a weed and threaded it through his fingers. "Do you . . . do you come here sometimes, too? At night I mean?"

"No. I haven't been down to the lake after dark, since, well . . ."

"Did you want to go down now?"

"Not anymore."

"Do you want a ride, then?"

"Yeah, all right."

We got up. My head felt lighter, almost airy. I drank more water. "The car's my mother's," Toby told me as he climbed in. It was a sensible sedan, very neat inside. I told him I was staying at Nadia's, just down the road.

I settled in, ready for a few minutes of awkward silence, but before we had left the parking lot, Toby spoke. "So are you ever going to tell me what's so awful about the changing stalls?"

"Nothing's awful about them."

"You said they had a reputation."

I glanced sideways at him just in time to catch his barely restrained smirk. His looseness loosened me—though the buzz I still had going undoubtedly helped—and before I knew it, playful words were spilling right out of my mouth once more. "The real story might be kind of terrifying."

"Try me."

"I don't know how to start."

"I thought you were a storyteller?"

I was an out-of-practice storyteller, but Toby made me want to meet his challenge. I took a breath, remembering the ghost stories you used to ask me to improvise on our family camping trips. "One dark and stormy night—"

"Is this the real story or a fake story?"

I skewed my head at him, brows narrowed. "As I was saying, one dark and stormy night many years ago a couple people came to Bottomrock Lake to get into some mischief."

"Like sex?"

"No. We're in a family park."

"Actually, we just left it."

I groaned. Every time he interrupted with a question, I became more determined to spin his yarn. "So, this was back in the seventies, and they came here to neck."

"Oh, I have so many problems with that. First, you said there was no sex."

"Necking isn't sex."

"Second, people didn't call it necking in the seventies."

"When did people say necking?"

"I don't know. The fifties?"

"Well, what did they call it in the seventies, then?"

"Maybe *jump your bones*. Which is scary-sounding, so it works better for an urban legend anyway."

I sunk into my seat. "You're such a backseat writer."

"So you admit that this is a fake story?"

"Never." But I stopped narrating, my momentum fading with the fog in my head. "It's that driveway on the left."

The front porch lights were on. As I unbuckled, I glanced at Toby and imagined that this was what it would feel like at the end of a date, with nervous butterflies flitting about in my stomach, as if at any moment he might lean across the seat to kiss me and I was waiting for the cue to meet him. But this wasn't a date, and Toby wasn't leaning over, and despite the fantasy that had flashed in my head, I did not want to kiss him.

"Good night, Toby."

"Good night, Teddy."

Still drunk, I zagged up the walkway to the porch. When I reached the door I turned around, expecting him to already be driving away. But Toby was still sitting idle at the top of the driveway, hands on the wheel, waiting to see me safely inside.

ELEVEN

Your Secret Partner

ON THE NIGHT BEFORE ONE OF YOUR BIGGEST SWIM MEETS, YOU
crawled into bed with me and ran through your worries. They
weren't about not doing well. They were about doing *too* well. What
if you set a record, gained a sponsorship, joined Team USA, won
gold medals, made history? What if you peaked at seventeen? you
asked in all seriousness, your face bunched up in panic. I promised
you that you wouldn't peak. You'd find something else to excel at
because you were built to trend upward.

You and I told each other the things we didn't tell anyone else.
You knew all about every crush I'd ever had. I knew that you only
read the CliffNotes for the books in our English classes. You were the
first person I told when a short story of mine won the Massachusetts
Young Authors' Contest, and when you got invited to the Olympic
trials, you actually burst into the bathroom and yanked back the
shower curtain so you could see my face as you relayed the news.
So how is it that you had your first relationship with someone, and
I didn't know? Maybe—hopefully, probably—that was what your
last text message had been about. But why not tell me right away?

You'd told Toby, for some reason, but not your twin. God, I wanted so badly to have one of your stupid apology letters. I knew exactly how you'd write it, too: They were always so curt and melodramatic. *Dear Teddy, I'm sorry I fell in love and didn't tell you. Will you ever forgive me?* I'd have settled for an old letter to reread, but lacking the power of foresight, I hadn't bothered to save any.

I probably owed you an apology letter, too, for not picking up on the waves of distracted happiness you must have been emitting. I'd been too busy scrambling to take every extra shift at Bottomrock I could, storing up my overtime pay to ensure we would have the best gap year imaginable.

Your phone was on the nightstand, on top of mine. The guest bed comforter puffed up around me as I rolled toward it. I started scrolling through your photos once again. This time looking for a cuddly selfie or an arm-in-arm pose. Something romantic.

One ominous question hung above all others: Why hadn't the secret partner come forward during the search for you?

Were they someone you'd run away with? Or someone you'd run away from?

I stopped flicking at a series of you in the woods, smiling wryly at the photographer. Bottomrock? I wondered. But no. Bottomrock doesn't have a forty-foot cliff jutting out over a quarry, nor a rusted crooked sign exclaiming NO JUMPING.

You were facing the camera, arms spread in king-of-the-world fashion, back to the sign. Then you were turned around, looking down at the water, your body steeled in determination. Then you were falling. Falling. Falling. The photographer hadn't gotten the exact moment you'd hit the water, just the splash afterward.

Do you have any idea how stupid that was? Mom yelled at you in the backyard. I'd just gotten home from work and was opening the window in the bathroom before taking a shower.

It's fine! I'm fine! you shouted, before swiveling away from her.

I'd meant to ask you what was so stupid. I couldn't now remember what stopped me.

I thought about you as I got ready for work, and on the walk there. You'd gone cliff-jumping last summer. You were adventurous, yes, but never reckless. When had you started playing fast and loose with rules? Who'd been your photographer? The secret partner? Toby? And would I have gone, if you'd bothered to invite me? You could convince me to do a lot of things, but jumping off a forty-foot ledge likely wasn't one of them.

The day after Pat's party was cool and gray, the kind of day with crisp air and layers of velvet clouds. With luck, the beach would be empty for most of the morning, if not the entire day. If it was, I'd soon have time to sit and continue looking through your phone.

I had no such luck. Derek sent me to the dock as soon as we arrived, where a pair of siblings wrestled and dunked each other on repeat.

My gaze bounced among the kids in the water, and I tried to remember what you'd told me about the Wahoo parties that summer. For an elite, private swim team with a national reputation, the Wahoos partied hard and often. You'd claimed you only cared about the parties as a kind of career networking. But suddenly there were all these Wahoo parties where you could have been shotgunning Natty Lights and leading faceless swimmers to empty bedrooms.

I sat cross-legged on the dock, my rescue tube balanced atop my knees. Waiting. Heart dropping as more patrons—four kids and two moms—trotted down the path. The moms set up folding chairs and the kids recruited Pat—who then recruited Nadia—to help them excavate a system of tunnels in the sand. Soon my kids in the water joined the excavation, and I was relieved of dock duty.

It was still brisk, still cloudy, and Derek told me that as long as the sand city was under the constructive supervision of Pat and Nadia, I could do as I pleased. He was going to take the rescue board out for some exercise. Which really meant he was going to paddle it to the middle of the lake and float.

"Where's Toby?" He hadn't yet gotten to work when Derek sent me out to the dock, so I hadn't seen him since last night.

"I sent him around the path, to pick up trash."

Trash collection was one of the "cleanup tasks" on Quimby's list, which after opening weekend had been promptly neglected on the guardhouse refrigerator. End of summer seemed so far away. I wondered why he'd given Toby—but none of the rest of us—some work to do, then figured that was my fault. Derek, too, had picked up on Nadia's coldness toward our newest coworker. "You didn't have to do that."

Derek shrugged. "It's no biggie." He hoisted the rescue board off its rack on the side of the guardhouse. "So, are you okay with this whole tree thing?" he asked.

Now it was my turn to shrug. My feelings on Petra's tree-planting idea were complicated. I knew she was getting something out of it, and I was glad for that. But attending another memorial for you was not exactly something I looked forward to. Last week we'd decided on a dogwood. Apparently their red berries were favored by birds, which we figured you'd like.

Derek took the board to the beach, and I plopped into a folding canvas chair on the sand and checked your personal Instagram. I was familiar with these posts, but now I would look under the lens of romance.

I went back more than a year pre-disappearance. Your posts fell generally into three categories. Category 1: our family. Mostly shots of the two of us, but also ones of you and Mom at some away competition or the whole family doing an activity, like that time Dad took us all bird-watching. Category 2 was friends, which was mostly shots of you, me, and Petra. At first, I didn't dwell on any of the photos in these first two categories. They couldn't tell me anything. But after a while, I began to linger.

On the "artistic" photograph you took of Petra's dropped ice-cream cone on the sidewalk along Revere Beach, with her pink-over-purple polka-dotted toenails peeking into the corner of the frame. The juxtaposition, you said, of the happy toenail polish and the sad melting ice cream made the photograph *award-worthy*.

On the incredibly out-of-focus selfie you took with Mom from the top of the CN Tower, posted as proof to Dad and me that you did actually take time out of your swimming schedule to be a tourist, as promised.

On the group shot of Petra, you, and me at the top of Mount Sunapee, right before you challenged us all to go down the double black diamond trail.

Interspersed among these, of course, were the photographs of Category 3: Wahoos. Most were group shots, but even among those, I hunted for evidence of flirtation. Eyes angled at some person instead of the camera. You and someone standing close together. A glancing touch. A targeted smile.

I flipped through photo after photo, my bare feet tucked into the sand. There were too many candidates, I realized. The Wahoos were a large team, taking the best swimmers from all across eastern Massachusetts. But some kids appeared over and over again—your closest friends on the team. I recognized their faces but knew few names.

Toby could give me names, provide context for the moments you'd posted. Where was he? Derek had sent him trash collecting a while ago. Even if Toby had decided to check the entire Lake Trail for discarded bottles, he should have finished by now. Tucking a walkie-talkie in the pocket of my shorts, I started off around the lake.

I weaved around the picnic tables and grills and rounded on the dirt path that marked the start of Lake Trail. The trees here were sparse, the trail only discernible by the cairns Derek and I had placed along its bends, two summers past. God, I had been so excited to tell you about that day. I'd spent half an afternoon with no one else but him! Even though nothing had happened—we were just looking for suitable rocks and constructing towers in literal silence—to sixteen-year-old me it had felt significant. When Derek and I had finished crafting cairns, as we were walking back to the beach, he'd chuckled and said, "Teddy, all of yours look like something out of Middle Earth," and that was true. I had been purposely placing all of my rocks in jagged, fantastical stacks, whereas all of Derek's were neat pyramids about one foot high. You and I spent a while lying across your bed, guessing as to whether he'd meant the comment as flirtation. When we finally settled that he must have been flirting, in the vein of "I find your dorkiness adorable," we'd then discussed how I could casually mention wanting to watch the trilogy again, to see if he would show interest in watching it with me. As you know, despite how you'd practically scripted our dialogue, I never worked up the courage to ask him.

You were always so good at talking to people. You could go right up to someone you'd never met and fall into conversation. You knew how to be comfortable anywhere, with anyone.

About a half mile away from the beach, Lake Trail crossed the dam that divided Bottomrock Lake from the river. Water babbled over stone. I found Toby sitting on the dam, feet in the lake, drawing.

So much for "trash collecting."

The leather cover of his notebook was frayed at the edges. The pages inside were beginning to curl. His hand flicked as he changed the direction of his lines, sketching a woman in a strange outfit. Like a spacesuit mixed with a soldier's attire. Sleek, conservative, and tough.

"Derek's going to want to see at least one empty can."

Toby jolted in surprise. "I have five." He jerked his thumb in the direction of a trash bag, laid at the edge of the dam. "And hello." He continued to draw a woman who didn't look quite human—her eyes too big and too far apart, her ears very small, near perfect circles.

"Someone you know?" I cringed inwardly at my terrible joke. I was still learning how to act around Toby. I wasn't angry with him anymore. Whatever had happened to you, I didn't think it was his fault.

"Sort of." Toby gave the woman what looked like a sheath for a slender dagger. "This is Moira."

"Ah. I understand perfectly now." I shuffled over dried leaves that coated the boardwalk.

"It's a character sketch."

"Like, for a story?" Your other best friend tells stories like me? Except I didn't write stories anymore.

"Mostly I get these ideas for characters and settings and stories and I draw them."

He stopped sketching when I sat down and dangled my feet above the water. They didn't quite reach, but Toby kicked some water up to wet my sandals.

"So do you do anything with the characters you draw?" I asked.

"One day I'd like to write a graphic novel. Except I'm better at drawing than writing."

"You could get better at writing. Or get a partner." I slid to the edge of the dam and stretched my foot until my toes dipped into the lake.

Toby laughed.

"What?"

"Nothing. It's just— Never mind," he said.

"It's something."

"It's not really. Izzy said something similar once, is all. About how she wanted to find me a writing partner." Toby looked at me, his meaning clear. Flustered, I flicked the water with my toe and gazed at some lily pads clustered along the shore.

"Can you help me with something?"

He slid his notebook into his pack. "I can try."

I showed him the photo I'd landed on as most representative of your Wahoo friends. "I thought maybe you could tell me who all these people are." It was a shot of you, him, and five others—three guys and two girls. You were all in your team suits standing in front of a pool. It was one of those shots that had been taken before everyone was ready, or maybe by several different smartphones, so no one knew which way to look.

"Well, that person in the middle there is your sister. And on the far right, that's me."

"Hardy-har-har. I know Bryce, too. But the others?"

"It's our practice lane." He pointed. "Kevin, Nico, Meiling, and Jasmine."

"Nico and Meiling are on either side of Izzy?"

"Yeah. What? You think she was dating one of them?"

"I have to know." Everyone was in a racing uniform, with water slicking over sleek muscles. Your eyes were angled to your right and slightly upward. Maybe toward Nico, but maybe also toward a camera in that general direction. Nico had a nick in one eyebrow that made him look dangerously sexy and a closed-lipped smile that looked like the smiles we used to make fun of when our parents brought us to Red Sox games and we saw the pictures of the ballplayers on the Jumbotron. Some players went for a happy, friendly look, whereas others aimed to intimidate. Our favorites were the ones that fell hilariously in between, too stern to be happy, too silly to be intimidating. That was the sort of smile Nico wore. On your other side, Meiling had gone for a full, toothy beam, a real ear-to-ear grin that looked genuine. She wasn't looking at the camera, either. I think she was looking at you.

"Well, it wasn't Bryce or Jasmine—they both only date guys. I suppose it could have been Nico, though he isn't really the boyfriend-type," Toby said matter-of-factly.

That was exactly why I needed Toby. "Okay. And Meiling?"

"Maybe. Why are you trying to figure it out by looking at pictures, anyway? I'm sure whoever it was, she must have been texting with them, right?"

I shook my head.

"Come on. She can't have been *that* determined to keep it a secret," Toby said.

"She had the occasional text with some other Wahoos, but there's nothing romantic. Or regular, like there would be with someone you're dating."

I looked again at your photograph. Meiling was tall with long limbs and wide shoulders that tapered to a narrow waist. The lankiness would have looked goofy on most people, but her dark eyes had a seriousness to them, while her happy smile read as friendly. Jasmine did look goofy. Her head was tilted, her eyes opened comically wide, and her tongue peeked from between her lips. Kevin had shaved his head so close to the scalp that he was practically bald, but I could see you liking that commitment to the sport. I realized, studying them all, that I didn't have any clue what type of person you preferred. "Tell me about them. Maybe if I know a little about them, I can guess who she might have liked."

"There were other people on the team, you know. Not just the ones in this photo."

"I know. But these are the people she knew the best, right? Look." I showed Toby more photos. Again and again, you had posted photos of people from your practice lane. Candids of Kevin and Bryce arm wrestling, of Meiling, eyes closed, headphones on, psyching herself up for a race. The whole group hanging off some large panther statue as Nico pretended to strangle it. These were your swimming friends.

"What if you could meet them?" Toby said.

"You want to bring me to practice?"

"I was thinking a party. You invited me to one, and I didn't show up. I figure I owe you." He blushed. "And anyway, most of them go to things like that. Plus the other people who aren't so photogenic. Maybe someone could tell you."

You had never invited me to a Wahoo party. I always thought it was because you knew I didn't like hanging out with groups of people I didn't know. But I liked the idea of attending one now. Besides providing an opportunity to uncover your mystery partner, it would give me a glimpse into the world you'd known apart from me. "When's the party?"

"Fourth of July."

This weekend. I could handle that. "Okay. Let's go." The sheet clouds were beginning to thin. The sun would be out soon, and that meant people would come to the beach. I was half-surprised that Derek hadn't called us back yet, but then I saw him still out on the water, lying flat on the rescue board with his back to the sky.

"Have you ever been cliff-jumping?" I asked Toby.

He laughed as he kicked the water. "Bryce can't even convince me to jump off the high-dive."

"Did you know that Izzy went? Last summer?" I showed him the photographs.

"A date?"

"Maybe." Also another secret. Another reckless act, from a girl who used to go out of her way to find a crosswalk before she'd cross the street. That summer was a cryptex, and your partner felt like the key.

If I was going to go down this road, looking for you with Toby's help, it felt like he should know the truth behind my curiosity.

"Her passport is missing," I blurted, too afraid to look at him. I'd already seen the pity—from Mom and Dad, from Petra—as they decided I was making a big deal out of nothing. I didn't want to see it on his face, too.

"What do you mean, 'it's missing'?" He kept his tone even, and I wondered—hoped—that he might actually be considering the clue meaningful, like I did.

"It's gone. I looked all over, right after she disappeared. It's not in the house. There are a few other things missing, too. Some camping supplies she bought that summer."

"And you think . . . she left the country?"

I nodded.

"So these questions you've been asking me . . ." Toby swirled his feet in the water. "About the person she was seeing. About the midnight meeting. You're trying to figure out really what happened that night, aren't you?"

I listened for skepticism on his voice. Hearing none, slowly, I said, "Yes," and waited for an interjection of judgment.

Instead he said, "I'm in."

"You're 'in'?"

"Something was going on with Izzy last summer. I should have seen it, but I didn't. So I'm in with you. All the way. Whatever you need, however I can help. I want to find out what happened to her, too."

I smiled. I'd started the day off with a new lead. Now I had something else I didn't have before: someone to help me find you.

IF YOU WERE going to tell your secrets to someone who wasn't on your swim team and who wasn't me, it would have been Petra. A part of me wanted to go over to Petra's house and have her admit that of course she'd known you were dating so-and-so, because then the mystery would be solved. But another part of me hoped you hadn't told Petra. I didn't know if I could handle it if you'd confided in her, too, when you had lied to me.

That night, I walked over to Petra's after dinner. Ms. Schaffer answered the door.

"Teddy, how nice to see you!" She hugged me. "Petra's in her room." She flicked her wrist down the hall as she bellowed to her daughter. Petra was expecting me, of course. I'd texted her. When I nudged open her door, she was deep in her closet, shuffling through dresses. A few had been tossed haphazardly onto the bed.

"What's all this?"

"I'm glad you're here. You can help me pick out something to wear." Petra's six-month anniversary with Karen was coming up. She threw a blue, flowery sundress into the pile on the bed. "So what did you want to talk about? My mom likes the dogwood idea, by the way."

"Izzy."

Petra lingered on a green strapless still hanging in the closet. "What about Izzy?"

"Do you think she was dating someone?" I sat beside the pile of dresses and traced my fingers over the dappled fabric of an orange halter top.

Petra passed the green dress and continued down the line. She took her time answering, which was how she had always been whenever I tried to talk to her about what had happened to you. "Why are you asking?"

"Toby said she was."

Petra stepped out of the closet and sat down in her desk chair. If she'd known, her face gave nothing away. Pulling her knees up against her body, she said, "And we believe Toby?" Right after you'd gone I had told Petra about my doubts regarding Toby's account of that night and how I thought it was possible, probable even, that you were still alive. She'd tilted her head at me, her face oozing sympathy and doubt.

"Yeah, I do."

"Well, who?"

"He said he didn't know. Just that at the very least, he thought she was dating, or hooking up with, someone from the Wahoos."

Petra swiveled the chair. Her fingers drummed against her shins. "Why would she start dating someone and not tell us?" So Petra hadn't known.

Unless she was lying to me, too.

Despite how we'd fallen away from each other this past year, Petra still knew how to read me. She stopped drumming her fingers. She sat up straighter. "You think she told me." It wasn't a question.

"Not exactly . . ."

"Yeah, you do." The words were a sharp slice through a thin veil. "Or at least, you think it's possible she told me. You think it's possible I've been carrying around this secret about Izzy. With the police looking for any information about what could have happened? You think I'd just sit on this big thing? God, Teddy!" Petra stood up, her face growing flusher with every octave her voice rose.

"No, I just . . . I had to be sure. I'm sorry. You're right, there'd be no reason for you to keep it a secret after she left if . . ." I trailed off because I saw Petra's pitying expression on the word *left*. She sat down again.

"Teddy," she said quietly. "I thought you'd stopped that."

"I did." She meant looking for you. I decided not to tell her that I'd started up again.

"Because, it didn't . . . I mean you didn't find anything before and . . ."

"I'm not looking. I found something out that surprised me and I'm curious. That's all."

She blinked at me.

"I swear."

Petra nodded, though I wasn't sure if she actually believed me, or was just pretending to. She resumed her nervous finger drumming. "Honest: If Izzy was hooking up with someone, she didn't tell me. But, I mean, okay. Don't take this the wrong way, but does it matter?"

Of course it mattered. I checked my annoyance before I spoke again. "It does. Because she was obviously keeping it a secret for a reason."

"Yeah but . . ." Petra's voice was so low she was practically whispering. "It's not like it's going to change anything."

"Of course it changes things," I said. "It might help us understand what happened."

Her fingers drummed some more. She was no longer looking at me. "Teddy . . . we know what happened."

"We don't know why," I said, skirting around her comment.

"Well, I mean. We kind of do?" She waited a beat as I stared at her. "We know she was upset. Because of trials. And she'd been withdrawing."

"She wasn't withdrawing, she was . . ."

"She told me she was too busy to hang out, like, every time I asked, for weeks before, and she would get quiet sometimes and just kind of go somewhere in her head and . . ."

Had you? I shook my head. After trials you were upset, yes. But you'd bounced back. You and I had spent hours in REI, picking out packs and a tent and moisture-wicking shirts. We'd mapped out our route. We'd signed up for a wilderness survival course. You'd been so excited about the things we were going to do: scuba diving and surfing and cage diving with great white sharks. And this was all for a trip that was still a year away.

I knew what Petra wasn't saying. What she thought you'd done that August night. I'd known other people thought that of you, but I hadn't known Petra to be one of them until now. I shook my head. You weren't so hell-bent on swimming in the Olympics that you wanted nothing else out of life. "Izzy didn't."

"I'm not saying that," Petra said quickly. "I'm just saying . . . she was sort of lost that summer. And it made her do something reckless."

"If she told you she was busy, maybe it's because she *was* busy. With this new relationship."

"Yeah, maybe, but, Teddy . . . even if you find this person, it won't . . . She'll still be . . ." Petra stopped. I knew what she'd barred herself from saying: *She'd still be dead.*

See, here's the thing that Petra didn't get: I knew there was a possibility you were dead. Of course I did. I simply chose to have hope that you weren't.

"I just need to know."

Petra bit her lip again. There was something else she wanted to say, something she was debating internally. You know how Petra was—growing up, she'd had trouble speaking her mind. But in the last couple years, she'd gotten better at it. Gained confidence. Found a little bit of footing to express herself.

"I'm not trying to be insensitive, really I'm not. I just . . . I don't think I can keep talking to you like this."

"Like how? About Izzy?" Most people did not want to talk to me about you. They got uncomfortable, they changed topics, they avoided eye contact. Even as Petra talked to me about planting your tree at Bottomrock, she was more focused on planning the event— what tree, where to plant it, who should speak and what they should say and whether there should be food or music—than she was on remembering you.

"About Izzy like she's coming back." Petra's face flushed as she broke eye contact. A few tears caught in her eyelashes, and she blinked them away.

"Okay, so we won't talk about that. You should go with the orange dress." A random selection on my part, but I wanted a response. I crossed my arms and waited.

"Yeah, maybe." Petra didn't get up to look at the dress. She just kept looking at me like she was looking at your ghost.

I wanted her to start up a conversation. Any other conversation. I wanted some gesture from her that she still wanted to talk to me, even without you. But she didn't say anything else, and I didn't say anything else, and after a few moments I told her I was tired from lifeguarding and had to go home. As I left her house and walked to ours, I moved my friendship with Petra to the list of all the things I had lost, post-you.

TWELVE

Independence Day

FOURTH OF JULY. BEFORE I COULD GET TO BRYCE'S PARTY AND ALL your potential partners, I had to contend with an entire day at Bottomrock. An entire sunny, hot day with a full and *busy* park. Whistles blared. Children squealed. Even Snappy surfaced in the swimming area, floating like a mossy log and igniting a ruckus. I was sun-zapped by the time we had to set up for the Greening Country Club's Independence Day Lobster Barbecue. It took us an hour to bulldoze sandcastles, add fresh charcoal to the grills, pitch canopy tents, and unfold tables and chairs. We had barely finished by the time the country clubbers started throwing lobsters on the grills.

In the outdoor shower, I power-washed off a day's worth of sunscreen, sand, and sweat. When I came out of the rickety stall, the lifeguards had set up the picnic table behind the guardhouse, and Pat had snagged us plates of grilled lobster and potato salad and Solo cups of white wine.

I turned down the alcohol, mindful of my long drive ahead to Bryce's house for the party. I had this idea in my head that it would just fall into place. Maybe I'd walk into the party, and someone would stare at me with widened eyes and slackened jaw, and I'd know immediately that *that* was the look someone would have if their missing ex-girlfriend's identical twin showed up unexpectedly. Or maybe I'd size up a few different people, and when I met yours, it would click.

This line of thinking was, at best, truly naive. But even though I wasn't writing stories anymore, I still had an imagination that wouldn't stop piecing together unlikely scenarios and convincing myself they were possible.

After dinner, Toby wandered over to the shore. Before I could follow, Nadia grabbed my hand. She swung it, once, in a wide arc, then released. Her face was ruddy from the wine.

"Want to hang out with Pat and me tonight? His brothers are launching fireworks."

I knew what Nadia would think if I told her I was looking into what happened to you again, which is why I hadn't. She wouldn't even have to actually say anything: Nadia was a master at telling people what she was thinking through facial cues alone. She'd rebuke me with one ridged brow and tightly drawn lips and I didn't want her guilt-tripping me ahead of the party.

I'd told Mom and Dad that I was hanging out with some Bottomrock guards after work and would be home by curfew. Not exactly a lie, since I was hanging out with one Bottomrock guard, and I did intend to be home by curfew.

"Can't," I said to Nadia. Toby ambled along the water's edge, kicking pebbles into the lake's lapping baby surf.

"You've been getting along with Toby lately."

"Uh-huh," I nodded, not in the mood to elaborate on that, either. Toby had been giving me a Who's Who of Wahoo swimming in our down moments at the park.

Nadia didn't push. "Well, have fun with whatever it is you're doing. I'm going to see if they gave us any more wine."

I started toward Toby again, and suddenly Derek popped around the corner of the guardhouse. "You know, I've gotten so used to seeing you in a red bathing suit, it's almost weird to see you in clothes." He smiled.

"Believe it or not, I have a closet full of items that aren't red one-pieces."

"You clean up good. That's all I'm saying." He smiled again. He was smiling a lot. I smiled back at him because, well, it was hard not to return a smile with Derek grinning at me like he was in a toothpaste commercial. I imagined you yelling at me to flirt back. Hadn't you coached me, trying to up my confidence so that I'd be ready for a moment like this? I used to take your advice about guys, even though you had no romantic experience, because you were so good with people in general, and I wasn't. I'm better now. I still probably overthink things, and I still rely on sarcasm, but your voice is in my head, helping me to not feel so alone.

Even though you had no experience. According to Toby, I was wrong on that front.

"So how do you like BU?" I said to distract myself.

"I love being in Boston." As Derek talked, I nodded along. I remembered how you'd called him G.I. Ken. The square jaw and stern eyes of a marine. The California-surfer swoop of his Barbie-blond hair. And then I thought of Toby, your friend, who you had trusted with at least some of your secrets and who I was trying so hard not to like because . . . It was getting a lot harder to remember why I'd promised myself that Tobias Smith was off-limits.

Derek was telling me stories about his freshman year of college, the wrestling matches he'd won and the parties he'd attended, and I halfway listened to him out of politeness, throwing in just enough commentary to keep him going. But I was also listening to the clubbers, the way I listened to park patrons from the chair, scanning conversations for anything interesting enough to pass the time.

When I heard your name, spoken by a couple of women who'd made the bold decision to wear high heels on the beach, I tuned out Derek entirely.

"And you know that this is the lake where poor Isabella Ware died last summer." *Isobel*, I thought, knowing if you'd been there, you would not have hesitated with the correction.

"I'd forgotten all about that." The second woman gazed out at the lake, as if suddenly expecting to see your corpse ascend from the weeds like a swamp creature. "Terrible accident, wasn't it?"

"I don't know that it was an accident at all," said the first woman.

"I thought she drowned?"

"They never found a body. And there was a young man here with her that night." My eyes darted to Toby, who had paused at the edge of the lake, gaze on the gossiping women, face pale.

"And he . . ." The woman trailed off.

"Who else? Boys can hardly be trusted."

Something strange and powerful took hold of me then. I stomped over to the women. "Enough. You don't know what you're talking about, okay? So just shut it."

"Excuse me, young lady—"

"No." My pulse was racing. My whole body shaking. I had never done anything remotely like this before. "The police never found any evidence that Izzy was murdered, okay? And they cleared 'the young man's' name because there's not a scrap of evidence that he did anything wrong. So stop yammering about a real-life tragedy like it's an episode of your favorite crime drama and just—"

"Teddy!" Derek hissed at me. "I'm so sorry, ma'ams." As Derek continued placating the women, I crossed the beach to Toby. He was still pale, but a small smirk had started to stretch across his lips.

"Thank you," he said softly.

"Yeah, well, you already know I think she wasn't murdered, so . . . No big deal."

"But I didn't know you could be so . . . Izzy."

I could feel my rage simmering down. "I didn't, either." I felt empowered. Energized. Maybe this person I was becoming—this one who could yell at insipid strangers, who could stand up for a friend—was the person I needed to be to dig up your secrets.

THIRTEEN

What We Talk about When We Talk about You

AFTER THE COUNTRY CLUBBERS LEFT, AFTER THE TABLES AND CHAIRS were folded and the canopies unpitched, after the trash was emptied into the dumpster and the guardhouse locked shut for the night, Toby and I lingered at my car, waiting for the parking lot to clear by mutual unspoken agreement before we would talk about our mission. The sun had only just begun to sink behind the hills, and the park was still shrouded in the pink hues of twilight. A nervous energy twined inside me, left over, perhaps, from the rush of defending Toby and your friendship with him.

As the last car crunched gravel, I asked Toby if he told anyone I was coming.

"I told Bryce. He said it was cool." He buckled in. I started the car.

"Does he think we're . . ." I glanced at Toby. He was looking at the trees illuminated by the car's headlights as we passed. His hand rested on the door handle, his finger picking at a patch of loose fabric.

"He knows we've been working together. I guess he thinks we're friends."

I nodded, adjusting my hands on the wheel.

"Is that okay?" Toby said, and I glanced at him again. He was watching me now, uncertain.

"Is what okay?"

"That I told him we were friends."

"We are friends."

Toby relaxed a little. His lips curled, a slight smile that waned before he spoke again. "Right. But he doesn't know that we want to, umm . . ."

"Interrogate people?"

"I was thinking we'd be more subtle than that."

"Honestly, I have no idea how to be subtle about this," I said.

"Maybe start by just talking to people. And eventually, you could just ask. I mean, if it's not the first thing out of your mouth, if you've got a conversation going . . . I don't see why anyone would lie about it."

"You don't?"

"No." He sounded surprised. "Do you?"

I saw a lot of reasons why someone would lie. Because you'd asked them to, and they wanted to honor that. Because they were afraid of what people would think, if it came out now that they'd been dating you that summer. Because they were involved, somehow. "I think the bigger question is why it started out as a lie."

"You don't think it was just because they were trying to be private?"

"*Private* means not making out in front of everyone. Not posting photos on social media. It doesn't mean secret." And you had kept this secret from Petra and from me. There had to be more to it than worrying about your teammates' gossip.

"Maybe she liked keeping it secret," Toby said. "Could be exciting that way?"

I bit my lip, considering, no longer certain of how well I'd known you. It was hard enough to accept you'd kept this secret from me. To then believe that you *liked* keeping me in the dark? I couldn't go there. "Izzy's practical. She does things for a reason."

"True. But she also did things for the challenge."

He had me there. You pushed yourself constantly, in more than just racing times. Your energy levels were almost inhuman. Sometimes I wondered if you'd leeched them from me, in utero. "What's the challenge in lying and sneaking around? We're sneaking around. It's not so hard." I glanced right just enough to catch Toby's grin. "Not like that."

"I didn't say anything." But the smirk was still there, a mellow sheen in his chocolate eyes that dulled the edge on my nerves.

"So you really don't know anything more?"

Toby rolled his thumb over the frayed spot on the door handle. "What do you mean?"

"What exactly did she say? When she said she was in a relationship?"

"It was a long time ago. But I don't think she used that word."

"What word do you think she used?"

"That she was with someone? Had met someone?"

"And she just flat-out told you this?" I tried to say this without jealousy. I didn't own the patent on being your confidante.

"No, no. It wasn't like 'Hey, guess what, I'm dating now!' It was . . . Okay, so last summer, I was seeing this girl Taryn from the team. And Taryn and Izzy were kind of frenemies? And Taryn was jealous of, like, any other girl I ever wanted to hang out with, so Izzy told me to tell her that it was okay for us to hang out because she was with someone, and I said I'm not going to lie to my girlfriend and she said, very adamantly, that it wasn't a lie."

"And you didn't ask any follow-ups?"

"I didn't memorize the conversation. We were in the middle of a practice set at the time. We had to start swimming again soon."

"But, like, later, you didn't want to know who it was? You said she said she met them at a Wahoo party."

"Yeah. Sometime after that I asked her if I could meet this person, and she got all coy and said maybe, and I asked if I knew them, and she got coy again and said something about how I might. So I asked her how *she* knew them, and she said they got together at a party."

"But this was when?"

"I don't remember. I'm sorry, Teddy. I really don't. Sometime last summer."

"And you never talked about it again?"

He shrugged. "She kind of left me with the impression she didn't want to talk about it. So I didn't bring it up." He paused to look out the window. "I wish I had. Because right now? Looking back at all this? It was really strange that she was being so coy."

On that, he and I wholeheartedly agreed. *Coy* was never a word I would have used to describe you. "I have some theories about why she would've lied."

"Like?"

"So Izzy wasn't telling *anyone.* Maybe because people might not have approved if she did."

"So who'd get widespread disapproval?"

"Someone older."

"Some of the alumni come around over the summer. Come to parties like this," Toby offered.

"So there's a theory. Or . . ." I paused. I had zero evidence for what I was thinking, but I couldn't stop myself from thinking it. The idea had sparked when I tried to think of who in your life you had spent time with but would lie about liking, and had burned slow since. "Maybe her coach."

"Connors?" Toby shook his head. "He's married."

"So?"

"He's in his thirties."

"So?"

"Izzy was seventeen. Barely."

"And she was probably the most exciting swimmer he'll ever coach."

For a moment I could see Toby's eyes flickering, considering. But then he said, fast and hard, "No. I know him, okay? Connors is a decent guy. Besides, no one is going to tell you anything if you start accusing him of . . . of what you're accusing him of."

"It's just a theory."

"It's wrong."

"Okay."

We didn't say anything for a few minutes. Toby asked if he could put on some music. He was scrolling through a playlist on his phone when I said, "Sorry. I shouldn't have suggested that."

"It's okay."

"It's not even my favorite theory."

He waited a beat before responding, probably still a little annoyed at me. "What's your favorite?" he said at last.

"That she was falling in love."

"Why wouldn't she tell you about that? That's a good thing, right?"

"Because Izzy was so focused on getting to the Olympics. I think she might have thought that if she admitted to anyone her priorities were shifting . . . and I'm not trying to say she was giving up swimming for love or anything like that, just that, maybe, she was allowing someone to share importance and that, I don't know, maybe admitting she was doing this would make it real. Would mean the thing she'd always said was her sole focus wasn't anymore. That she was just like every other dumb teenager. And if Izzy was scared of anything—"

"She'd have been scared of letting herself be ordinary," Toby finished.

"Yes, exactly. And then if Izzy Ware was suddenly in a relationship, everyone—me, my parents, her friends—we all would have been like, whoa, this person must be special, must be important, we'd better pay attention! I think she was getting tired of attention." Here's what my favorite theory about you and your secrets boiled down to: After all that time in the spotlight leading up to trials, maybe you'd craved time in the shadows.

"I like that theory," Toby said softly. "It seems like something she would've done."

Something lifted in me, having Toby agree with my assessment of you. We were on the highway now. "Have you considered what it means, if we find out who she was dating?"

"You want to ask them if they were there that night."

"And if they were there . . ." I'd been trying to avoid dwelling on this part, focusing instead on the first part of the equation. But if you'd met up with your person that night, after sending Toby around the lake, and this person didn't come forward to say they'd seen you . . . some of the reasons I could come up with for keeping *that* secret were very dark.

Toby didn't say anything for a moment, his face solemn. "The police never found any evidence of foul play," he said softly.

I nodded, agreeing. Another quiet moment passed before I had to change subjects. "Do you talk about her?"

"What do you mean?"

"I mean, with other people, your teammates, do you ever just talk about Izzy?"

"No."

"That doesn't seem fair."

"It's not. I wish . . ." He trailed off. I wanted him to keep talking. To not become one of those people who couldn't stand to bring up your name. My grip on the steering wheel tightened as I waited, trying very hard not to push. His hands flitted nervously across his lap. "I wish they would. Not like all the time. Just. So, for instance, last week we were doing suicide laps—"

"I'm going to need you to explain what those are."

"Back and forth across the pool"—he mimed the motion with his hands—"the short distance, very fast. Lots of turns. So we were doing these laps, and Jasmine asked when the last time was that someone actually made Coach's intervals, and Meiling said that she didn't think anyone ever had. But Izzy had. And I'm pretty sure Mei knew that."

You'd tagged Meiling in a number of your pictures. The lane-mate Toby had pegged as the smart, quiet type. I wondered if she'd be there tonight. I wondered if she'd see me and think for a second she was seeing you.

"Are people going to get weird, with my coming?"

"Little late for that, Teddy," Toby said in that droll tone he favored for humor.

"I could always take us duckpin bowling instead."

"I'm game if you are."

For a moment, I was tempted. Scrap the party and the investigation and bury your mystery once again. I'd been doing well, all things considered, these last few months. What was I thinking, trying to sleuth out answers to your secrets? Maybe your secrets had been kept secret for a reason, and I should trust that. Trust you.

But if I took Toby at his word, and I did, then you had lied to me. I wasn't ready to go the rest of my life wondering why.

"We're going to this party." I said this with as much gusto as I could muster, and I think I did a pretty good job of convincing Toby that my enthusiasm was real. "If people are weird, I'll deal."

"It's a weird situation, so yeah, probably some *will* be weird. At least a little, at first. But everyone loved Izzy and it's not like they're all refusing to talk about her. They just don't go out of their way to, you know?"

I did know. More than I wanted to. "We could talk about her."

"Haven't we been?"

"Not about what happened or why she was hiding things. Just about her."

"In general? Or now?" he said.

"Both. I don't know. I'm not trying to force it. So I guess, in general."

"Sure. We can do that." He nodded thoughtfully before he said, "Did you ever do that thing with her where you try to describe the plot of a book based only on its cover?"

I smiled, remembering. "It was a creative exercise. We used to do it during her swim meets when we were little. When we got older, she tried to make a game out of it. I always won."

"Wait. How could you make that a game? It's all subjective!"

"She made a scoring chart. Points for originality, for humor, for cohesive plots. Et cetera."

"Well, now we have to play sometime, using the chart." He smiled. We let the silence settle between us again, and then Toby said, "So tell me the rest of that changing stall story, with the necking." He waggled his eyebrows until I laughed.

"Which story: real or fake?"

"You're already ruining my suspension of disbelief."

"Well, we can't have that." I paused as I exited the highway. "So I think I said it was a dark and stormy night, a long, long time ago, back when necking was a thing, and two people named Tony and Thea—"

"Love the names. So creative." He smirked at me.

"Came to Bottomrock to jump each other's bones. And Tony was a bit scared of being in the woods at night, but he sucked it up, for Thea's sake."

"Nice twist on traditional gender norms. Go on."

I rolled my eyes. "This commentary isn't very helpful."

"Do you want me to stop?"

I shook my head. "Anyway, they were halfway undressed when they heard this sound—"

"What sort of sound?"

"Like a gurgling." At my gurgle, Toby laughed.

"Your sound effects are very effective."

"I'll make sure to use more of them when I finish telling the story later."

"You're leaving me in suspense?"

I nodded, just as the car's GPS announced that we'd arrived.

FOURTEEN

A Midsummer Night's Kegger

WHENEVER I MET ONE OF YOUR SWIMMING FRIENDS FOR THE FIRST time, I would get the *pause*. For a fraction of a second their eyes would open a little wide and their lips would part a sliver as they gazed upon an imperfect version of you. Same hazel eyes. Same flat cheeks narrowing to a divot in the bottom of the same rounded chin. But where your arms were toned and powerful, mine were strings. Where your stomach was taut, mine was soft. I have a curve at the hip that you don't and shoulders that curl like the corners of an aging paperback, where yours are straight and strong. My body was the way yours would have grown had you not devoted yourself to sport.

Of course, my worries about the inevitable *pause* had an added layer now that you were gone. After you, I got the *pause* a lot more often. In the months immediately after, some people, especially people who'd known you better than they'd known me, looked at me like I was something dug out of a grave. Petra had done it, and not so long ago.

Toby and I didn't say much as we walked from the car. I vacillated between imagining that your secret partner would reveal themselves immediately and imagining that Bryce would end up kicking me out for making his guests "uncomfortable." When we climbed Bryce's front porch, with dance-pop blasting from somewhere inside, I clutched Toby's hand. I was about to dive into your world, without you. He laced our fingers together and gave a small squeeze of solidarity.

The house was full of familiar faces, and I began to catalog those that I'd known from you and those Toby had told me about. Jasmine—the backstroker on your IM relay team—was standing in a corner of the living room, talking to a dark-haired, dark-skinned girl I recognized from some of your Instagram posts and whose name I was pretty sure started with a *K*. Other people drank and shouted over the music, laughed, played games. All these beautiful, energetic, competitive people. Toby led us through the hall in search of Bryce, who found us first.

"T!" Bryce made his way through a throng of people in the kitchen and joined us in the narrow hallway. His long, blond hair was slicked back and water dripped from matted strands, down his bare chest and damp board shorts. I wondered if he was perpetually scantily clad and soaked. I knew Bryce, a little. You'd talked about him often, and I'd met him at a few meets. But even if you had harbored a little crush on Bryce, he wouldn't have returned your feelings. Not in that way.

Bryce hugged Toby, then he hugged me, too, scooping me up a little. "It's so good to see you, Teddy," he said after letting me go. I hadn't seen him since that summer. The curves of his boyish cheeks had angled into a pointy jawline, shadowed by fringes of facial hair that were too sparse to shave. His shoulders were fuller, and he was taller than he'd been in the photographs—by a couple inches, at least. I'd been looking at your pictures, which had been taken at least a year ago. I buried the pang as I realized that of course your friends wouldn't look exactly as they had when you'd known them. Of course they would have grown.

Bryce asked, "Can I get you guys anything?"

"My usual, if you've got it. Teddy?"

"Oh, nothing for me."

"Got it. Be right back." Bryce dipped into the throng once more.

A few curious eyes peeped in our direction. "So this is a Wahoo party," I said.

"Everything you'd dreamed it would be?"

"And more." Really it had the same too-loud pop music, the same red cups, the same little micro-groups of people milling around, just like every other party I'd ever been to—which, to be fair, isn't exactly a huge number, but it's also not exactly a tiny one, either. I don't know what I was expecting. People in Speedos doing keg stands, perhaps.

Bryce returned with a cup filled with what looked like rum and Coke and another filled with a clear, fizzy liquid, which he handed to me. "Izzy's go-to," he clarified when I started to shake my head because I wasn't planning to drink. "I thought you might want to try it." Immediately curious—you'd had a mocktail of choice, who knew?—I sipped the drink. Sticky sweetness of a cherry-lime soda and pineapple juice overwhelmed me. And also, somehow, calmed me. It was as if having your drink in my hand was a little bit like having you there to break the ice. I thanked Bryce and took another sip. "So, Bottomrock, huh?" Bryce said. "How's Derek? Is he still working there?"

Toby told Bryce that Derek was head guard, and somewhere in the back of my mind I remembered Derek used to be a Wahoo, once upon a time. Bryce and Toby chatted a little more, but when I didn't have the buzz of alcohol to soften my self-consciousness, I was terrible with small talk. So I didn't even try. I simply blurted: "I want to know who Izzy was going out with."

Bryce's brows tapered, like he wasn't sure if he'd heard me correctly. "What'd you mean?"

"She was going out with someone before— And anyway, she was lying about it. To me, at least. Toby thinks it was a Wahoo."

Bryce pushed air through his lips in a silent whistle. "I didn't know."

"Welcome to the club." Toby patted Bryce on the back. "We're just curious." He glared at me, probably because I was being the opposite of subtle, which was not how we'd discussed handling tonight.

Bryce invited us to hang out on the back porch, which turned out to be halfway consumed by a crowded hot tub, water brimming at its edges. More people lounged in some wicker furniture, passing around a vape pen. A musky marijuana haze filtered slowly out through the porch screen. It wasn't a scene I was expecting. According to you, smoking was a direct attack on a swimmer's most valuable asset: their lungs. I guess I assumed that your teammates would have felt similarly.

Gazes drifted in our direction. Most alighted for a few seconds, curious and uncertain, before flitting away again. One person shot up from the wicker sofa he'd been slouched in and rushed at us, saying, "Izzy fucking Ware."

And then Nico, your lanemate with the sexy dangerous scar on his eyebrow, scooped me off my feet and kissed me on the mouth.

"Uh, not Izzy." I touched my lips as my feet found firm ground and Toby's steadying hand found my shoulder. The uninvited kiss had been relatively chaste, and its deliverer was up-in-the-stratosphere high. Still, that his reaction to me had been a sweeping embrace . . . maybe your partner was announcing himself, after all.

"Making friends?" Bryce chuckled while Nico at least had the decency, even in his state, to look aghast. "Oh shit, oh fuck, of course you're not Izzy."

"Because Izzy . . ." I wanted him to fill in the gap. *Izzy's in Australia, duh! I helped her run away and I'm still madly in love with her!*

"Would have had my balls for sure if I *ever* tried to kiss her. Not cool to just assume. So. Not. Cool. But you know how weird this is? Like, two seconds ago I was thinking about how your sister was like the best beer-pong partner and now *you're* here! The twin!" He laughed. Did he just say you had played *beer pong?*

"Hey, man." Toby shook his head lightly in warning. Nico's smile dropped. I'd never seen someone's excitement go from sixty to zero so fast. Nico said, "That was totally inappropriate, wasn't it? I'm a douche, a rude fucking douche."

I told him it was all right, and he relaxed, offering me his vape pen. I shook my head. "I have to drive later, so."

He nodded. "Want to be my beer-pong partner? You don't have to drink. I can drink for you. I did that for Izzy sometimes, too."

"Sometimes?" I stumbled over the word.

"You know how she didn't drink for, like, the days before a big meet." Nico shrugged.

Five minutes at this party and I already knew something new. You drank alcohol. Not as a rule, but sometimes. I told Nico I didn't want to play and crossed him off my suspect list.

Toby and I began to mingle our way through the party, working into a rhythm of subtle interrogation. It was still awkward as hell, but most of the people who'd known you were curious enough that they wanted to talk to us. And it felt natural for me to say, after pleasantries, "So tell me about Izzy the swimmer," and then Toby and I would listen to them reminisce about races you'd won by a fingertip, challenges you'd undertaken in practice. Apparently you'd spent a lot of time last summer accepting whatever athletic dare someone threw at you. At first you would suggest them yourself, "Do you dare me to . . ." but soon you didn't have to. It became a game on the team: Come up with a dare that Izzy can't beat. The dares got increasingly challenging, borderline risky. You swam fifty yards entirely underwater. You did backflips off the starting blocks. You treaded water with weights tied to your ankles. Honestly, learning about all these dares gave Toby's story about the midnight challenge a lot of credence, but it still didn't tell me why you were pushing your limits so regularly.

After a while I would ask who you'd been closest to on the team, and the person I was talking to would rattle off the list of names I already knew: Toby, Jasmine, Bryce. Meiling and Nico. Kevin, too, though his name didn't come up as often as your other lanemates'. And I would say, "So which one was she into?" like it was a joke and they'd laugh, too, and say something like, "I know, right? She could have had her pick." I was beginning to wonder if Toby had been wrong, if maybe he'd misunderstood or maybe you'd lied to him to keep his girlfriend from getting jealous, but there had been no secret relationship. Until Jasmine confirmed it.

"I asked her who like three times, and she just kept saying nobody special. I can't believe she didn't tell you, either. I was hoping you'd be able to fill me in!" Jasmine laughed. I tried to match her casual tone, but really, I was getting frustrated.

"Why even bother telling you in the first place, right?"

"She didn't, exactly. I caught her putting on makeup after practice one day, and when I asked her if she had a hot date, her face got all red, so I was like, Oh my God, you do! And she nodded. She had this big goofy grin on her face. I swear I'd never seen her giggly. Can you imagine?"

The answer: no. You hadn't shown me that side of you. Was there something wrong with me, that made you think you couldn't?

We bumped into Meiling in the kitchen—I don't know where she'd been all night; I'd been keeping an eye out—as she refilled her beer. She gave me the *pause*, more obviously and elongated than anyone else.

"Meiling, right?"

She nodded.

"Hey, Mei." Toby patted Meiling's shoulder. "You having fun?"

Meiling shrugged. "Tired from yesterday still."

"We did suicides for a half hour yesterday," said Toby, filling me in. As they talked for a few minutes more about swim practice, Meiling kept looking toward the door, her feet shifting around like she was waiting for the first opportunity to bolt. I thought, *This was your person.*

"You and Izzy were pretty close, right?"

Meiling bit her lip, looking at me out of the corners of her dark eyes. "No, not that close," she said softly, the way someone says something they regret.

"Huh. Well, she talked about you a lot."

From Toby, I got a glare. He knew I was lying. But from Meiling, I got one stretched, hopeful word: "Really?"

"I think she might have liked you." I ignored Toby's dagger

eyes. I did feel bad—an actual twinge in my gut, brought on by how Meiling had perked up at the idea that you'd spoken to me about her. But I had to try something different—wheedling my way around to asking about your crush wasn't working, and Meiling was the first person at this party who actively wanted to get away from me.

Her eyes darted to the floor. "No, she didn't." She took a long sip from her drink.

"What makes you think that?" said Toby, steering us back into truthful territory.

Meiling finally met my gaze full-on. She pressed her lips together. "I'm sorry. I'm staring. It's just . . . uncanny." And then she told us how she'd stayed late after practice, pre-trials, when you were swimming extra laps. She'd swum with you, and in between sets you started joking around as you practiced finishes, blocking each other from reaching the wall. With two hands stretched above your head in a powerful butterfly stroke you hit her dead-on in the chest, right on the breastbone. When you pulled your head out of the water, you were laughing, and she had tried to kiss you. You dodged. You told her you were sorry, you had someone. At first, she thought you were just making an excuse because you didn't like her the way she liked you, but the way your face flushed when you said it, the big, goofy smile. The giggles, from a girl who didn't giggle. She believed you.

Meiling didn't actually say this much. A couple sentences, and I got the gist. I could see on her face how badly she missed you.

I teetered back. Meiling smiled sheepishly and walked away with her beer. My heart was hammering, too much sugar, probably, from your overly sweet mocktail. There was a bowl of punch on the counter and I served myself a cup. I drank deep.

"Teddy that's . . ."

"I know."

There was probably more alcohol than punch in the punch bowl. I filled a second cup and took it with me outside.

"Teddy—" Toby said at my heels. He pushed a path through some people to get to me.

"She met someone *before* trials," I said, swigging the punch. All this time, I'd been assuming the secrets started after trials. When you'd lost your shot at the Olympics, it had messed you up. I figured that gave you some leeway to act contrary to character. But before trials you'd been excited. Energized. Hopeful.

Before trials, you had no reason to lie to me.

Toby reached for my hand as I swirled on the lawn. When he caught my wrist, he reeled me in. I needed so badly to be comforted that I didn't second-guess it, I simply huddled against his chest while he held me.

"You really ought to just tell her," someone said from behind us.

A small congregation of people had followed us into the yard. Bryce and Nico and Jasmine, and a few girls I didn't know, including the blond who had spoken.

Toby dropped his arms. "Taryn," he warned, just as I said, "Tell me what?"

Toby's ex-girlfriend took a couple crisscrossed steps in our direction, swaying enough to send a spurt of beer over the rim of her cup. "You've been trying to figure out who your sister was with? But it's obvious, isn't it? You're standing right next to him."

Confused, I stepped back from Toby as Nico jumped forward, catching Taryn on the elbow. "Let's leave them alone, hey?"

She shook free. "Why does everyone still love that pompous bitch?"

"Okay, that's enough, now, let's go inside." Jasmine was at her side, too, gently tugging her other arm. Taryn relented.

"Is she right?" I spun to Toby.

"No. She's drunk. It wasn't a good breakup. She quit the team. I didn't know she'd be here tonight." He ran a nervous hand through his hair.

"Why did you break up?"

"Because of Izzy." I arched my brows, and he clarified, "Because Taryn thought there was something going on between Izzy and me."

"Was there?" I had to ask again. This time, he hesitated. "No."

"Then why do you look like you're lying?"

He said nothing.

I pushed away from him and stormed back into the house. Leave it to me to have to cross a sea of your drunk teammates before I could return to my car. My head was spinning a little, but I'd only had a couple drinks. Taryn's words echoed. *You've been trying to figure out who your sister was with? You're standing right next to him.* Odds had to be on the guy you'd talked about more than any other person on the team. The guy you'd called gorgeous. The guy you'd brought to the park for a midnight swim. Yet. I believed Toby when he said it wasn't him. Maybe simply because I didn't want it to be him.

Something else needled me about what Taryn had said. *Why does everyone still love that pompous bitch?*

Miss Pompous was one of WhisperingWahoo's nicknames for you.

Suddenly I wasn't trying to go home anymore. I was going to confront Taryn.

I found her on the front porch, clustered along the railing with a gaggle of girls, vaping. They all looked younger than me, by a year or so. Taryn's three friends glommed around her, a protective shield.

"You should apologize," I demanded.

She held her head at an angle, half her face hidden by a pane of hair. She breathed in on the pen before handing it off to one of her friends, who passed it along without taking a hit. "What for?" The words snapped.

"For the things you said to Izzy that summer."

She made a show of rolling her eyes. "I barely said two words to her that summer."

"You said a lot online."

"Can you go now?"

"I want to know why you said what you said."

Taryn stepped forward, emerging from her alcove of friends. "About Izzy and Toby fucking?"

The harshness of her tone forced an image into my head that I did not want, for many reasons, though the most paramount in that moment, as my head buzzed, was a sharp jab of jealousy. It was quickly followed by anger. That Taryn, after spending a summer harassing you online, would say something now so clearly meant to rile me. That she would think I'd roll over and let her. In the not-so-distant past, I would have. But I didn't have you to fight my battles for me any longer. "And that's why . . ." I trailed off as a wave of dizziness twirled my brain. "You said all those mean things? Because you think Izzy was fucking Toby?" As the words squirreled their way out of my mouth, I started to snicker.

You: who until tonight, as far as I'd known, had only ever kissed someone on a dare. You: who had told me once that you didn't get why everyone went so gaga over sex—why kids our age rushed headlong into it, why there were so many movies and TV shows that involved characters doing a plotted will-they-won't-they dance, why certain people made it their life's mission to keep other people from having it. *This* you, fucking Toby in the shadows.

"Oh my God, you're mental," Taryn said. "You're laughing about this? He's probably the reason she's dead—"

At the word *dead*, I shoved Taryn hard enough that the drink fell out of her hand. Everything hung in place then, like a video tracking frame by frame. Taryn's dropped jaw. Beer dripping off her fingertips, soaking into her distressed jeans and in between the straps of her wraparound sandals. A red cup drawing a slow circle of booze on the porch boards. Her friends, wide-eyed and maybe slightly amused, but stunned into silence. I'd never shoved anyone before.

"Crazy bitch." Taryn spat the words. She shook her hand, flinging drops of beer into the air. I wondered if she was going to shove me back, maybe throw a slap, and we'd end up fighting. But too much time was passing. Taryn stalked inside, flanked by all but one of her friends.

The girl who stayed behind had brown skin; a small round nose; and short, dark hair lightened by a streak of magenta that fell across her forehead. I'd seen her earlier in the night, talking to Jasmine. She looked out into the street, like maybe she wasn't sure if she should be talking to me. "I'm sorry she said that." The girl's whisper was nearly lost to the party music bleating through the open windows.

"It's okay. I shouldn't have . . ." I stopped. There were a lot of things I shouldn't have done tonight. I didn't need to enumerate them all.

We stood still and quiet, watching the last of the beer trickle out of Taryn's cup and soak into the porch. I wasn't sure why she didn't just go inside after her friends. Maybe she'd decided it was time to get new ones.

"I was pretty new to the team when your sister . . ." The girl stopped, nervous, like she thought I might shove her, too, if she said the word. *Died*. It pinged in my head in all its forms. *Die, dead, died*. "I'd just joined that winter," the girl tried again.

"You don't have to be nice to me." It felt like that's what she was doing. Lingering out of guilt over having been mean by association to the girl with the missing twin. I didn't want her charity.

Flushing, the girl tucked a strand of hair behind her ear, only to have it pop back out and curl over her eye. "I'm trying to say—I was new, but I did know your sister a little. And . . ." She stopped again. "Well." Another pause. "Izzy . . . she made me feel really welcome," the girl said at last, and it wasn't just something randomly comforting to say. I could tell from the glisten in her eyes that she meant it. You would have been welcoming. That was your nature, and your enthusiasm for your swim team was infectious. "And also, I know that Taryn is full of shit sometimes," she added, and I laughed. It came out as a hiccup.

"I just mean"—and now her words rushed out, like she was eager to be done speaking with me—"she says Toby was cheating on her, but she says that about almost every boyfriend she's ever had. I doubt half of it's true. Okay?"

I nodded.

The front door opened. Toby looked at me, then at the dark-haired girl, but before he could say anything, she patted my hand once, awkwardly, then slipped quickly inside. He dawdled in the doorway, his lips parted slightly as he worked up to whatever it was he had come to say. I didn't have the energy to be angry with him anymore. I looked at my watch. It was almost midnight, and I was going to be late for my curfew. I started off the porch.

Toby asked me to wait. "Where are you going?"

"Home."

"You're not driving." He swiped the keys from my hand in some sort of ninja move I had not anticipated. I tried to get them back, but he fisted them so neatly I couldn't get purchase.

"I have to be home by midnight."

"Or you'll turn into a pumpkin?"

"Or my parents will think I'm dead." I hadn't meant to be so blunt, but I was tired of watching my words. Toby kept the keys fisted tightly even after I had swatted his knuckles four or five times.

"If you have to be home, I'll drive you. You're drunk."

"I'm not drunk. I had two drinks."

"Two Everclear punches that are only starting to really kick in now."

"You've been drinking, too."

"I haven't, actually."

"I saw you with one."

"It was just Coke. I don't drink."

I was still swatting his hand. He made no move to dodge.

"If you drive me, how will you get home?"

"I'll sleep on your couch."

"My mom won't like that."

"And she'd rather you drive drunk?"

"She'd rather you not be in our house."

"Why?"

"Because you're a souvenir."

"A souvenir?" He said it softly. He didn't ask me to elaborate; he just stayed quiet for a moment. Light whistled across the sky and then exploded in an array of pink and red. Toby spoke again, calmly. "Then I'll borrow your car and go somewhere else."

"Why?" I stopped trying to peel his fingers away from the keys. Even with my cloudy head, I knew that I'd hurt him.

"Just let me drive you home, Teddy. Please."

I surrendered, too drained to keep pretending he was the reason I had gotten so upset. The day felt so long ago, but when at last I crawled into the backseat and lay down, I was devoured by my exhaustion—from the sun and guarding, from the gossipy country clubbers, from Meiling and Taryn and the version of you that I hadn't known at all. I didn't want to think anymore.

"Seat belt." Toby climbed into the driver's seat.

I boosted myself up just enough to buckle the seat belt.

"Teddy, hey, you can sleep, but first, I need your address."

"What?"

"I don't actually know how to get to your house. I'll look it up on my phone."

"Just use the GPS."

"That's what I'm going to do."

"No. The car one. It remembers." I slumped backward once more. "Don't mess up my seat settings."

"I'm, like, five inches taller than you, I have to move the seat back." The gears whirred softly as the seat slid back. I heard him fiddle with the GPS.

Toby roused me when we reached home. He'd unbuckled my seat

belt, and was sliding his arms underneath me, one at my shoulders and one under my thighs. I started.

"Hey, sleepyhead." He lifted me out of the car.

"Where are we going?"

"You're going to bed."

"You're carrying me."

"I see your deduction skills remain intact."

Mom and Dad had left the porch light on, I could see insects buzzing around it, but all of the other house lights were out. They had finally stopped waiting up for me.

"Set me down."

As he lowered me to my feet, he kept a hand on either side of my waist, steadying me. The porch light spotlighted his face. Five weeks of regular sun had lightened his hair and shaded his skin. The small crescent scar on the underside of his chin moved as he swallowed. A moth flew between our faces and fluttered around the light.

"Can I borrow your car?" His fingers pressed lightly against the small of my back.

"Yes. But don't go yet, okay?" I tugged him toward our porch swing.

It rocked side to side as we crashed onto the cushions. Ungraceful as I was, I had dragged him on top of me. He had one foot still on the porch, but his other leg was wedged between mine. His chest skimmed mine with every breath. "You're still drunk." Which one of us he was reminding, I don't know.

I watched his eyes flick back and forth as he tried to figure out what to do with me, and then I slithered backward so our faces weren't so close and his thigh wasn't pressing between my legs, stirring up a thirst that I had no idea what to do with. He sat down on the other end of the bench, by my feet. I flipped around and edged toward him. Fit my head in the soft place where his shoulder met his chest. "I don't want to be alone right now."

He slipped one arm over my shoulder, anchoring me in his warmth. "That's funny," he said. "I don't want to be alone right now, either."

FIFTEEN

Your Purloined Hours

Mom's gasp yanked us both from sleep at dawn. The swing wobbled as we fumbled apart, making it harder to unthread ourselves. Mom barked a solitary command to each of us in turn: "You, go home. You, inside." Then she marched inside herself. I told Toby to ignore her and follow me in.

"How do you think it feels to walk down the hall and find out you never came home last night?" Mom snapped as soon as I got inside. Toby's shadow extended down the hallway.

"Maybe I should wait here?"

"I told him to go home." Exasperated, she started to pace.

"Mom, that's stupid. He's not going home."

"Why not?"

"Because we have to be at work in a couple of hours and he has no car." I was getting dizzy just watching her.

"What's he even doing here, Teddy?"

I couldn't tell her about the party, because she would want to know why I'd gone to a Wahoo party in the first place, and explaining *that* would mean explaining why I was once again searching for you, which I was definitely not about to do. So I abbreviated the truth. "He drove me home."

"Why?"

"Mom." I looked at the floor.

"She was tired, Mrs. Ware." This from Toby, who I could sense shifting behind me, awkwardly waiting out my daughter-mother spat.

"Well, maybe your curfew shouldn't be so late!"

Maybe it was the way Mom pretended I was the one who'd spoken, or maybe it was the way she pinned her scrutiny on me, so obviously and purposefully ignoring the boy who stood at the threshold between in and out, but I needed her to know that Toby wasn't the bad guy here. That he'd done a good thing, the right thing. "It wasn't because I was tired. I was drunk." I wanted to deflate her anger at him, and it worked. She stopped pacing and scowling and looked at Toby with something akin to relief.

And then quite abruptly, she was hugging me. "What's my one rule, Theodora?"

Even though I'd grown slightly taller than our mom, she had my head pinned down. I spoke into her shoulder. "Be home by midnight?"

I knew her anger had truly dissipated when my sarcasm garnered a chuckle. "Okay, my other one rule."

"If I'm going to drink, I'm sleeping over."

"No driving after drinking. No getting into cars after drinking." Her head shifted upward, eyes now on Toby.

"Toby doesn't drink." I wiggled out of her embrace in time to see Mom's skeptical eyebrow raise.

"It's true. My dad was killed by a drunk driver." This was news to me. I wondered if it would be news to you, too. At what point did or would Toby and I become better friends than you and he had been? When Toby confessed this, Mom touched her fingers to her lips and told him she was sorry.

"Next time, come inside when you get home?" Mom fingered the end of my hardly-held-together ponytail. "You nearly gave me a heart attack. And we'll have to talk about your drinking with your father."

I nodded. Up until now, our parents had been fairly cool regarding my alcohol consumption. When they found out I was drinking (Petra's mother told them, after we'd gotten carried away with a bottle of swiped wine in her basement, about a month post-you), they didn't forbid it. They did what a lot of our friends' parents were doing: sat me down, told me that they loved me, that they wanted me to be safe, and we had a pretty lengthy discussion about the dangers of alcohol and how my brain was still developing and I shouldn't overindulge too often, and well, I'm sure you can imagine the rest from there. It was one of the first growing-up moments I experienced without you.

Mom set me up with Advil and a giant glass of water in the kitchen. We ate cereal at the counter while she hovered, her gaze ping-ponging between us. Then she asked Toby whether his mother knew where he was. She did. He'd sent her a text last night, though he doubted she'd seen it. She was working an overnight shift at Mass General and was probably in surgery. Mom got quiet for a moment, uncertain, I'm sure, how to comment on this revelation, though I could see in her eyes she thought Toby's mother should be more involved in his comings and goings. But she pushed past that and asked Toby about the Wahoos. That she would willingly land on a conversational topic so close to you absolutely floored me. That's when I realized what she was doing with all the small talk: She was trying, like really trying, to put what had happened with you aside and treat Toby like she would a boyfriend, or at least potential boyfriend, a thought that made me fidget. Taryn's accusation still stung, and Toby hadn't fully accounted for why his ex-girlfriend was so convinced there had been something between him and you.

And yet, there *was* something between us. I mean, we had fallen asleep in each other's arms, which was brand-new territory for me. And I couldn't even dwell on what it meant or why it had happened or how I felt about it because Mom was watching us like she thought the second she left the room, we'd lunge for each other, and she hadn't yet decided how she felt about the idea of her remaining daughter caught in the thrall of Tobias Smith. So I didn't so much as glance at him as I shoveled cereal into my mouth, and Toby prattled easily about his most recent swim meet.

Dad came down and mussed my hair and only paused for a moment upon seeing Toby sitting at my side before he said hello like it was no big deal that the boy who'd watched you disappear was in our kitchen eating breakfast, though I saw him give Mom that look you called "married ESP." They'd have a conversation later and it would probably touch on why I was having unannounced sleepovers with a boy and it would definitely include the subject of how welcome Tobias Smith should be in the house.

But all of that could wait. For now, both of our parents were on their way to work, and Toby and I had time to kill before we were due at Bottomrock. I put our empty bowls in the sink and told Toby to follow me upstairs.

Your bedroom door was open. Mom must have looked in there for me. The door rasped as I pulled it closed. I pivoted fast and nearly crashed into Toby. Or, more accurately, into Toby's chest, inches from my face, close enough I could see the strained cotton fibers where his shirt stretched over his butterfly shoulders. I tried to ignore the hitch in my heart, and the memory of his body breathing against mine.

I continued past him. As I threw myself across my bed, the latch on my door clicked into place. Toby had closed it. "I think I need more sleep," I said, my face pressed into the bedspread, but I heard Toby shifting.

"Okay," he said. And then, "Should I go wait in the car?"

"Aren't you tired? It's, like, six a.m."

"It's after eight."

"Well, you're welcome to take a nap."

"Here?"

I rolled over. My brain was finally starting to process what I was saying. "Don't look at me like that. It's only practical. Because it'd be weird for you to nap in any of the other beds in this house."

"And it's *not* weird for me to nap in your bed? With you?"

"We just spent the entire night sleeping on a porch swing. This bed is far bigger and more comfy." To prove it, I rolled again, giving him room to sit beside me. And I *was* just being practical, I reasoned. As well as magnanimous. Inviting him to lie down next to me said *Thank you for driving me home and maybe saving my life.* The least I could do was make sure he had a comfortable place to rest until we had to leave for work.

Toby sat down on the edge of the bed and pulled out his cell phone. Bafflement doused the edges of my fatigue. I watched him play a phone game for about ten seconds before I said, "You're not sleeping."

"I'm not sleepy. You can sleep."

"How can you not be sleepy?"

"I'm well hydrated and used to early hours."

"So you wake up early even when you don't have early-morning practice?"

"I have practice this morning. I'm just not there."

I propped myself on one elbow. "You have practice," I said slowly, incredulous. "The morning after a big party?"

Toby tucked his phone away. "Coach doesn't care that yesterday was the Fourth of July. Practices after big parties are usually the best ones, anyway. Because everyone is extra groggy and surly."

"And that makes them the best?"

"When everyone is groggy and surly, Coach lets us warm up with watermelon wars."

"What the hell is a watermelon war?"

"Watermelons float."

Intrigued now and definitely less heavy-eyed, I pulled myself to my knees. "Go on."

"So if you grease watermelons up a little, they get slippery, right?" He mimed greasing a watermelon. "Then you throw them into a pool, so they're really tricky to hold on to. We split into teams, and we fight over the watermelon to try to bring it across to our side of the pool."

"And this is fun?"

"It's amazing."

"You're not messing with me?"

Toby shook his head. "Izzy hated it. She wasn't very good."

"At holding on to a greasy watermelon?"

"To be fair, no one's good. That's kind of the point. It's just stupid and hard."

You would have hated it, then. Pointless activities were never your forte. But Toby hadn't hated it. Even though he was smiling, and even though he was telling me all about watermelon wars in his playfully mocking voice, I knew he was missing out. Because of me. "You should be there."

Toby shrugged. "How would I get there?"

"You didn't have to take me home. That was never the plan."

"I wasn't going to let you drive."

"You could have called me an Uber. Or my parents. Or taken my car to practice this morning. Watermelon games aside, I know how big a deal it is to miss."

"But it's not a big deal. This was my first missed practice in two years, which is totally rare. *Everyone* skips every once in a while."

"Izzy never skipped."

Toby pressed his lips together and stayed quiet.

"She skipped?" I wanted him to tell me I'd misunderstood, but I knew that I hadn't. And quite honestly, I wasn't shocked to learn yet another thing you'd kept from me. I should have felt sorry for Toby: He kept giving away all your secrets by accident, while you weren't there to guard them for yourself. Instead I felt hurt, once again, by you.

"How often?"

"Not often," Toby said quickly. "Seriously. As far as I know, it was only two or three times. After trials."

"Did she tell you what she did, when she skipped?"

"I didn't ask. I figured she stayed home."

"It's weird, though, isn't it? That she skipped but told me and our parents that she was still going?"

"I guess it's a little weird. For Izzy."

"You think she skipped to see . . . whoever?"

"I really, really don't know, Teddy."

I collapsed against my bed pillows and folded my arms over my face. You'd lied about whatever relationship you were having *and* you'd lied about where you were going. What else had you lied about that summer? And how could I not have known? That was the most painful part. Your lies twisted me up inside, but my own obliviousness . . . that wrenched me completely.

Sometime before you'd gone away, you'd stolen hours for yourself. A seventeen-year-old skipping a handful of practices shouldn't be a huge mystery. But this was you. And you know the way you were. So you can see, can't you, why I was so unmoored by the news that the you I'd thought I'd known wasn't really you at all.

"Teddy?" Toby's hand rested on my elbow. "Are you okay?"

I wasn't, but I was working on it. Underneath the crook of my folded arms, I did a few breathing exercises. "I'm just thinking."

He pulled his hand away and shifted beside me. "All of this, it's about before," I said. Toby agreed. "And it's vague. Rumors. I wish there was some way to figure out where she went when she skipped." As soon as the words slipped through my lips, I realized there was. I sprung up and hurried downstairs. After snatching the car key off the hook by the front door, I thudded off the porch and tossed myself into the Avalon. A moment later Toby hopped into the passenger seat beside me.

"Where are we going?"

"We're not going anywhere." I booted up the GPS.

In the months immediately post-you, I'd done exactly what I was doing now: scrolled through the GPS's trip memory. Nothing seemed off to me then. Just as I imagine, if the police had done this same thing, nothing had seemed off to them, either. You hadn't gone anywhere strange or suspicious. You'd hadn't gone anywhere regularly that wasn't expected.

But I knew something now I hadn't known then.

"Maybe there's a little Holmes in you after all," Toby said as he realized what I was looking for. I was on the edge of my seat, literally and emotionally, hoping this computer had a memory large enough that it still retained the data from last summer. When the screen showed trips from a year ago, I calmed and focused.

"Has your practice schedule stayed pretty much the same summer to summer?" I asked Toby.

"Yeah, I think so."

I began to look through the trips for times that matched up with practice. Toby pulled up a calendar to help match up dates with days of the week. I started in June. Our favorite bubble tea shop on Woburn. That Italian restaurant we'd gone to as a family to celebrate Dad's promotion. That lake in Maine that Dad had taken us camping at. Each new item on the list was a memory of the last summer I'd spent with you. But none of these trips were ones taken while you should have been at swim practice. That fit with what Toby had said: You'd only skipped a few times after trials. I started into July.

The first skipped practice was one week after trials. On a Wednesday evening, you'd driven to Cambridge. I googled the address, but it was just a parking garage. The Wahoos practiced in Cambridge, of course, but you didn't need to park in a garage. The second missed practice—a Sunday afternoon—you'd gone to a beach in Ipswich. I knew the beach well. It was Mom's favorite. She loved walking the trails that snaked around the dunes. And eight days before you disappeared, you'd driven to a lake in Maine.

Dad had taken us camping in Maine a few times, but the name of this site, Lake Bear, wasn't familiar in the slightest.

"Why would she go here?" I looked at the Google Maps image of a kettle pond in the center of Maine. Dark water flecked with lily pads and ringed by spruce and maple trees. I opened a new browser to see images of the lake. There were hiking trails and campsites and a cliff that hung over the water, with a familiar sign that read NO JUMPING.

The week before you disappeared, Mom had just started taking me to colleges. She was excited to look at schools for their academic programs as opposed to their swim teams. I checked my email to match the dates of one of our early trips. Mom and I had been in Pittsburgh while you'd gone to this lake, jumped from this cliff. I didn't think you'd have gone with Dad. If you had, surely he'd have told me all about it. And he never would have let you jump.

But clearly you'd gone with someone.

I glanced at the clock. Toby and I had about ten minutes until our shift started at Bottomrock. Needless to say, we were going to be late.

WHEN WE ARRIVED at the park, Nadia was hanging life jackets up by the canoe launch.

"Has Derek said anything?" I asked her, already shooting up the steps into the guardhouse.

"No, he's too busy teaching Pat how to get himself beaten up." She rolled her eyes.

Sure enough, Derek had Pat's arm wrenched behind his back, locking him in a wrestling hold.

"Hey, guys!" Pat eked out as he squirmed ineffectively against Derek. Caught off guard, Derek let go. "You're late. Both of you," Derek said. Pat rolled his shoulder and flexed his wrist, red from Derek's hold. Derek's gaze flicked to Pat. "Next time I'll teach you how to get out of that."

"Aye-aye." Pat brushed passed us.

I shoved my bag into my cubby. "Sorry."

At my apology, Derek softened. "It's not a big deal. Slow morning. But don't let it happen again, okay?" He eyed Toby, who was wearing the same plaid shorts he'd left the beach in last night and a lifeguard shirt he'd clearly borrowed—I had a few that were oversized for me but fitted on him. Toby grabbed an extra bathing suit and excused himself to change.

"You doing okay?" Derek asked after Toby had left.

There was that question again. I was charged—I had a new lead in my search—and angry, at you for lying, and at myself for not knowing you well enough to catch you. Both left me with an antsy energy that was far from okay. "Yeah, fine, why?" I smeared sunscreen on my face.

Instead of an answer, Derek handed me his phone. He had Instagram open to WhisperingWahoo's account. There was a new post. A photograph of Toby and me in Bryce's backyard, right after our conversation with Meiling. Bathed in the glow of the porch light, the embrace looked sweet. The captioning, however, was anything but.

I guess sluttiness runs in the family. #WahooWhore #IsItIncestIfIBoneMyTwinsEx

"I figured you'd have seen it. Though by your face . . ." He ran a hand through his hair as he placed the other on my shoulder. "I'm really sorry, Teddy. Some people are jerks."

"Yeah," I agreed, feeling far away. The nerve of Taryn. "Some people are."

"Can I help you with that?" Derek gestured toward the sunscreen I was clutching. I turned around to let him get my back.

When Toby returned, I felt suddenly self-conscious that Derek's hands were kneading sunscreen on the back of my neck. I stepped forward, saying, "Good?"

Derek nodded. "Good."

Though it was a warm, clear day, Derek had been right when he'd called it a slow morning. A few toddlers waddled at the edge of the water, not far from their parents' arms. I twirled a stick in the sand and tried not to think about Taryn's latest post. Instead I focused on the trip you'd taken to Maine. It was too far for a day hike. You must have camped there. Is that why you'd bought those camping supplies I couldn't find? The only logical someone you would lie about camping with was whoever you'd been lying about liking/dating/hooking up with. You were seventeen. On a camping trip with a partner. So yeah, I can surmise what that meant. Romantic location, a tent, a sleeping bag for two, and not a whole lot of sleeping. Could there be another reason why you'd sneak off to some random lake in Maine? And now the cherry on the top of your deceit: You'd been serious enough with someone to go off on a sex trip, and still you'd been keeping it from me.

I thought of Taryn's allegation and dismissed it.

Nadia pulled up a folding chair beside me. "So, how was your Fourth?"

"Good," I said automatically.

"You sleep with Toby?"

"Yeah," I said, and Nadia practically fell out of her chair.

"Really?" She looked startled, maybe a bit concerned.

I came out of my own head and realized what she'd said. "I mean no, but . . . why did you even ask that?"

"Because I didn't think you were listening. You looked far away."

"Sorry. I'm . . . Tell me about your Fourth." I didn't want to talk about mine, and given the grin that threatened to burst from her constrained lips, I could tell she wanted to talk about hers.

"Pat and I hooked up."

"Seriously?"

"Just a kiss. On his back porch. His brothers were launching bottle rockets and when they were focused on setting them up, Pat said to me point-blank, 'Can I kiss you?' and I just nodded like some kind of robot and then he kissed me and said, 'Cool,' and ran down to the lawn to help his brothers. So I'm really glad you didn't smash Toby last night because that would have totally overshadowed my news."

"Ha, yeah," I said, remembering how we had spent the night together, swaddled. "So are you two like together now?"

"No? It's weird."

"Why?"

"Because we're both going to college in, like, less than two months and now is so not the time to get a boyfriend."

"Isn't he going to UMass? And you're going to Tufts?"

"Yeah, but it's still . . . I don't know." I'd never seen Nadia have this much trouble with words. She was flushed. I looked over my shoulder and saw Pat ambling back up the beach. He zigzagged to let a little kid chase him with a plastic shovel.

"So . . ." Nadia swatted my shin with her fingers. "Why *did* you and Toby show up together today?"

"Coincidence." I shrugged, feeling only a little bit guilty over the lie. I was growing more used to telling them, kind of like you. "Can I ask you something?"

"Absolutely." She leaned closer, like she thought I might tell her a secret.

"Have you ever gone out of town and not told your parents?"

"I've probably gone into Boston, or someplace like that, without telling them." She plucked a few weeds from the sand. "Why? Are you going on a trip?" She eyed me coolly.

"No," I said quickly. Then I amended. "Probably not. It's all hypothetical."

"Okay, where are you probably not hypothetically going?"

"Nowhere." I stirred a divot in the beach with my twig.

"All right. You don't have to tell me, I guess. But you know that this is like when you say you're asking for a friend. Nobody's hypotheticals are that specific." She waited a beat, giving me the opportunity to change my mind. Maybe I should have told her, not just about the lake in Maine, but about everything I was learning about you. Instead I kept my mouth shut and thought about how you'd gotten away with the Maine trip. A trip to Maine was not a lie by omission. Even if you hadn't stayed the night, the six-hour round trip would have meant a cover story, for Dad at the very least.

Nadia got up after a minute or so of my silence, and I heard her giggle as she joined Pat playing on the beach with some kids. I felt bad for shutting her out, but I couldn't tell her the truth. Nadia was—all of the Bottomrock guards were, really—one of the few people who treated me like I was still me. I didn't want to lose that.

—

BOTTOMROCK, AS ALWAYS, diluted time. As the beach got a little more crowded and sunbeams cut the clouds, we went up to a two-guard rotation. I took the chair while Pat swam out to the dock. Three small children toddled at the shoreline, their toes splashing up sand and water. A boy, tenish, in the deeper water, dove and resurfaced on repeat, bringing up some new wonder from the bottom of the lake each time he reemerged, only to drop it after a few seconds of inspection in the sunlight. An elderly man, Mr. Consuelo, swam slow laps of breaststroke in between the docks.

I couldn't push you and your trip to Maine out of my thoughts. I tried—God knows I wanted to stop thinking about it. Because what could I do, now, a year later? There was next to zero chance that I could learn anything about where you were now from going to Maine, because assuming the trip *was* in some way related to your disappearing act, which it definitely might not have been, any evidence that you may have hypothetically left behind would be long gone, washed or weathered away after almost a year. Going there wasn't going to tell me who you went with. This *logic* didn't stop me from scripting out another story. How you could have set up a campsite. Pitched a tent. Stored some clothes, some food, in one of those bear-proof bins. Stayed there for a couple of weeks, off-grid while the search for you was under way. And I know this theory was ludicrous. You weren't a fugitive in a mediocre crime thriller. You were a seventeen-year-old runaway in an age when our every move ends up documented online.

But what if. What if you'd done something ludicrous? And what if I could follow you, somehow? Retrace your steps, as best as I could, in the week before you'd disappeared. Why hadn't I thought to do this before?

Because I'd been so focused on after.

Of course, I understood that retracing your steps in the weeks before your disappearance was a long shot. But the mystery of you was morphing. It was no longer just about where you were. It was about who you'd been.

With thoughts of you churning, I counted heads in the water, my usual method for staying focused on the swimmers. The elderly man between the docks. The diving boy. Two kids wading. There had been a third, I was pretty sure. I scanned the beach, wondering if she'd gotten out to play on the sand. But she wasn't there. I looked back to the lake, panic rising as I scanned for her tiny form.

A dripping wet head popped up from under the water. Laughing and splashing. The panic that had reared for a millisecond receded. Though my pulse was still galloping over what might have been, if I'd gotten too lost in my thoughts of you.

Toby climbed up the side of the chair and sat beside me. "How's your head?" he asked.

"It's been better. It's been worse."

"Here." He held out two Advil in his palm. With the two of us sitting side by side, I couldn't see Toby's face, but I could feel the edges of him.

"Thanks," I said as I conked my knee against his.

He laughed. "Come on now, don't get handsy, there are children here!"

I turned just enough to catch the glint of amusement in his candy eyes. "I'm not getting handsy. I'm getting kneesy."

Mr. Consuelo was now climbing out of the lake, foggy goggles perched on his forehead.

"Did you see what your ex posted about us on Instagram?" I

asked. The diving boy shucked some lake weed out of the swimming area.

"She posted about us on Instagram?" He took out his phone and scrolled. "I don't see anything."

"She's WhisperingWahoo," I said.

"Doubtful," Toby said.

"She basically admitted it last night."

But Toby shook his head. "You must have misunderstood. WhisperingWahoo posted a bunch of photos of her trashed at a party when we were dating. She got really upset about it."

"Maybe she did it herself for attention."

"Maybe. But this . . ." Out of the corner of my eye, I could see the photo of him and me tucked into each other on his screen. Uncaptioned, it was a sweet moment. "This is particularly mean, even for WhisperingWahoo."

I nodded. We continued watching the water, sitting side by side in silence, and I made a decision. "I know what we have to do next."

"Oh?"

"Want to come with me to Maine?"

SIXTEEN

The Road Trip

MORE AND MORE, I WAS STARTING TO BE IN AWE OF YOU. NOT *AWESOME* awe. Stunned, slightly afraid awe. The kind of awe a person gets when watching a thunderstorm roil the ocean.

I wrote down another memory in my catalog of you. It's from the Speedo Junior Nationals in Texas. One of the few trips that Dad and I went on because you and Mom had finally racked up enough miles for us to get free flights. The air in San Antonio that weekend was like walking into a mist of warmed honey.

That night we played Never Have I Ever with some of the girls from your team. I didn't know then that it was supposed to be a drinking game. You were all chugging blue Gatorade.

So we sat in a circle halved by the gap between two starchy hotel beds and played the game.

Most of the Never Have I Evers were inside jokes. *Never have I ever tasted Meiling's purple power drink. Never have I ever gotten lost at another team's pool.* My fingers stayed perpetually up. But then, inevitably, the truth-challenging sprouted barbs. *Never have I ever snuck a peek at the guys in a shared locker room. Never have I ever lied about why I was missing practice. Never have I ever taken steroids.*

None of you admitted to the last one. And you, my golden sister, didn't admit to any of these edgier acts. At the time, I didn't think anything of it, because that's who you were. A white-bread, straightlaced, pedestal-worthy girl with a laser focus on an Olympic medal. Now I wondered when that picture-perfect you began to crack.

You'd spent at least a summer spinning lies and veiling truth. I'd been keeping secrets for a few weeks and I was already exhausted. To get to Maine, I had to lie. On Toby's next day off, I told our parents I had to go into work early for a special training, and that after work I was going to Nadia's. Early that morning I sent Derek a text: *Running a fever. Can't work today.* Toby and I were planning to do the drive there and back in a single day.

We didn't talk much on the ride north. Toby drove and I tried to sleep, though I was too anxious to really relax. Instead I imagined your own trip. A faceless driver. The two of you talking all the way up, about the food you'd buy at one of those country general stores, the upcoming closing ceremonies, the places you and I were planning to travel in our gap year. Your fingers frequently swept their arm, their knee, the back of their neck. I'd never seen you flirt before, but you were always so expressive with your body, accentuating speech with wild hand gestures, dancing through your excitement, quick to scowl, pout, or glare when offended. So I figured you were a physical flirt, and I imagined the anticipation of what was to come seeping through in light, almost-absentminded caresses.

We were driving up to Lake Bear on instinct and hope. What could we possibly find there, after all this time? I wasn't sure, but my gut said it was the place to go. And even if we found nothing, I wanted—*needed*—to see the lake. You'd kept so much of that summer from me. I was taking some of it back.

Before we'd left, I'd checked out Lake Bear on Maine's parks and recreation website. Swimming, hiking, and boating were all at your own risk. The cliff-jumping wasn't mentioned on the site, though some further sleuthing revealed there was one incident, about five years back, where a teenager shattered his legs while jumping. Had you known this, when you'd decided to jump? Had the jump been your idea, or were you goaded by your photographer?

Camping at the lake was first come, first served. The ten-dollar-per-night fee was supposed to be deposited in lockboxes at each individual campsite. Honor system, essentially. Maybe they'd have a guest log. If they did, there was a fair shot you'd have signed it, since you'd always liked to sign them in vacation spots. "Think about how cool it would be if you saw that one of your favorite authors had signed one of these guest books," you'd said to me once. We were at a hotel in Baltimore, for one of your meets the spring before trials.

"Or Michael Phelps?"

"Exactly. Someday, someone could get that excited about us."

It was over an hour before we crawled free of North Shore traffic and crossed the border into Maine, nearly another hour before we were off I-95, winding along progressively smaller and more desolate roads. As the space between the trees dwindled, their shadows began to shroud the car.

Toby glanced my way. "You're awake now?"

"Never really slept," I said. "Thanks for driving, though."

"I like driving."

"So do I. Izzy always viewed it as more utilitarian, though." I paused. A subject change was needed, and we still had plenty of time to kill. "So you want to draw comics when you grow up?"

Toby laughed lightly. "Yeah, actually. I do. I mean, I'll probably end up sketching logos or making infographics or something. But my program is pretty good at helping you make connections, so maybe I have a chance."

"Program?"

"I'm going to art school in Rhode Island this fall."

"They have a swim scholarship?"

He shook his head. "I could have gotten one, somewhere else, but . . . it's not like I'm going to do anything with swimming." He brushed his hands over the steering wheel. "So are you going to school for writing?"

"I got into UMass Amherst. They have a pretty good creative writing program." I squinted as the sun reflected against the windshield. Petra and Nadia were the only two people who knew about my definitive plans to head to Australia. Well, also the admissions board at Amherst, who'd accepted my deferred enrollment request. "But I'm taking a year off to go backpacking in Australia."

"Like you were going to do with Izzy?"

I shot him a look, though I don't know why it surprised me that he knew. "Yeah. Mostly." He didn't ask the next obvious question, the one that I didn't really know the answer to: Was I going to Australia to find you?

At first, yes. Absolutely. Now? I hoped you were out there. I wanted to find out where. But did I really think, deep down, that I'd discover you in the outback as if some mystical twin force had drawn us together?

"The trip's a little different now," I told him.

"Like how?"

"Well, for starters, I'm probably not going to go swimming with sharks."

Toby laughed.

"I'm signed up for this walkabout. It's guided, but it's basically six intense weeks of hiking and camping through the outback."

"Sounds fun."

"I'm hopeful."

"Not long now." The GPS estimated fifteen more minutes. The car curled around a hairpin curve, providing a glimpse of the lake. Lush aspen and ash trees were mirrored in the water, there and gone in an instant as the road carved a path in the forest and cut away. Then the lake was back in view, bits of silver glittering where the sun hit the surface. Unlike Bottomrock, a pocket of nature tucked inside residential suburbia, this lake was nestled fully in the wilderness. I had only a weak signal on my cell.

Lake Bear wasn't staffed like Bottomrock. Its small parking lot sat at the end of a dirt driveway, and a worn-out sign pointed to a ranger's hut recessed from the road. There were no other cars in the lot, so we weren't surprised to find the ranger's hut empty. A sign on the door said the ranger was in on weekends only. I jiggled the door handle, but the cabin was locked.

"Let's go for a walk," I suggested, shifting my backpack from one shoulder to the other. We were here, and you'd been here, too, and my imagination churned with stories about this place. Here towering trees crafted seclusion, and nature insisted on being heard in the insects that rubbed their delicate wings, and the wafts of air that rustled leaves and whistled through the duckweeds. It was the setting for two different types of tales: a romantic interlude or a horror story. "We should check out all the campsites," I added.

From a weather-worn map under Plexiglas, we learned that the trail marked by white blazes zagged its way around the lake. Most of the campsites were along this trail, so we followed it. The hike was mostly flat terrain marred by the occasional root yawning out of the earth.

I swatted at whatever was nipping my ankles as we approached the first campsite. Had you pitched a tent here? Alone or with someone else? Had you grilled burgers over charcoal or packed sandwiches and homemade trail mix? I looked for what was so forbidden about this place that you'd been compelled to hide it from me, but I didn't see anything.

Off to the side of the clearing, a picnic table had been carved out of a pair of fallen trees. Its wood was completely etched. Initials surrounded by hearts. Dates and names. A few expletives like *fuck mosquitoes* and even a few lines of bad poetry. I scanned it, knowing that you weren't the type to incise graffiti, but unable to stop myself from checking, just in case. Could I discern your handwriting from a carving? Did I even remember the way it looked anymore? I thought you had a swoop to your descenders, a bit of drama that was at odds with your practicality. It didn't matter if I was right, though. None of the names or initials were yours.

We spent a few more minutes poking around. There was a box nailed to a tree to collect camping fees, its U-shaped lock severed and dangling, a lonely ten-dollar bill inside. There was a booklet inside, too, and my hopes lifted. Then disappointment dropped. There were only a handful of names in the book, and yours was not among them. We moved on.

"So did you guys go camping often?" Toby asked as we hiked.

"Every summer. My dad and I love it. Mom kind of tolerates it for the family-togetherness aspect. But Izzy . . ."

"She didn't like it?"

"Not so much. Which is why it's strange that the walkabout I'm doing was her idea."

Toby drew back a branch that had reached across the trail, holding it aside until I passed.

"At first, I thought she was nuts. Like, I *like* camping and hiking and being in nature, and I thought it sounded too intense. But she said that's why she wanted to do it."

"Because it scared her?" Toby asked.

"Yeah." We hiked up a short incline, then quickly shot back down.

"What else are you going to do out there? After the walkabout, I mean."

"I'm signed up for this program that does conservation work. You travel around the country cleaning up trails and beaches, going out on boats to collect trash from the ocean, and other stuff to protect the ecosystems."

"It sounds amazing. Izzy never mentioned that part."

"That's because Izzy was all about having this grand adventure where we scuba dive in the Great Barrier Reef and learn how to surf and all." You'd said we'd be too restricted if we committed to a volunteer program, that we wouldn't be able to travel around as freely or as often as you wanted, but I liked the idea of working outside. "And it's not like I don't want an adventure, it's just that I also feel like I should be doing something . . . useful."

"And this way you get to have an adventure that makes the world a little bit better. That's incredible. You're making the rest of us look bad."

I laughed lightly at that. I didn't think of my trip as admirable. To me, it was inevitable. You had set the trip in motion, and I had to see it through.

We paused, catching our breath, cooling as a breeze swept over us. Toby watched me with his big brown eyes, that mischievous grin of his forming at the corners of his lips, and for a moment I couldn't break away. We could have been any two people on a hike, getting to know one another and enjoying the day. But that's not who we were, and I didn't want to forget it. I shifted my pack and looked down at the crumpled leaves under our feet. "We should keep moving to the next campsite."

"Right." Toby started hiking again. "So, if Izzy didn't like camping . . ."

"What was she doing here? Yeah. That got me, too. Like, did she come here explicitly to cliff-jump? Or was that a spontaneous thing and she came here to camp? And it's not like she hated camping. She liked being outside and bird-watching with Dad. And she was definitely willing to bear hiking if it got her to cool views. Basically, she didn't like sleeping on the ground. Sometimes we stayed in one of those camping cabins. You know the kind I mean?"

"I've never been camping."

"Well, she liked that better."

Our conversation carried us to the other campsites, which were more of the same: names carved into logs, metal signs reminding visitors to CARRY IN, CARRY OUT. Not every campsite had a booklet. In fact, most didn't. I kept hiking, determined to do the loop around the lake, because it seemed like something you'd have done. When we passed a spot where the woods peeled away from the shore and the lake offered itself to the trail, I walked over to the water. I could see almost the entire lake from this angle. It was the sort of view you'd have liked. There was a sign that said SWIM AT YOUR OWN RISK nailed to a tree.

I plopped onto a bed of moss, chin on my knees, and looked out at the water.

Across the lake, the mountain sloped upward. Somewhere on that side a rock face edged out between the trees and jutted over the lake, but I couldn't pinpoint the opening. I knew from what I'd read online that the jumping spot wasn't part of any trail. There were sketchy instructions on how to find it. Leave the trail at the giant birch. Cross the stream with the three little waterfalls. Pass the boulder that looks like an old man. You could geotrack it if you were lucky enough to get a cell signal. Otherwise, finding the right spot to jump was part of the challenge. I could imagine you liking this part. The puzzle of it. But to actually jump, in a location where at least one person had suffered severe injury? It was stupid, and you weren't stupid. I had to think you'd been pressured into it—dared perhaps? Like your teammates had been doing all summer long.

"Lunchtime?" Toby asked. That wasn't why I'd sat down, but I pretended like it was, and nodded, unzipping my bag to pull out my sandwich.

Toby joined me on the embankment. In typical Toby fashion, he had a thick grinder stuffed with ham, cheddar, and a rainbow of peppers. I'd seen him eat lunch almost every day for a month now, and I still found the quantity and quality of the food he ate impressive. He was like you, in that way, only with far fewer protein shakes.

"Okay. I have to ask: Did you force some poor deli owner to open shop early just to make you that?"

"No, I made it."

Looking again at the French loaf swollen with crisp peppers and a healthy mound of meat—had he actually carved the inside of the loaf to better fit the sandwich contents?—my brows arched. "You make these sandwiches yourself?"

"Didn't you make your sandwich?"

"Obviously. Look at it." My cheese-and-turkey on white bread sulked in its shriveled shrink-wrap.

"You can have some of mine, if you want." He offered half of his grinder.

I shook my head. Slowly, I peeled back the plastic. I wasn't actually hungry, but I picked at the sandwich anyway. As I gazed out at the lake, I asked Toby where he would travel, if he were to take a trip like mine.

"The American Southwest. Or any desert, really."

"Why the desert?" I pulled back a piece of crust and nibbled it. The lake was flat and calm. Trees were reflecting on the surface, stretched and distorted like in a funhouse mirror.

"Deserts look like other planets. Or how I imagine other planets look, anyway."

"For your space soldier stories?"

"I don't really have a story for her. She's just a character in my head." Toby took a bite of his sandwich and eyed me as I continued to pick some pieces off mine and slowly chew them. After a few minutes of quiet, he said, "Hey, Teddy? You all right?"

"I'm fine."

"Detective-ing—now, granted I have very little experience, but I think it probably involves following a lot of leads that don't pan out."

"I know." And I did.

"But we had to come here, I think," Toby said. A breeze overturned the leaves on the trees, lifting their veiny sides toward the sky. Toby slipped the second half of his grinder back into its bag.

"Because now we don't have to wonder if there was something here," he said matter-of-factly. He wasn't indulging me by helping with this investigation. He wasn't just *doing a nice thing* for the sister of his missing friend. He was in this with me. He'd come all this way, knowing it probably wasn't going to yield any new clues, because he understood the tug of your mystery. Maybe just as well as I did.

I almost kissed him. Instead I broke our gaze and tried to banish the impulse. But it lingered in the knot of anticipation unspooling in my chest. I needed something else to look at, but Toby was so close, I could already feel my eyes flitting back to his boyish, goofy, gorgeous face. And if I looked at him, I'd think about kissing him, and if I did that too much, then I would just kiss him, and that would be weird because we hadn't come here to start a tryst in the woods. So I settled on the SWIM AT YOUR OWN RISK sign that I could see tacked to a tree over his shoulder. I looked at it without really seeing it for a few moments before it came into focus.

I stood up. There was a small black spot in the bottom corner of the sign. Only the black spot wasn't a spot, but a hole. Slowly, carefully, I stuck my finger through it. The edge was ringed with sharp spikes, each flayed outward like something had punched its way through the metal. Something like a bullet.

There were plenty of innocent reasons why this sign might have a bullet hole in it. Hunters. Kids taking potshots. This bullet hole could have been there a year, or it could have been there ten. It had nothing to do with your trip here, yet it unsettled me. Toby followed me to the sign and stood close behind.

"Teddy," he said.

I touched the pointed edge of the torn metal, felt the sting as it pushed into the pad of my finger.

"Teddy," he said again. This time his hand settled on my shoulder. I jolted. Twisted toward him. But he only redirected me, turning my shoulders so that I faced the bullet hole once more. "There are cabins over there." He pointed beyond the sign and across the lake, where two log cabins were just visible behind a row of trees. "If she did come here to camp . . ." Toby started.

"She'd have stayed in one of those," I finished.

We started hiking again, following the lake as it slithered around the forest. The cabins would peep into view one minute—dark logs and peaked roofs barred by tree trunks—and slide from view the next. For the twenty or so minutes it took us to reach them, I wondered if they could possibly be a mirage. They weren't, of course. They were each nestled into their own little clearing and set back a dozen yards from the water, with a bear-proof box for storing food and a few stools carved out of stumps. One of the cabins even had a makeshift fire pit of cool, dusty coals haloed by rocks the size of my fist.

I walked into the first cabin with a mind full of *ifs*.

If you'd come here to camp.

If the cabins had a guest log.

If you'd signed it.

If the log hadn't been lost, or stolen, or replaced, or somehow rendered illegible in the last year.

There was no door to the first cabin. Instead, it was entirely open on the lakeside. A peninsula of architecture. The floorboards gave to my weight when I stepped inside. A loud creak escaped.

With no windows, the lighting inside the hut was dim. To my left and right were bunks built into the wall, each long enough for an adult to lie down and wide enough for two people, if they snuggled.

Along the back wall, a small tabletop stretched outward and hovered in the room like a beggar's palm. If there were chairs once, they were here no longer. A CARRY IN, CARRY OUT sign was nailed to the back of the hut, centered over the table like wall art.

"So what's the point of a place like this?" Toby ran his palm over the hard surface of a bunk.

"A little elevation. A little protection from the elements. Some people like to sleep in the open air without worrying about rain." I tapped the flashlight app on my phone and shined it along the walls, looking for etched names. Found a few here and there, but none that were yours. Toby and I poked around for longer than necessary. There was nothing in the cabin to be found.

The second cabin was a mirror of the first, except this one had a single wooden stool tucked away under its table. I was still scanning for graffiti because I couldn't leave without crossing off every possibility, when Toby said, "Hey, come look at this."

He was on his hands and knees, his head ducked under one of the bunks. His shoulder rolled as he reached for something.

He emerged with a leather booklet that had a broken chain dangling off the spiral binding and the emblem for the Maine Department of Agriculture, Conservation, and Forestry stamped on the front. Underneath the ornate circle, in gold lettering, were the words *guest log*. Toby handed it to me.

The papers were stiff and blotchy and wrinkled. This book had been here for a while. And there were names, a lot of names, paired up with two other columns for date of visit and comments. We brought the book outside for better lighting.

I traced the log backward in time. Three pages in, and I was back to last year. Four pages, and I'd found August. I didn't need to scrutinize any further. Your handwriting—the swooping g's and p's and y's that I remembered—was like a beacon to my eye.

I & K August 20 Happy Anniversary

"You think that's her?" Toby's voice tickled my ear as he looked over my shoulder.

"It's her handwriting. Her initial. The same date from the GPS."

"Hell of a coincidence."

"Yeah." I touched the dried ink. You'd used initials. Why? And K? Who was K?

You'd been celebrating an anniversary.

Kevin. One of your lanemates was named Kevin. "How many Wahoos have K as their first initial?" I asked Toby, turning to face him.

"There're two Kevins, but one of them joined too recently. There's a Kyle, but I'm pretty sure he's gay. There's Kiernan. He's a little older. Wasn't at the party. But he would have been around last summer. As for girls, there are a lot more. Two Kristens, three Kaitlins, a Kathleen. And . . ." He trailed off.

"What?" Whatever Toby was thinking pained him. He glanced away, putting both hands in his hair and teasing strands toward the sky. Finally he pressed his palms against the top of his head.

"Coach Connors." He closed his eyes. "His first name is Keith."

SEVENTEEN

K Is for Keith

"IT'S NOT NECESSARILY HIM," I FOUND MYSELF SAYING, DESPITE THE chill that rocked me when Toby said his name. If you had been sleeping with a married adult, of course you would have lied about it. Toby and I sat on a log bench. The guest book was splayed open on my lap. Wind rippled the lake and ruffled the trees.

"I know that." Hands on his knees, he leaned forward, trying to catch his breath. This was the first time I'd ever seen your laid-back, smirky friend as anything other than calm. Even in the moments when he'd seemed sad, he had still seemed calm. And I don't know why—maybe because I didn't really know your coach, and so it wasn't so discordant for me to think of him as a sleazy, borderline pedophile; or maybe it was because, if K was Keith Connors, then I finally had a reason I could understand for why you'd lied to me, to everyone—but in that moment, I was calm. Sitting outside the cabin where you'd had your tryst, I didn't worry about your story. I worried about Toby. His mentor. Your possible lover. I placed my hand on his.

"Maybe it was Katie Ledecky," I said.

Toby laughed, a blithe, airy chuckle. "They did meet for, like, twelve seconds in Singapore."

"The most romantic twelve seconds in the history of USA Swimming," I quipped.

"So Katie goes on the list," Toby said lightly before his smile faded. "But we can't discount Coach Connors."

"I know." I dug the toe of my sneaker into the dirt. I wasn't discounting him. Just then, he topped the suspect chart. "So—and I totally don't mean this in an I-told-you-so way—you think it's possible?"

"I didn't, before. But it makes sense. Why she wouldn't tell anyone. Why she . . . And, I mean, it was such a big secret that she didn't even write out full names in here." He tapped the book, right under the initials *I & K.*

"Yeah." I didn't know what else to say. Your coach. Your married, grown-up coach. I wasn't even sure what he looked like. Though I'd met him a handful of times over the years, I'd never paid much attention to him. I conjured up a youngish face covered in scruff. Dark hair slicked back like he was fresh from the shower. Did Keith have kids? I thought he did. One, maybe two. Babies. "I think we have to—" I started to say.

"Bring this to the police," Toby finished, except that hadn't been my thought at all.

I was already shaking my head. "What would the police do? Is it even illegal? She was seventeen. That might, technically, be old enough."

"But he was her coach. An authority figure."

"I didn't say it wasn't creepy." I looked down at your missive. The longer I regarded the writing, the more I recognized your hand. I began to write the scene in my head. You sat on the cot in the cabin, the log balanced on your thigh as you etched this memento, adding a whimsical loop on the ampersand, stretching the tails on your y's. Your lips curled as your eyes angled from the page to the person sitting beside you. You'd been at this camp, maybe even on the same log I was on, not a week before you'd vanished. My nerves clenched as the prospect of that midnight meeting grew sinister. Was your affair with him the thing that had caused you to do so poorly at trials? Maybe he'd broken it off sometime between this camping trip and your disappearance, and that's why you'd been so upset.

Maybe you had arranged to meet with him that night, to run away together or to talk, but something had gone horribly wrong.

I shut the book.

"I still think we ought to tell the police," Toby said.

"Tell them what, exactly? That we found this book with initials in it and we think Izzy wrote it and we think the *K* stands for Keith Connors?"

"The police can look into it, at least. Decide if it's relevant."

"And if it's not? If we're wrong?"

Toby waited a beat, looking at me, before he responded. "We'd ruin him."

We sat silent for a moment, our fingers still linked.

"Besides, I'm pretty sure the police won't take anything I tell them seriously." Although, I thought, maybe Officer Kelly would. He'd always thought there was something to my theory, even if he'd been unable to prove it. If I found something, something real, I promised myself I'd take it to him.

"Why?"

I drew in a breath, slowly, deeply, my shoe slotting once more into the groove I'd made in the dirt, but I did not let go of Toby's hand. "I spent the first few months after she disappeared looking for her." I kept my face trained on the campground. Soil compacted by the soles of so many hiking boots, laid barren from use. "Like, obsessively. I think it started because she sent me this text, the day before."

I paused, but Toby gave no indication that he knew about the text. "I was out of town, and she said she had something she had to tell me when I got back. I couldn't stop thinking about what that might have been. I got this idea that maybe she had this grand plan to run away and that was the thing she was going to tell me, and then I couldn't find her passport or the camping gear she'd bought and they found her earring across the lake . . . I yelled at the chief. When she stopped her search. My parents had to come pick me up, and they were so furious. And still I didn't stop looking, for a while."

"Why did you?"

I remember the moment I realized I had to give up. Mom and Dad had found me in your room, in the middle of the night, systematically entering possible passcode combinations into your phone to try to unlock it. It's their faces more than anything that sticks with me. They both looked lonely, and scared, and so much older than their forty-six years.

"Because I could see what I was doing to my parents."

"Do you want to drop it now?"

From the tenor of his question, I could tell he hoped the answer would be no. Now that we'd started down this path, he wanted to see it through. Not because he hoped to find you—I don't think he believed there was a you to find any longer—but to find out what was going through your head, that summer and that night, when you'd walked out into the lake for that midnight swim. I wondered, if I said yes, would he stop for me?

But I didn't want to drop it. The idea that you were living off-grid in Australia was feeling less and less plausible. But even if we couldn't find you, we might find out what had happened to you. And besides, your secrets were about something more now. They were wrapped up in the person you were becoming. The person you'd been so determined to hide from me. The person I'd been too distracted to see.

"I don't want to stop. I just want to be sure."

Toby squeezed my hand. "So we'll keep looking. Into Keith. And Kiernan and Kevin and all the Kaitlins and every other K-named person Izzy knew, whether they were on the Wahoos or not. But maybe we should promise each other something else." With his free hand, Toby tilted my chin up. Our foreheads nearly touched. I could see the shadow of stubble that fringed his jaw. I could see the pale streak across the bridge of his nose where his sunglasses rested. And I saw something in his eyes, compassion or hope or guilt or some messy tangle of all three, that tugged at me. "We have to promise we won't get obsessive."

"I'm not sure I can promise that," I whispered. Then Toby's thumb brushed my cheek, and I thought that maybe, with his help, I could.

TOBY AND I CAME up with a plan on our way back from Maine. We were going to ask Coach Connors to share his practice attendance records from that summer. With the records, we could see who else had missed practice the same days as you. It would give us a list of potential suspects. Somewhere to start.

We thought about trying to steal the records like spies, with Toby creating a distraction so I could sneak into his office, sleuth around his computer. But that sort of plan would only work on a TV show. Really, your coach had no reason to refuse to share the records, especially given he didn't know what we wanted them for. And I was willing to bet he'd grant a lot of leeway to your suffering sister.

I visited your training pool a few days later. Your coach didn't match my fuzzy memory of him. His beard was full, not scruffy, and speckled heavily with gray. His dark hair was combed back, but not wet or greased. Fit hands moved across a smartboard in his office, collecting the names of your teammates into groups of four, erasing some and replacing them with others as he glanced between the board and his iPad. Creating relay teams, I realized. His office had a glass wall overlooking the pool deck, so I could observe without going in. He had pictures of his wife and two little kids on his desk. There were trophies on a built-in bookcase, medals and plaques on the walls. Photographs, too, of swimmers. Action shots and team shots. I spent a while—too long, probably—scanning them for you.

"Teddy?" Keith opened the door, his head cocked in curiosity. His voice was even, without so much as a tinge of shame, like I'd imagine any decent human being would have if the twin of his mysteriously missing lover showed up at his office unannounced. But it also lacked excitement. I wasn't a happy surprise. Then again, like most people in your swimming world, he'd known me for my face more than anything else. I wished, not for the first time, that I could read people as well as you.

"Can I help you?" Keith Connors glanced around, as if checking for someone else who might have accompanied me, perhaps to speak on my behalf.

Suddenly our simple plan to "just ask" seemed incredibly naive. I shifted. "Hi." The word squeaked out. This was not the greeting I'd planned. I'd hoped for confidence and certainty, not indecision and timidity. The greeting was too me and not enough you. What if he was K? He'd kept your secret for so long, I didn't know what he'd do to make sure it stayed quiet permanently.

It was very early morning—before my shift at Bottomrock started—and his swimmers, Toby included, were in the weight room. Our conversation resonated across the empty pool deck.

"Did you want something from me?" He slipped the smartpen behind his ear. One hand gripped the doorknob, the other hooked his pocket with his thumb. Not inviting me inside. Not dismissing me, either.

"Yeah." I shifted again. He was good-looking, I suppose, for a guy with close to twenty years on me. He was still in shape, if maybe a touch heavy at the waist. He wore a short-sleeved, navy polo shirt, tucked into faded jeans. A simple but orderly look, not unlike the way you liked to dress. His arms were hairy, which some people liked. Maybe you had.

And I was spending way too long trying to eyeball what had drawn you to Keith, when I didn't even know yet if it'd been anything at all. "I wanted to talk to you about Izzy."

"Sure. Come in." He walked to his desk. "It's good to see you, Teddy." He smiled slightly as he gestured to the chair facing his own. "How are you?"

"I'm all right. I . . ." A photograph of you hung on the wall. I hadn't been able to see it from outside the room, but it was clearly the collection's centerpiece. You were doing butterfly, your head and shoulders vaulting from the water as your arms cycled back to it. Your expression was determined. *Here I am. Come and get me.*

Keith saw me looking. "Singapore, I think. Right before she—"

"Tied the world record." I hadn't ever seen that shot. It was professionally done, for sure. The detail was exquisite. I could make out droplets of water sliding off your skin, beading on the edges of your goggles. The photographer had captured not just your determination, but your vivacity. I felt like you might leap right out of the frame and back into my life.

"So what did you want to talk to me about?"

Something insistent in his voice drew my attention. He had one hand pressed flat against the cover of his iPad. I imagined this man suggesting the two of you jump off the cliff at Lake Bear. Maybe he was one of those people who was into extreme sports. Maybe, with your coach's encouragement, jumping would have seemed more cool than risky.

"Last summer," I said bluntly, watching his reaction. I think I saw him swallow.

"What about it?"

"I know Izzy skipped a few practices. I've always wondered if you knew why."

There was a definite pause before he answered. "She didn't tell you?"

I shook my head. Keith lifted his hand to curl his fingers, and the imprint of his palm rebounded from the supple fabric of the iPad case. He said, "Stress, probably. What happened, the way she performed at trials, I mean, it really got to her."

"Because she didn't make her times?"

"She didn't even come close." The sentence was a verbal shrug.

He thought he was telling me something I already knew. But you hadn't told me much about trials. Only that you hadn't been fast enough.

"Right." I was too embarrassed to let on that there might be yet another thing you'd kept from me. "She told me it was terrible, but she didn't really go into details."

"And that's why you came here today? For those details?" he asked, and I swear, on the ends of those questions I heard relief. I nodded. "Yeah."

"It wasn't just her speed. Everything was off. She botched her starts, she was slow on the turns, sloppy in her form. It was like she was suddenly a different person. Like her head wasn't in it at all. I swear, if I didn't know any better, I'd say she was trying to tank."

"She wouldn't have—"

"I know that. But she was under a lot of pressure . . . a lot of stress . . ." With each pause he glanced down. "I wish I'd realized how much." He spoke softly into his lap, and I knew, just as I'd known with Meiling, that this man missed you fiercely.

I almost asked him flat out if he'd been sleeping with you. The question was in my head, poised for release. But I couldn't edge it out. Because what if I was right, and he had been having an affair with you, and he lied to me, now? I had no reason at all to believe he'd be candid with me here. And if I was right, and I played my hand, then he wouldn't give me the attendance records, and he certainly wouldn't tell me anything more. He'd probably start getting rid of whatever evidence might be left. He'd send me out the door in mock outrage because how dare I impugn his honor? If he sent me away, I wondered whether I might be able to distinguish indignant rage from camouflage.

And what if I was wrong? His grief was not like that of our teachers, who pooled sympathy in their eyes when they said they were sorry and then whispered things like, "That poor girl," when they thought I was too far away to hear. It wasn't like that of our neighbors, who dropped off food and stayed to chat with our parents about the Red Sox, because they didn't know how to talk about a maybe-dead daughter. For most of the adults in our life who weren't related to you, their grief was genuine but finite. It was the kind of thing that tightened their chests and made them give their own loved ones a hug before it dissipated. An acorn loosed from a tree, falling quickly to rest. Apart from our parents, Keith was the first adult I'd met who still felt the lack of you one year hence. What if he was just a man who had loved you like a brother or an uncle, and I tainted him with my paranoia?

I stuck to the plan. "You're right. It was probably stress. Still . . . I wondered if you might have attendance records for the practices that summer? I'd like to take a look at them."

"Sure," he said quickly. Glad, I think, to have something concrete to do that might send me away. "I can email them to you." He slid a piece of paper across his desk, along with a pen. I wrote down my email address.

I thanked him, then left his office and went to Bottomrock.

QUIMBY'S CLEANUP list, in preparation for your tree dedication, had been pinned to the refrigerator in the guardhouse since opening weekend. But today was the first cloudy day we'd had in a while and Derek decided it was finally time to cross some things off. I was glad for the distraction—I couldn't stand the idea of just waiting around in the guardhouse, checking my email every thirty seconds to see if Keith had sent the attendance records yet.

While Nadia and Pat sorted through life vests and discarded unsightly ones in a junk heap, Derek scrubbed the boats clean and I took a rake to the beach to clear the sand of sticks and leaves and bits of trash blown free of the dumpster.

Toby joined me once he'd arrived. "How'd it go?"

"I don't know." I lifted the rake to pluck leaves from its cracked teeth. I was still processing my little tête-à-tête. Keith had been kind, yet guarded; open, yet hesitant. I couldn't quite wrap my head around him, and that was disquieting.

"Well, did he give you the records?"

"He said he'd email them."

"So that's good." Hope laced his voice. "Did he ask why you wanted them?" Toby had his own rake, but it was largely for show. I'd already done most of the work. He had the head of the rake in the sand, and he clung to its handle like a cane.

"No. But I was pretty openly curious about her behavior that summer."

"And how did he react to that?"

"I don't know." I hated saying something so empty, but it was all I had. I wished Toby had been there with me.

Toby began supplying me with words. "Nervous?"

"Maybe."

"Concerned?"

"Possibly."

"Confused?"

"Stop with the adjectives!" Frustrated, I jabbed the sand with my rake. "I'm not very good at this."

He balanced his chin on his rake's handle and watched me stir up the sand. "What's your gut saying?"

"That he has something to hide." And there it was. Toby had coaxed out the thing that had been bothering me since I'd left Keith's office. Your coach may have told me the truth, but he hadn't told me all of it.

"Do you have an idea what?" He straightened, waited, his gaze sniping.

Just then, your phone pinged in my pocket.

I whipped it out fast, heart lurching. But it was only an alert. WhisperingWahoo had just posted something on Instagram. A photograph of me in the coach's office that morning. The image was blurred by the windowpane, but Keith looked distraught. The caption read: *As thirsty as her twin? #DontStandSoCloseToMe #WahooWhore #MissPompousII*

Whoever had taken this photograph was at practice that morning. Taryn quit the team last summer, so unless she was stalking me, it wasn't her.

But whoever it was had a vendetta against you. And now, me.

"I'm sorry, Teddy." As Toby reached for me, Nadia said, "Sorry about what?" and I jerked away.

She had come around the bend to stand at the crest of the beach, one hand on her cocked hip. "Whoa. Didn't realize I'd been using my ninja sneak. Derek sent me to see if you two needed help but *clearly* this beach is debris-free. So . . . what's he sorry for?" She glanced between us and squinted in the morning sun.

"He has nothing to be sorry for," I said quickly, stuffing your phone into my pocket. I would ignore this bully, as I'm sure you had. It was hard to do: I was bursting to stand up for you, but that would do no good if I didn't know who I was standing up against.

"Ah." If there was one face I could always read, it was Nadia's. Skepticism seeped from her very pores. She knew something was up. "Well, Derek wants Toby to help with the canoes, and we're supposed to collect trash from the trails."

"I can pick up trash, if you'd rather work on the canoes," Toby offered, but Nadia shook her head. "Thanks, but I'm all right. Teddy, let's get some gloves."

"Sure." As Nadia strode off, I foisted my rake off on Toby. "I'll let you know when I get that email."

Nadia and I were well into our task, picking up empty Dorito bags and crushed beer cans, when she finally confronted me.

"What's going on with you and Toby?" she demanded, putting a hand on my wrist. I stopped walking. "No. Wait. I take that back. What's going on with *you*?"

"Nothing."

"You say that, yet you and Toby clam up so fast whenever anyone else nears, it's like you're discussing state secrets."

"Well, we're not."

"Well," she droned, teasing me. "Why can't I know, then?"

A breeze swayed the recycling bag in my hand. The cans inside it chimed. "Someone's posting mean stuff on Instagram about Izzy and me. That's all."

"About Izzy? That's . . . vile, even for the internet. Who is it?"

"Anonymous account. Someone on her swim team, though."

"Ugh. I'm sorry, too. And why are they doing this now?"

My eyes locked with hers, then darted away. It was enough, though, for Nadia to see that I was dodging the question. "Teddy." A name said in its own sentence like that is almost never good. It's a prelude to bad news. A signpost signaling a conversational turn to solemnity.

"What?"

"You're not . . ." Her gaze moved to the space between the trees, where sunlight sparkled off the lake. "Looking again?"

I shifted, knowing that the longer I took to answer, the more my silence said. But I didn't want to lie. "What makes you think that?"

"I've heard you and Toby say *Izzy* several times when you're all huddled together having your secret chats, and you asked me that weird question about a lake in Maine, and you called in sick when I know you weren't because the next day you were totally fine, and, now someone is harassing you about Izzy online, and well, Toby seems nice and all, but something happened that night, and . . ."

"Don't be like that." I started walking again, heading for a crunched juice box at the base of a birch just slightly off trail. Nadia huffed as she followed me.

"Like what?"

"Suspicious. 'Cause he's not."

"But he's probably damaged."

"So am I!" I snatched the juice box and dumped it in with the cans.

"That's trash," Nadia said.

"It's cardboard. Cardboard's recyclable."

"Not when it's covered in sticky corn syrup."

"Fine." I dug it out and handed it to her. "Happy?"

She turned the box about in her gloves. "Teddy," she said slowly. Softly. "You're not damaged."

"My sister disappeared. Why wouldn't I be damaged?"

"What I mean is . . . I think it's different, for him. I don't know what happened that night, but I think it's weird he's working here. How much do you really know about him?"

"What—you think he's WhisperingWahoo? Because things were said about him, too."

"I think he's not telling you the whole truth."

"I know he's not afraid to talk to me about my sister."

"And I am?"

"Petra is."

"She won't talk to you about Izzy?"

"Explicitly. She told me to stop."

Nadia bit her lip. "You guys had a fight about it?"

A fight, sure, that was one word for what had happened between us. Though the dissolution of our friendship hadn't happened in one fight. It'd been happening slowly ever since you'd gone. Apart from some emails she copied me on regarding your tree dedication—the dogwood had been ordered and at least one person had volunteered to read something—I hadn't spoken to her in almost a month, and she hadn't contacted me, either.

My only response to Nadia's question was a nod.

"You know you can talk to me about Izzy, if that's what you need."

"It's not the same." I couldn't shake the dismissal from my voice. "You didn't know her."

"No. I didn't," she said softly. "But I'd like to, if you would bother to let me." Nadia waited, the juice box still clutched in her hands, watching me like I might suddenly start spilling everything I had never told her about you. When I failed at that, she spun on her flip-flops and walked back to the trail. I watched her go, my recycling bag dangling at my side. I began walking parallel to the trail, wanting to give her space and keep some for myself.

The empties and other garbage grew more frequent as I walked, and I realized that I'd wandered near to the backcountry campsite where the police had found your peacock earring. Now I followed a makeshift trail along the ridge until I reached the clearing. In its center, stones circled charred coal and twigs to create a fire pit. Two large logs had been dragged onto either side, complementing two stumps, so that together, they formed a ring of seats. The ground was compact from so many sneakers treading over it. And stapled to one of the larger trees at the edge of the clearing was a lockbox, not unlike the ones that had housed guest books at Lake Bear.

Ignoring the broken shards of beer bottles I should've been collecting, I walked over to the box and lifted its lid.

It was empty. Of course I'd done this before. So had the police. The idea that I might find something now was absurd.

I sat down on a stump, thinking I should either clean up the site or head back to the beach, but failing to do either. Was this the site of your midnight meeting? The one that may or may not have happened? That may or may not have been with K? I used to imagine that you'd come here as a pit stop of sorts, after crossing the lake. You could have stashed your gear here, picked it up before going wherever it was you were headed next. I imagined your earring falling off as you drew a fleece over your head.

All of your secrets: I couldn't help but feel they were leading someplace dark. Maybe the earring hadn't been innocently knocked loose during a wardrobe change. Maybe it had come off in a struggle.

I took your phone out and pulled up WhisperingWahoo's feed. Why did this person care what I did? The comments, though aimed at me, still centered around you. By now I'd read through IzzyWareSwims, and while WhisperingWahoo had posted a lot of nasty things along these lines, you hadn't once replied. Which seemed odd, when I thought about it. You were confident enough to stand up for yourself. So why hadn't you?

I searched your phone for all instances of WhisperingWahoo's handle, and that's how I found your deleted messages.

Because nothing's ever really deleted, it was easy enough for me to restore them. There were dozens.

You: I know who you are and I want you to stop.

Who am i?

You: A lying troll.

Lying? i have a little video i could post that says otherwise

By the time stamps, three minutes passed before you replied.

You can't.

Stop being such a greedy whore and maybe i wont

You didn't say anything else, but you'd opened the harassment floodgates. Messages like:

ure just a slut who doesnt deserve her life

and

1 day the world will see u for the entitled bitch u r

and

Why dont u go die, ugly bitch?

This last one, sent on the morning before you disappeared, was the only one that you'd replied to: *Why don't you say that to my face?*

Maybe I was looking at this all wrong. Maybe you hadn't arranged to meet your partner at Bottomrock at midnight. Maybe you'd arranged to meet WhisperingWahoo.

Maybe that's why you'd never come home.

I didn't stop to think about my next move. I could do exactly what you did. The thing that had maybe gotten you killed.

I sent WhisperingWahoo a message.

EIGHTEEN

Technically, I Never Lied

I ECHOED YOUR WORDS EXACTLY: *I KNOW WHO YOU ARE AND I WANT YOU to stop.*

Two days passed and nothing happened.

No reply from WhisperingWahoo.

No attendance records from Keith.

And I was on edge about both.

You'd known, apparently, who WhisperingWahoo was, but you hadn't recorded the name anywhere that I could find.

As for Keith, I began to worry he wouldn't send the records at all. Maybe he'd forgotten, or maybe he never had any intention of sending them. Maybe it was just a thing he said to get me out of his office. Or maybe he was taking time to doctor them. But what could I do? Go back and ask again? Not when only two days had passed. Initiate the stealth operation Toby and I had mused about? It was too soon for that, too. I was impatient for answers, but I had no choice other than to wait.

At home, Mom and Dad had yet to force "the talk" they'd vowed re: my alcohol consumption. Instead, they seemed to have decided on another track: They kept trying to get me pumped for college.

At dinner, Dad began waxing nostalgic about how he and Mom had met on the stoop of their college library, where she was reading the book he'd been unable to find because she'd checked out the last copy just moments before. You and I had heard that story a million and one times before, but it felt different this time. Like there was a lesson there, if I could only tease it out.

It occurred to me then that I was being cruel, keeping them in the dark about my plans. Wasn't that precisely the thing you had done to me?

"I have to tell you both something," I blurted. Since you'd been gone, we'd taken to sitting at the end of the table closest to the kitchen. Dad in his usual place, at the end, but Mom in your seat, across from me. The other end of the table was empty. Unset and a little dusty. The funny thing was, now that we had fewer people, we ate together a lot more often.

Dad pushed his glasses up higher on the bridge of his nose. He looked a little hurt that I'd interrupted his reminiscing.

Mom set her fork down. "What is it?"

"I deferred."

Mom simply stared at me, blinking, until finally she said, "What do you mean, you deferred?" while Dad harrumphed, "So that's why we haven't gotten a bill."

"I mean I filled out the paperwork in May to defer enrollment until next fall."

"Well, undo it," Mom said.

"I don't think I can."

Dad was watching me with this expression on his face that was sad but knowing and also a little bit relieved. Like a man who'd been wondering something for a long time, and even though the answer was not what he wanted, at least he finally had one. "You're still going, aren't you?"

I nodded.

"What on earth are you—" Mom's face swapped anger for fear the moment she realized what my plans must be. She pursed her lips that way she always does when she's annoyed and thinking. "Australia?"

Once more, I nodded.

"And you knew?" She turned to Dad now, her voice halfway between accusation and a plea.

"I didn't know. But . . . all those hikes with Petra. She hasn't been talking about college at all. And then we didn't get any paperwork from UMass. . . ."

"Why didn't you say anything?"

"I didn't want to think she would lie to us," Dad said.

I felt a pang of regret but still managed to say, "Technically, I never lied."

"No." A verbal fist pounded onto the table. Though clearly annoyed with Dad, Mom was more upset with me. "None of that smartass crap right now, Teddy. You promised you were done with Australia."

"I *never* said I wasn't going. I just stopped talking about it."

"Why?" Mom said.

"Because it was making you uncomfortable."

"No. Why do you still want to do this? Back when your—" She stopped there.

"You can say her name, Mom. Izzy. Your other daughter. When Izzy was going to go with me, it was a fine idea."

Mom flinched at the mention of your name. She had one hand wrapped around her water glass, but she didn't lift it. "It was never a fine idea. It was a tolerable idea, for the two of you to go off together, and besides you were younger then and we always assumed it was just a—a . . ."

"Fantasy," Dad supplied.

"Exactly. Because Izzy wasn't really going to want to take all that time off training, she was going to want to go straight to a college swim team and—"

"We were going to do this only if she didn't make the Olympics. Which, news flash, she didn't."

Something dark flickered in Mom's eyes. "I'm well aware," she said, her words both firm and soft.

"But now you're going alone?" Dad asked. Ever the diplomat, trying to defuse the tension.

"I'll meet people there."

"Teddy . . ." My name was a tsk. Because I'd always been the more reserved of the two of us. The listener, not the talker. The storyteller, not the adventurer. The follower, not the leader. In the film of our lives, I was the comic relief to your starring role.

"I have to grow up sometime, Mom."

"So do this, then. When you've grown up more," she said, oblivious to the insult inherent in her words.

Dad cleared his throat. "Now, Teddy, surely this trip would be more fun if you waited. If you asked a friend? If you had more money saved up? Maybe next summer I could take some time off work and—"

"We're not paying for this," Mom said.

"I didn't ask you to pay for it. I have my own money. And I have Izzy's money, too."

"We gave that to you for college."

"You didn't stipulate. Izzy was going to use it for this trip."

"Teddy, be realistic! You can't just fly around the world and hike off into the outback! You're going to get yourself killed!"

"No, I'm not."

"For starters, you're not in shape for all that backcountry trekking—"

"I *am* in shape. That's why I've been taking all those hikes with Petra."

Dad jumped in now. "You need to have certain survival skills—"

"And you know I took that wilderness survival class."

"But what if you get hurt?" Mom said. "Bitten by something or sprain an ankle or—"

"I'm not actually going alone. I'm going on a tour, with a guide. I'm being adventurous, not suicidal."

The room suddenly got so silent I could hear the refrigerator humming. Dad flicked some carrots around on his plate. Mom finally released her water glass. Our half-eaten dinners were growing cold.

"How long will you be there?" Dad spoke almost rationally, though there was still a hint of unease on his voice. Mom was glaring at me.

"The tour is six weeks."

"And then you'll come home?"

"No. I'm signed up for this conservation program in Brisbane. We'll do projects that help the environment."

"Don't you need a work visa for that?"

"No. It's volunteer. The work focuses on coastal areas and the ocean. Food and lodging is provided." I stirred my rice, watching the different shapes and colors of the microwavable variety pack swirl together. I took a bite—it was on the cold side of lukewarm—and

risked a peek at Mom. She hadn't said anything since I'd said the
S word.

"No," she said as soon as my eyes landed on her. I wasn't sure
if it was denial or command.

"Mom—"

"No, Theodora." She had a hand braced on either side of her
plate. "You are not going to Australia. Absolutely not. You can't do
this to us." Her eyes gleamed with fresh tears.

"Mom, I'm sorry if this upsets you, but I'm not doing it *to you*.
I'm doing it *for me*."

Mom shook her head. She looked at Dad, "Henry, do something."

When he said, "Do what?" Mom left the room.

Dad frowned at me over the rim of his glasses and said, "Well,
kiddo," like that was all that needed saying.

"You can't stop me."

"I know that. But you have to fix things with her before you
leave." He picked up his fork, two pieces of steamed carrot still
pierced on its tines, and put them in his mouth.

FOUR DAYS AFTER I visited Keith Connors in his office, Whispering-
Wahoo still hadn't replied to my text, but Keith did share his Google
spreadsheet with me. There was a message attached.

*Sorry this took a few days. I had to figure out how to separate
this from my records of everyone's personal information. Which, for
obvious reasons, I can't share with you. I hope this helps you get some
peace. All the Best, Coach K.*

K. I already knew he had the right initial, but somehow, seeing him call himself K was an arrow to my gut. Had he really just given away his own secret identity?

The spreadsheet he'd shared, while lacking the personal information of your teammates, as Keith had pointed out, was more than just attendance records. It had meet times; personal bests; relay groupings. It had a schedule for which drills to use on which days to ensure the proper rotation of muscle workouts. If I hadn't already been suspicious that Keith Connors was K, I could have guessed you'd fallen in love with him by this spreadsheet alone. It rivaled the ones you used to keep, tracking your racing times, cataloging your caloric intake, budgeting time for swimming, weight training, stretching, and schooling.

Of course, I was at Bottomrock when it came in, and the spreadsheet was too elaborate to easily take in on my phone screen. I showed it to Toby, and we made plans for him to come over after work to look at it together.

Dad was the only one home when Toby and I got there. Mom was teaching a remedial summer session of English lit. He was in the kitchen, collecting vegetable scraps from whatever he'd been cooking for the composter. I yelled that Toby was over, helping me with a work thing, and dragged Toby upstairs.

My phone buzzed as I was opening up my laptop, but it was just a text from Nadia, providing an update on her hangout with Pat (he put M&M's in the popcorn!). I set it aside and tilted the laptop screen so Toby and I could both see it from where we sat on my bed.

"August twentieth." I named the day you'd claimed as an anniversary and scanned the date column until I found the right one. My hopes were immediately tanked. "It says practice was canceled!"

Toby leaned back. "I remember that now. A chemical thing. They put too much chlorine or something in the pool, so no one could use it for a few days. Must have been then."

"How convenient," I said.

"What, you think Coach overchlorinated the pool on purpose? Isn't that a little over-the-top?"

"How often does a pool get overchlorinated, anyway?"

Toby shrugged. "It's not unheard of. And if he wanted to miss a practice, he didn't have to sabotage it. He could have just missed."

"Fine. But if practice really was canceled, then anyone could be K." I leaned back, too.

"What about the other days?" Toby asked.

"Keith was at practice on the Sunday she went to Ipswich. Two people are marked as absent that day, besides Izzy. Darren and Lila. No K's."

"Maybe she went alone? What about the one right after trials, when she went to the parking garage?"

It took me a moment to scroll to the date. "It says Coach Dwyer ran practice that day. Keith was out for 'personal reasons.'"

"Where was the garage again?" Toby flicked through something on his phone.

"Cambridge."

"No, the address. Put it into Google Maps."

I did. Toby leaned toward me, his chin hovering just above my bare shoulder, his cheek nearly brushing my neck, as a pin popped up on the screen. "What are you looking for?" I asked him.

He didn't answer. Instead he continued to scroll through his email until he said, "Got it. Okay, let me see that." He took the laptop and typed. After a moment, he turned the screen back to face me. There were two pins on the map now, half a block apart. "What's the second pin?"

Toby was somber-eyed as he sunk into the bed. "Coach Connors's apartment building."

I think we probably stared at each other for a full minute before we were broken apart by a knock on the door. Dad poked his head in without waiting for a response.

"You two scurried up here fast enough," he said. "Hello." His eyes moved from Toby, to me, to the laptop that shared a perch on our side-by-side shins.

"Did you want something, Dad?"

"I made soup for dinner. There's enough for Toby, too, if he's staying."

It felt absurd to be discussing soup after what we'd just learned, but maybe we needed some time to process. I turned to Toby. "You want to stay for soup?"

"Sure."

Dad had made tomato soup and grilled cheese. The sandwiches were warmish and only very lightly grilled, but they soaked up the tasty soup. I had my phone out on the table, waiting for WhisperingWahoo's reply. Nobody said anything until, halfway through the meal, Toby asked Dad about this bird he'd seen on his windowsill, which he described as muddy-colored and shiny and round and narrow and with a head that was cocky like a rooster's. I wondered if he'd just made the bird up, because whatever it was, he stumped Dad, who got up to retrieve his bird guide.

"Is there really a bird that hangs out on your windowsill?"

"Yes."

"And you just happen to have regular access to some rare specimen of bird for the eastern Massachusetts seaboard?"

"I think I'm just terrible at describing birds."

Dad returned with his book. "We'll get to the bottom of this mystery yet, Tobias. Now what would you say was the dominant color? The color on top, not the underbelly?"

"Brownish. I think."

"So your standard LBJ," Dad hmmphed.

"The president?" asked Toby.

I shook my head. "He means 'little brown job.' "

Dad gazed at me over the rim of his glasses as they slipped down the bridge of his nose. He had the guide pried open with one hand. His other held a spoon, which he used to swirl some of the steam out of his soup. "Oh, so you *do* listen to me sometimes." He looked at Toby. "LBJs are tricky. Because they're so common, you see. Did it have any distinctive markings?" He flipped through several pages.

"Definitely a Robin mask."

"You think it was a robin? Could be a female . . ."

"He means Robin as in Batman and Robin. Right?" I slurped some soup, barely concealing my grin. Neither Mom nor I had shown interest in discussing birds with him since you, and I knew he'd been starved for bird talk. I liked seeing Dad engaging with Toby, even if Toby didn't really care about bird identification. He wasn't being patronizing about it; he was just . . . being friendly. Trying his best to peck away the awkward.

"Yeah. He's like a superhero sidekick bird."

"That sounds like a cedar waxwing, then." Dad tapped a photograph in the guide and angled it at Toby. "Is that it?"

"Yes! With the rooster head!" Toby took the guide. "You know, the Mohawk feathers?"

"Ah, the crest. So that's what you meant by the rooster's head." Dad was smiling.

"Thank you," I said to Toby as we walked upstairs after dinner.

"For what?"

"For helping my dad be okay with . . . this."

"This?"

"*This*. The weirdness of you being here, helping me, when you were also, you know, there. With her."

"Good thing you want to be a writer. You really have a way with words."

"And now you're insulting me." I shook my head, amused. We'd reached the junction of my bedroom and yours. One door open. One door closed. I entered my room, leaving yours behind.

My phone buzzed again, and I didn't hesitate to check it.

"Why do you keep looking at your phone like you're expecting nuclear launch codes?"

"It's just Nadia," I said, but when Toby lifted his brows in skepticism, I added, "I'm expecting a message from WhisperingWahoo." He was too good at reading me, though I really had little reason to keep this a secret from him.

"And why would you be expecting that?"

My cheeks flushed. "Because I messaged them." I divulged the rest—how I'd found your deleted, mostly one-sided conversation with the anonymous troll, how the messages grew more openly hostile to the point of threatening. How you'd messaged them back on the morning of the day you'd vanished.

"And what are you planning to do now, Teddy?" There was a bite in his voice that I hadn't heard before.

"See what response I get. Maybe try to meet them."

"Alone?"

I said nothing.

"With the person who sort of threatened and maybe met up with your sister in the middle of the night on the night she was never seen again?"

"It's not like I'd do it at midnight in the woods!"

"And you're not going to do it alone!"

I bristled, but Toby wasn't being chauvinistic; he was being smart. Smarter than me. Maybe smarter than you, too.

"Don't you get that I want to help?"

"Yeah."

Sweetness returned to Toby's eyes, warmth to his voice. "Will you let me?" He stepped closer. I only had to shift my hand an inch and I could touch his fingertips.

"I'll let you know as soon as WhisperingWahoo replies." Immediately I felt relief. I wasn't alone, the way I had been since you.

"So." I took a breath. "We think she went to Keith's house the day they both missed practice."

"She could have gone somewhere else. There's a movie theater not too far from that garage. And, like, dozens of restaurants. Or she could have gone to someone else's house. A lot of the people on the team live in Cambridge. *I* live in Cambridge."

"Less than a two-minute walk from that garage?"

"It'd be more like fifteen."

"According to the spreadsheet, everyone else was at practice that day, anyway."

"But what about all the other places she might have gone?"

"I don't think we want to bank on the theory that Izzy skipped practice to go to the *movies*."

"She skipped practice to go to the beach," Toby pointed out.

"Yeah, but why not just go to a closer movie theater, if that's what she was doing? I'm pretty sure in detective books they follow their most promising leads first. And everything still points to Keith."

Toby inhaled. "I know. I just . . . I'm open to it, I am. I just have trouble seeing it."

"So we'll make ourselves see it." I jiggled the mouse, waking the laptop screen. Two red pins still sat side by side on the map. "We need something more concrete than a missed practice."

"When you were doing your—" Toby paused, searching for a word. "Research," he said finally, carefully. I appreciated his delicacy. "Before. You searched Izzy's room?"

"Yeah. I told you I didn't find her passport."

"And that was your first clue? That something weird was going on?"

I nodded. "Sometimes I . . . You're going to think this is stupid."

"Try me."

"So when I couldn't find her passport, I started to get these stories in my head of Izzy out there somewhere in the world. And she's okay and she's happy and she's just . . . traveling. And for the first time since she disappeared, I felt—"

"Hope," he said softly.

The word hung on the air. "Yes." Toby understood what no one else seemed to. People had told me there's no point in having false hope—if that's even what this was—but I disagreed. Hope was how I managed to go on. "I know all the scenarios I've imagined are just stories. I know what other people think happened. I know what *you* think happened. But this . . . it makes things easier."

We looked at each other across the bed as my revelation settled.

After a moment, Toby broke the silence. "Have you searched her room again, since we started learning all this stuff?"

I shook my head.

"Well, back then, you were looking for where she'd gone. Not who she'd been spending time with before she ran away, right?"

"So maybe there's something in there, something I missed before—"

"Because you didn't know its importance," Toby finished.

That's how we came to search your room again.

Going into your room was not something I did often or lightly. I'd spent a lot of time in there while I was "researching" and then for a while I didn't go in there at all. In the last few months I'd been in there more, mostly to pull stuff out of your closet for Australia. You had a really high-quality wetsuit, and I'd worn most of my wicking shirts to threads, but yours were practically new. Stuff like that was strewn on your bed. Otherwise, the room was as you'd left it, right down to the stacks of folded laundry on your dresser. Over the winter, I'd overheard Mom and Dad arguing about what to do with your room. Mom had wanted to sort through your belongings, throwing some stuff out, donating other things. Dad had said he wasn't ready. For parents who rarely fight, their voices got pretty loud, but seeing as all your stuff was still here, untouched, Dad must have won. I hadn't heard a peep about clearing the room out since.

As we entered your room, Toby skimmed the small of my back with his hand. The gesture said more than words could.

I started with your desk and had Toby take your closet. I shifted through your journal, checking the dates we now knew as significant, but you only ever wrote about your diet and exercise, and the dates in question were no exception. On the Wednesday after trials, when you'd gone to Cambridge, your meals for the day looked normal, for you. Three egg whites and a turkey sausage for breakfast. An orange as a midmorning snack. Eggplant parm sandwich on whole wheat for lunch. Protein smoothie as an afternoon snack. And tuna casserole for dinner. I knew you hadn't eaten that at our house, what with how Dad feels about tuna. But if you'd skipped an evening practice, you'd probably had dinner somewhere. Casserole sounded homemade. "Have you found anything?" I called to Toby.

"It's just . . . all Izzy's stuff." He shrugged as he came out of the closet and lowered himself to the edge of your bed. "Are you guys ever going to do anything with all this?"

"What would we do with it?"

"Donate it, maybe. Keep some of it for yourself."

"I have some of her stuff. On the bed there? It's for Australia. Most of her other stuff is swimming related."

"I mean like her clothes. Or jewelry."

I shook my head, dismissing the thought of claiming your things like an inheritance.

"I bet she'd want you to have something. Like a little thing, maybe? Her favorite necklace or earrings?" He toed the carpet.

"Why do you care?"

"I don't know." Toby rose. "It was a bad idea." He started for the closet, then stopped. "It's just . . . I think Izzy would have wanted her stuff to get used."

He had a point. Probably the same one Mom had been trying to make to Dad. You always did hate waste. "The earring the police found, that was one of her favorites. A little blue-and-gold peacock feather. Intricate. Delicate. I was kind of surprised she liked them so much. They weren't her usual style." I flicked through your collection of silver studs. "They were new, last summer, I'm pretty sure. I never really thought about where she got them before but—"

"You think they were a gift," Toby finished my thought.

I nodded. A gift from someone with more grown-up tastes and means.

Every new piece pointed at Keith, but none of it was definitive. None of it was proof.

We went back to searching. I kept rifling through your desk while Toby shifted about your closet hunting for love notes, doodles, photographs, trinkets. Anything that seemed odd, different from your usual taste, too expensive, too adult. How could you possibly have had a relationship with someone and not left anything behind?

I drummed my fingers on your laptop.

At the chime of your computer booting up, Toby emerged from the closet.

"You're thinking she had photos?"

"No, I've been through those. There's nothing useful. I'm going to pull up her email." You had too many emails in your account to go through them one by one. But with the right search criteria, I could find something more particular. An email exchange with your coach, close to trials, wouldn't have seemed suspicious the last time I went through your things.

Toby looked over my shoulder as I searched Keith's email address and narrowed the dates. His breathing hitched when we saw you'd sent Keith an email the day after your trip to the parking garage. There was nothing in the subject line. I clicked to expand.

Thank you for last night. You have no idea what it meant to me.—I

"That's it," I said. "They skipped practice together. She went to his house."

Toby straightened. "Did he reply?"

I shook my head. "No."

"So what's our next step? We confront him?"

Because Toby was standing, I stood, too. "Not we. Me."

"Why—"

I stepped closer to him. "For a few reasons. One: If I botch this, and we still think he and Izzy might have had a thing but we don't know for sure and he's no longer willing to talk to me, then you can swoop in as backup investigator."

"As comic-booky as that plan is, I'm not going to let you go do this alone, either."

"This is totally different than meeting up with Whispering-Wahoo. And you didn't let me get to reason two. Because he's your coach."

"And I've already accepted that he's probably a creeper."

"But what if he's not? What if there is some other explanation for all of this? If I accuse him of having an affair with my missing sister, he'll chalk it up to me not thinking clearly because my twin is MIA. And we'll never have to see each other again. But if *you* and I accuse him, and we're wrong . . . do you think you'd be able to look at each other the same way again?"

"You've thought about this a lot, it seems."

"I have to talk to him again. Without you." I reached between us, taking his hand. His fingertips were chilled, so I curled mine around them, lending him my warmth.

"Just let me know when and where you're doing it. So if he murders you, I have some information to give to the police this time."

I knew Toby was joking, and I moved to swat his shoulder and hopefully the smirk right off his face. Even so, a chill danced down my spine.

NINETEEN

In Which I Go to the Home of Your Coach

I STOOD ACROSS THE STREET FROM KEITH CONNORS'S TOWN HOUSE, looking up at the shuttered blinds of the third story, where your coach lived with his family. It was a nice building: untarnished blue paint, clean white trim, a hexagonal tower of bay windows rising up on the right side. A family of four couldn't live here on a swim coach's salary. I didn't know if they owned or rented, but I figured the money must have come from her. I wondered how well you'd known Mrs. Connors. I wondered if it was her money that had bought you the peacock earrings.

I was acting on the assumption that Keith Connors was K, but every clue Toby and I had uncovered had led me to these white-washed steps. I crossed the street and rang the buzzer for the third floor.

An intercom clicked on. A woman's voice asked, "Hello?"

I almost ran off the porch. It was four o'clock in the afternoon, on a day when Keith had morning practice. I'd been hoping his wife would be out working and he'd be home with the kids. Toby had told me he handled a lot of the child care.

"Hello?" the woman asked again, this time with a bit of annoyance on her voice. I spoke before I could talk myself out of it.

"It's Teddy Ware. I'm Izzy's sister." A year since you'd been her husband's star swimmer, but she must know your name. Who could forget the near-Olympic athlete who'd been coached by her husband and had tragically disappeared into the bowels of a dusky lake?

"Teddy?" the woman echoed my name, her annoyance now replaced with confusion. Maybe I was getting better at this reading-people business. Or maybe I was simply hearing whatever I wanted to hear. "I'll buzz you in." Another click. When I tried the door, it opened.

A petite brunette with a toddler on her hip met me on the stairs and led me up. The toddler drove a toy car over her shoulder and down her back, vrooming as he went. A teakettle was hissing as we entered her apartment. "Sorry, I had just started a pot. Do you drink tea?"

"Not really." I closed the door behind me.

She plopped the kid into a playpen in the middle of the kitchen and moved the kettle from the stove. In another room, a television was on. Action music from a children's cartoon blared. As Mrs. Connors poured hot water into a mug that had been set out and prepped with a tea bag, she asked me if there was anything I would like to drink.

But she had yet to ask me why I was there. Maybe she knew. Maybe Keith had come clean about the affair and they'd patched things up.

Maybe she'd helped him get rid of you.

"I could use a glass of water," I said.

She smiled kindly and opened a cupboard. The child stood up and shook the side of the playpen.

"Mrs. Connors," I started as she handed me a glass of water.

"*Dr.* Connors." Then she amended as I started to apologize, "Common mistake. When you go through as much schooling as I did, you feel ownership of the title." She smiled again. It was a small smile—just a slight upturn at the corners of her lips—but it was comforting. Yet I wasn't sure why I was being comforted.

"Aren't you wondering why I'm here?"

"A bit," she admitted. Then she called into the other room. "Jamie, will you turn the television down?" Back to me: "Sorry. It's Spider-Man. Her favorite." Dr. Connors sipped her tea.

"It's okay." How could this woman stand in her kitchen chatting with a teenage stranger and not ask what I was doing there? She watched me, and I got the feeling she was letting me take the lead. To talk, or not. To stay, or leave. It was my show, and she was content to play the audience.

"Is Coach . . ." I stopped because he wasn't my coach. "Is Mr. Connors here?"

"He stepped out to get some groceries. He should be back soon, if you want to wait."

"Right." I sipped the water. If she knew, she was being surprisingly cool about my coming here to dredge up old news of her husband's creepy affair. And if she didn't know, I was about to ruin this woman's life.

"Was there something you wanted to talk to him about?" Something about the emphasis she placed on the word *him* seemed strange to me. Who else could I have come there to talk to, if not the man who'd coached my twin sister to the Olympic trials?

"Yes." Despite this odd doctor and slightly hectic, very real home, I needed answers about you. Affair or not, you'd come here for some purpose. That much, I knew. Keith had the answers.

But maybe Dr. Connors did, too.

"Did you know my sister at all?"

She sipped her tea before answering. "Yes."

"You came to the meets, then?"

"Some of them. Not too many. Often I'd be with the kids or my patients." She noticed my curiosity at this and added, "I'm a psychiatrist. I see patients at a clinic in Cambridge and an office in Ipswich."

I blinked. Ipswich. "Near the beach?" The question was hardly more than a whisper.

"Yes, quite." Dr. Connors still smiled her soothing smile as she watched me with what I now knew were her psychiatrist's eyes. My own therapist had often looked at me like that: a friendly grin to encourage comfort and confession; a cocked head to portray close listening; all the while, she would read me with her wide, intelligent eyes. Dr. Connors was reading me now, trying to puzzle me out.

"Izzy was your patient, then." This I now knew, too.

"Not officially."

"But unofficially?" The words stuck in my throat on the way out.

"There is such a thing as doctor-patient confidentiality."

"But she wasn't officially your patient."

"No, she wasn't."

"And she's . . ." I stopped. The word I wanted to say—*missing*—would engender skepticism and pity. And I wouldn't say the other word, the one that Dr. Connors would undoubtedly assume filled my blank.

"Yes, she is."

"Can I use your bathroom?"

"Of course. Down the hall." She gestured. "But, Teddy—are you okay?"

I nodded.

In the bathroom, I braced my hands on the sink and looked in the mirror. Your face stared back at me. Of course, it wasn't really *your* face. It was mine. But for a moment the red tinge in my hair from the sun faded into the brown and my slightly crooked nose smoothed into your aquiline peak and my freckles, so many this summer, fanning out like wings under my eyes, just like Toby had said they did, disappeared against my sandy complexion. I gazed at you and me until a knock forced me to break away.

"Teddy?" It was Keith, returned from his food run. I stared at the door until he said, "Please answer so I know that you're okay."

I opened the door. Keith's face was tilted slightly, his cinched brows and wide eyes stricken with concern. "I'm okay," I told him.

He looked me over. "You sure?"

I nodded.

"Laura said you wanted to talk to me about something."

I nodded again.

"Come on, then." I followed him down the hall to an office. There were pictures in this office, too, but they were mostly of the family. Except for one. On a bookshelf behind the desk, Keith was in his Wahoo coaching polo with his arms around two uniformed swimmers: Bryce and you. You were both in swim caps and shimmering from pool water. Everyone smiled.

Keith closed the door and sat down at the desk. There was another chair, in the corner, sort of like a dining room chair. I took it.

"My wife's home office, mostly," Keith said. "But we share."

I nodded. Apparently, I'd lost touch with words.

"I know we don't know each other very well, but I sort of feel like I do know you," Keith said.

I managed an eyebrow raise at that. "Because we look so much alike?"

"No. I mean, you look similar, sure, but I'd never mistake you for her. You move differently."

"I *move* differently?"

"It's hard to explain. Carry yourself? Your sister liked to make herself known. Physically, I mean. You're not like that."

I didn't say anything, too busy trying to determine what it meant that Keith thought we moved differently.

"It's not bad. I'm not criticizing. It's just . . . God. I'm rambling, aren't I?"

I shrugged. Seconds ticked by as I looked at the picture of you and Bryce and Keith on the bookshelf. I considered how you'd been Dr. Connors's patient, too many questions flying through my thoughts all at once. Did that mean you *hadn't* been having an affair with Keith? Did Mom and Dad know you'd been seeing a psychiatrist for . . . something? Had they been keeping secrets from me, too?

"Teddy." Keith said my name cautiously. "Why did you come here?"

I fingered the ridges in my chair's armrest, following their curves. "Thank you for last night. You have no idea what it meant to me." It wasn't hard for me to recite this line. It had been running through my head like lines of a script since I'd uncovered the email. When I glanced up, Keith was looking at me like I'd grown a second head.

"It's from an email she sent to you, the day after you both skipped practice."

He fidgeted in his chair. His hand brushed across his stubble. "That's why you wanted the attendance records?"

I nodded.

"What are you trying to find out?"

I looked at him straight-on. Keith was definitely on edge. Even more so than when I'd spoken to him in his office. His rambling was evidence of that. But where did his wife fit into all this? Where did K?

"She came here? Not long after trials?"

"Yes," Keith said without any hesitation.

"Why?"

"For dinner. She wanted to talk to my wife."

"She wanted . . ." That didn't make sense. You had come not to the home of your coach, but your . . . therapist?

"She knew what Laura does. Her specialty, I mean, and she asked me if I could set something up."

"Because she's a psychiatrist?"

"Would it be okay if I brought Laura in? She can talk about this better than I can."

At my nod, Keith left the small room. Why would you need to hide talking to Dr. Connors? It actually made sense to me that you'd need to talk to someone, given the stress you'd been under leading up to trials. And then after you failed to make the Olympic team? I'm honestly surprised Mom and Dad didn't *insist* you see someone, and I'm positive they would have said yes if you'd suggested it. So why the charade?

My mind went to the word Keith had used when I'd asked why you'd wanted to talk to his wife. *Specialty.* How his eyes had shifted away when I'd sought clarification that you'd wanted a psychiatrist, like that was it, but also not quite right. I whipped out my phone and googled *Dr. Laura Connors, Ipswich.* I found her website.

Dr. Laura Connors specialized in helping adolescents overcome trauma. I reread her credentials and philosophy until the words on the page blurred. There was only one that really mattered: *trauma.*

Suddenly your response to Toby's *Everything OK?* text struck a heavier note.

Keith returned and I quickly tucked my phone away. He opened a folding chair, and Laura sat down next to me.

"Izzy wasn't seeing you because of stress," I said as my heart picked up speed and my mind spun newer, scarier stories. Trauma was abuse. Trauma was assault. Trauma was something that happened to soldiers and people who were present for violent catastrophes and natural disasters. It was for people who grew up with drug-addled parents. For children who were touched by an uncle or a priest or a random pervert in a public restroom. *Trauma* was not a word that belonged to you.

"The answer to that is fairly complicated," Laura said in reply.

Keith drummed the desk with his fingertips, four taps in quick succession.

"Then uncomplicate it! Why did Izzy need to talk to a trauma specialist? What happened to her?"

"Teddy, please understand—"

Dr. Connors stopped talking when her husband held up his hand. "Can you listen, for a second?" Keith said before telling me a story. A few days before trials, he had found you swimming extra laps. Not just swimming. Plunging. Like you were in a race. Like you were already at the Olympics. He stopped you at the wall and reminded you that you should be tapering, you were going to overwork your-self, and you said you *had* to swim, it was the only thing keeping your mind clear. You were about to shoot off again for another lap when he reached to stop you, he claimed, but when he touched your shoulder, you jolted backward. You began to flail. Your breathing came in fast, heavy puffs. Your legs reached for stable footing that was too far underwater to do any good. You started to cry. And you were shaking so badly and so suddenly, your face dipping below the surface, that he jumped in the pool to buoy you. He put his arms around you and at first you thrashed, not wanting to be held or even touched, but he stilled you anyway, gathered you up, and carried you out. He got you a towel, and you were still crying, incoherent, shucking breaths as he steadied you. He asked you what was wrong and you said you didn't know. He said if it's nerves, you don't have to worry, you'll be fine, you're ready. You said it wasn't nerves. So then he asked you if something had happened, and you said yes. He asked you *what* had happened, but you shook your head and changed your story, saying nothing happened. You said, "I'll be fine. Please don't tell anyone. It's nothing I can't handle." You went to the locker room and he knew he should call our parents, but he didn't because you had begged him not to. So he watched you over the next few days and you seemed okay, until your performance at trials revealed you were *not* okay, something had gotten into your head, jostled your focus, wrestled away your drive. And he thought again that he should tell our parents, but he didn't because you had asked him not to and because he'd already waited and you'd already missed your chance at these Olympics. But something was still off. Something had scared you. A few days after trials you came to his office and asked about Laura. He said he'd make you an appointment and you balked. You just had some questions for her, you said, eyes shifting downward in a way that was entirely un-Izzy. So he invited you to family dinner, and you came.

Keith shook—audibly, visibly—as he recounted this tale of your panic attack. When he finished, he pressed a knuckle into the corner of his eye.

"And that's it? You never found out why she was so upset?"

He looked at his lap and I knew from that evasive, guilty glance away that he was still hiding something. "Izzy never told me," he said.

"But she told you?" I turned to Laura, who had been silent during her husband's confession, though I had felt her watching me keenly.

"I don't think she told me everything."

"What did she tell you?"

Laura looked at Keith. Then she looked at me. "I'm sorry, Teddy." The words weighed on her.

"You're not going to tell me?" I pressed, even though I already knew my answer. She'd been prepared for me. Keith had probably told her I'd come to his office, and ever since then, she'd been thinking about whether she would tell me your secrets, should I come calling.

"Izzy wanted it kept private."

"But she was a kid! Don't you have to, legally, tell her parents?"

"Actually, no. In Massachusetts, anyone aged sixteen or older can consent to mental health treatment without the permission of their guardian."

"But you said she wasn't officially your patient?"

"I said that because I didn't charge her. Practically, though, I offered counsel under the condition of anonymity."

"But she did see you again? At your office in Ipswich?"

"Yes. Once."

"Did you ever think that maybe whatever it was that she talked to you about could have something to do with what happened to her? Did you even bother to tell the police?" I was panicking now, thinking that maybe, if they wouldn't tell me anything, I could get them to tell someone. Officer Kelly would act on this news. Surely he would.

"Of *course* we did," said Laura. "Honey, we told the police that first week. They know all of this."

I snapped my mouth shut on my next protest. The police knew that you'd unofficially seen a psychiatrist. They knew why you'd seen her. But that information hadn't been shared with me, despite all of the other parts of your case they'd allowed me to know. Why?

"Was it . . ." Besides trials, the only thing I could think of from last summer that could have troubled you was the cyberbullying. The first taunt was in early July, a few days before trials. Had I been so wrong? Had this been the thing that had rattled you so much your coach had had to jump in the pool to comfort you? "Was it because of WhisperingWahoo?"

"Whispering . . ." Confused, Laura looked to Keith.

"It's an anonymous Instagram account," he said, filling her in.

"Someone on your team was harassing her all summer!"

Keith and Laura shared a look, like they hadn't known, but weren't surprised.

"It would have been another stressor," Laura said, to her husband, not me.

He ran a hand through his hair as he drew a breath. "I didn't know," he said to me.

"And . . . that's it? That's all either of you can tell me?" I looked back and forth between them, but it was Laura who spoke.

"Teddy, I wish I could tell you more, but ethically, I can't. Absent any immediate danger, doctor-patient confidentiality can only be broken by subpoena."

"Even after . . ." Again, I stopped, unable to say the word.

"Yes, even then." Laura's voice and eyes and even her posture radiated useless pity.

"I'm sorry, too." Keith's hands rested on the desk. He could no longer look at me. "I should have spoken out before trials. I was just trying not to make things worse for her."

"It's not your fault," Laura said to her husband. "It seemed like things were getting better. And I thought—we thought—that bringing in anyone else, against Izzy's wishes, wouldn't help her."

Keith nodded. He inhaled sharply, calming himself. As he lifted both hands and ran them through his hair, he loosened some strands so a few coiled across his forehead, making him look younger.

These two were acting as if I had suddenly evaporated from the room. "*What's* not his fault?"

Laura said, "He blames himself."

"I should have told someone sooner how upset she was. I should have pushed her to keep seeing Laura. And I'm so, so sorry I didn't." His head dropped. As I sat across the desk from him, watching him mourn you, I realized why his silence had smothered him in guilt: He thought you had drowned yourself.

That was not the information I had come here to find. I couldn't think about the story he'd shared—about whatever it was that had fucked with your head and made you screw up at trials, about how the police knew Keith and Laura's version of events and hadn't found it relevant, about you demanding once again that something be kept secret from everyone—so I stuck to my script, following the narrative I was already pursuing. "So you didn't go with my sister to a lake in Maine eight days before she disappeared?"

"What?" His confusion seemed genuine. So did his wife's.

"And you didn't give her gold peacock earrings?"

"Teddy, what are you—"

"Were you supposed to meet with her that night?"

"Of course not. Why would I—"

"Nothing. It's . . ." I'd come here hoping to solve for K. I'd thought I was well on my way to tying up the threads of your mystery, but instead, they were unraveling in my hand. I looked at Keith with his nerve-mussed hair and Laura with her understanding eyes—two people who had seen your pain and tried to help—and all I wanted was to wish the day away. "I think I'd like to go home now."

TWENTY

So I'm Kind of Mad at You

TOBY WAS OFF-LOADING HIS LUNCH INTO THE FRIDGE WHEN I WALKED into the guardhouse the next morning. Everyone else was already on the beach. We had lifeguard training. Quimby wanted us to practice our water rescues.

"Hey," he said.

"Hey," I echoed.

"Your text last night wasn't very detailed."

"Sorry. I was kind of tired."

He nodded. "Did you . . . learn anything?"

"Nope." Not true, not true, not true. And Toby knew I was lying. But I wasn't ready to admit out loud the things that I had learned.

Saying nothing more, I dropped off my things and dashed out of the guardhouse to join Nadia on the beach. Quimby had us enacting scenarios in the lake all morning as he called them out. Pat flailed in the shallow water, and I used the rescue tube to swim him back to shore. Nadia fell out of a canoe, and Derek paddled out on the surfboard to retrieve her. Through some creative positioning, I managed to evade Toby, avoiding even his gaze, and the hurt clouding in his eyes. Keeping Toby so purposefully in the dark was mean.

You'd kept me in the dark about so much, and here I was being a total hypocrite. Except I knew I would tell Toby everything. Eventually. When I could manage to get the words out. When I'd had more time to process it.

But we were a small guard staff, and I couldn't avoid pairing up with Toby forever. When it was my turn to play the victim, Quimby wanted us to practice deep-water backboarding. He told me to swim past the docks and pretend to drown.

"I can do it." Nadia stepped toward the water.

"No, no," said Quimby quickly and obliviously. "You just went out there. Toby's going to be the primary rescuer. Derek will be secondary. Then we'll do the whole thing again and switch up the roles." He crossed his arms over his bulbous belly and waited.

"It's okay," I said, steeling myself. There was nothing scary about having to pretend to drown in the deeper water, though my nerves begged to differ.

I picked a spot away from the lily pads and flopped backward, doing my best to float lifelessly as I listened for the sounds of rescue. Toby blew his whistle hard and loud. Sand whooshed into the air as he jumped off the guard chair, then feet flapped against the water. The splash of his strokes was fast at first, then slow as he neared me. Textbook. We're taught not to create turbulent water around a victim with a potential neck injury, but I've always wondered why the precaution mattered. All I was doing was waiting. I kept my lungs full of air, making my chest into a little life jacket. If I were really injured, I wouldn't be doing that. I'd be sinking. I'd be drowning.

My toes touched the weeds.

"Hey." Toby's voice was a little broken. He brought my arms up beside my head and used them to brace my neck. He treaded, his only job now to keep me still and afloat. Derek would bring an extra rescue tube and the backboard. "So . . . you doing okay?"

"Broken neck is all," I tried to joke, but I was shaking too much to pull it off. You'd been sneaking therapy. You'd been traumatized.

You'd been broken.

"Quimby shouldn't have . . ."

"It's all right."

Toby's presence was starting to have its usual, calming effect. With practiced ease he supported my body as we enacted the drill, waiting for Derek and the backboard to arrive. Toby's breathing wasn't labored, like mine would have been, were our roles reversed. I could feel the water swirling gently beneath me as he treaded. His hands were warm on my arms. His wide butterfly shoulders, exposed, shimmering, mere inches from my side. Every part of me within his easy reach. I had to say something or risk Toby being able to read the sudden hormone-laced thoughts etched on my face as clearly as an open page from my journal.

Toby sucked in a breath. "Teddy, about yesterday—"

I was saved from having to explain by Derek, who rocked the water around me with his arrival and dipped a rescue tube underneath my knees. My feet suddenly lifted out of the water, and I shivered. Derek brought the backboard up smoothly beneath me. His fingers dripped water onto my face in a teasing way.

I twitched. "Stop that!"

"Good, you can feel," Derek whispered in my ear. "That means you're not dead yet." He gripped my chin with his right hand, stabilizing my neck and grinning at me as Toby maneuvered my arms out of the way to install the foam pads that would support my head. They had switched places now, with Derek keeping my head afloat and cozy and Toby moving around to secure my body with the straps. His hands skimmed my breasts as he tugged the first strap taut. He glanced away as he did it, his cheeks a little flushed. I was flushed, too. I'd been strapped into backboards before, obviously, and had the straps tightened by all of the other Bottomrock guards, even Derek. I'd never considered it a sexy act before, but as Toby's hands moved across my body, I couldn't help but squirm. When he buckled the strap that went over my wrists, I quivered as his fingers skirted across my waist. By the time he made it to the final set, the one that hugged high on my thighs, I made myself stop watching him. I could still feel his fingers, though, gentle and brief.

Lying there, immobilized, all I could do was look skyward. A storm was coming. It had been brewing all morning. Clouds congregated in a deep purple mass. Wind swirled through the trees. The air was thick and heavy and smelled of rain.

"Hanging in?" It was Derek who popped into view and smiled over me. As he trailed off, he stroked the rim of my ear. I tried to lean away but the restraints held me in place.

Toby drew his hands back as he finished with the straps. They started to swim me carefully toward the beach. Tied as I was, if they let go, and the board tipped, I'd drown. This was the first time I'd been on a backboard and noticed how helpless I was.

Then Derek commanded, "Lift on three! One, two, three!" and my entire body rose with the backboard as they lifted me out of the water and carried me ashore.

We ran through a few more drills before Quimby left. Shortly after, the sky finally burst in a deluge and we all ran for the guardhouse to take cover.

But as everyone else ducked inside, I slipped off into the woods.

Rain pattered against the peak of the guardhouse roof and fell in staccato drips off the sides. Despite the chill it brought, I'd always particularly liked Bottomrock in the rain, and not just because it meant a quiet workday. The rain seemed to enhance the lake smell, of skunk cabbage and silt, algae and water lilies. I loved the smell. I loved the look of the trees with their leaves all weary. I loved the way rain patterned the sand. The way it made the water ripple. I knew Toby wanted me to talk to him. Every minute I kept him in the dark, he was becoming more and more convinced that Keith was K. I had to tell him, soon. It was cruel of me not to.

Last night I wrote down another memory in my catalog. About when Landon Adler asked me to homecoming freshman year and then changed his mind the day of the dance and asked someone else instead. You distracted me all weekend and then on Monday, in gym, we were doing a unit on weight lifting and you challenged Landon to a contest. Said you could lift more than he could. You even let him pick the machine. And then you won, lifting weight effortlessly that caused Landon's face to pucker and blush, and even though I knew it'd been easy for you, I also knew you'd embarrassed him for me. You were there for me when I needed you, always, so I couldn't for the life of me figure out why you hadn't let me be there for you. I thought I deserved the chance. And maybe that's selfish. But so is lying. So is leaving.

I'd reached the picnic table behind the guardhouse when Toby caught up to me. "Teddy!" My name cut through the rain, but I almost kept going. Almost. I swiveled. "He's not K," I said.

Toby stopped midstride. "He's not?"

"At least, I'm pretty sure he's not." The words had to force their way through a logjam in my throat.

"Then what happened?"

"She didn't trust me."

"Teddy—"

"It's true. The universe is practically screaming at me, 'You guys weren't that close!'"

"What did the universe tell you yesterday?" he asked gently, capping the remark with his characteristic smirk. He meant to cheer me up, but it didn't work.

I told him what I'd learned about you from the Connors. "And the thing of it is . . ." I stopped there, my feet sinking into the mud.

"What's the thing?" Toby lifted a hand to my chin and tilted my head, leaving me no choice but to look at him. And looking at him, I could do nothing else but tell him.

"I'm mad at her." I paused, scanning his face for signs of judgment, but all I saw were the raindrops caught in his eyelashes and one on the very tip of his nose. He hadn't balked. "For not telling me." It was a relief to finally voice what had been eating away at me since last night. And, if I'm being honest, what I felt then was only an echo of a feeling I'd had off and on since you'd gone. "Izzy was so wrecked by something that Keith had to jump in the water with her to calm her down. Whatever it was probably messed her up so bad that she couldn't focus at trials. She started seeing a therapist. And instead of being horrified that she was in pain, I'm mad at her for keeping it a secret from me!"

Tears I'd been storing up for nearly a year welled in my eyes. My knees crumpled, and my body began to shake, and then suddenly Toby had me wrapped in his arms. His hand cupped the back of my head. His cheek pressed against my forehead. "Hey," he said, softly, not a greeting or an accusation, but an acknowledgment. That he was there. That I wasn't alone. His chest was bare and warm despite the dampness from the rain. I could hear his heart thrumming, fast at first, and then slower, slower, calming, as I did.

"There's another thing," I said into his chest as the rain continued to pelt us and my last shudder faded into a sigh.

"What's the thing?" His fingers twirled my hair at the nape of my neck.

"I'm mad at me, too. For not seeing it. For . . . ignoring or being oblivious or . . ." I started to choke up again, and he held me tighter.

"Hey, I didn't see it, either, okay?"

"That's not the same at all."

"No, but I did see her three hours a day, six days a week. And whatever was going on, I missed it, too."

"That makes me feel, like, two percent better."

"And the fact that a year later, we're struggling to find any scrap of information about what was going on with her last summer? That tells us she was trying not to be seen, right?"

"Now I feel, like, three percent better." But I laughed into him, soaking in the warmth of his body despite the cool rain and lake breeze.

"She texted you, right? She said she had to tell you something? Maybe it was about all of this."

"Maybe." I should have read between the lines and called you. I should have known when you sent me that text that whatever it was you wanted to tell me, it couldn't wait for me to come home.

"Can we recap?" Toby's chest vibrated against my cheek as he spoke.

"Recap?"

"Run through what we've learned about Izzy that summer. Maybe, putting it all together, something will click."

"She was seeing someone," I started.

"And she wasn't telling anyone about it," Toby went on. "Plus, she skipped practice and also didn't tell anyone, and she saw Dr. Connors secretly during two of those skipped practices."

"She saw Dr. Connors *for trauma*," I added as I pulled away from him.

Toby's fingers slipped down my back as he, too, stepped away. "But not because some online troll was harassing her. Since Coach and his wife didn't seem to know about that?" He looked to me for confirmation.

"Right. So far, the harassment seems unrelated. Except that she texted them—challenged them—the same day she went to Bottomrock."

"And she had that note about a midnight meeting."

"A meeting that may or may not have happened, and may or may not have been with either the mystery partner or the mystery troll," I said. "It would help so much if at least one of these people wasn't anonymous . . ." And as Toby predicted, something clicked. "There's a video."

"A video?"

I took out your phone to show him the recovered conversation between you and WhisperingWahoo. "See, they reference a video that's proof they're not lying. But no video was ever actually posted."

"You think . . ."

"WhisperingWahoo was mostly slut-shaming Izzy. So the video—"

"Is probably of Izzy and whoever she was seeing," Toby finished my thought.

"Which Izzy wouldn't want posted, because she was keeping the relationship a secret."

"So if we find out who WhisperingWahoo is, we'll probably find out who the partner was."

"And then we can finally know if either of them went to Bottomrock that night. If they talked to Izzy or if they . . ." I didn't want to voice what I was thinking. That you might be truly dead, but not because you'd drowned.

TWENTY-ONE

How to Catch a Troll

I FULFILLED THE PROMISE I MADE TO MYSELF AT YOUR LAKE IN Maine: When I found something real, I brought it to a professional.

Officer Kelly had been assigned to the high school after your case was "deprioritized." Maybe his dealings with me had proved he had a rapport with young adults. Or maybe he was just the youngest officer in the department. In any event, I knew where to find him: floating around the grounds, forcing any would-be pill-poppers to take their drug habits to more secluded places than the parking lot or baseball diamond.

"Teddy?" he sputtered through a mouthful of grinder. A dribble of mayonnaise trickled down his chin, and he quickly wiped it away with a paper napkin. He was sitting on the bleachers by the tennis court, having lunch.

I couldn't help but think, *This is how you needed to reallocate your resources, Chief Anderson?*

Officer Kelly's eyes then drifted to Toby, who stood beside me. "What are you both doing here?"

"I got into her phone." I didn't need to say your name. Officer Kelly knew the moment he'd noticed me why I approached.

"And you found something?" Was that hope that lifted on his voice as I slipped your phone from my pocket and handed it to him, the conversation with WhisperingWahoo already pulled up? I waited a moment as he read through the messages before I blurted, "They threatened her. And that last one? When she suggested they meet? It was sent the day she disappeared!"

"That's suspicious, you're right." Officer Kelly handed your phone back to me. "But it's not enough."

"Not enough? Isn't it at least worth talking to WhisperingWahoo? Can't you get a court order or something to find out who they are?"

"It's almost impossible to get a court order that will force a big tech company to reveal the identity of a private account. And even if we were able to get a court order, which I don't think we can get on these messages alone, the tech companies fight them. It's just not viable."

"What about the video they say they have? Izzy was seeing someone. Did you know that?"

Officer Kelly squinted. "No, I didn't know that."

"And this video might tell us who that person was! Isn't that relevant?"

"Possibly. But that doesn't matter if we can't get ahold of the video."

"So that's it?" Toby said. "We find some real evidence and you're just going to say, 'Oh, well'?"

"I'm not saying, 'Oh, well.' I'm saying, legally, this isn't proof of anything. There is no reply from the recipient, so we don't even know if they agreed to meet. From this conversation, it seems like they *didn't* meet up. And by *your* own testimony, no one else was there that night at the lake." Officer Kelly took a breath. He climbed down from the bleachers, until he stood on even ground with Toby and me. He looked at us both, then zeroed in on Toby. "You've been helping her? Look for Izzy?"

"Yeah, I have."

Kelly nodded. His gaze switched back to me. "Teddy, I think you need to consider other possibilities," he said softly.

And that's when I knew: He'd been turned. My ally in the department. The one officer who had thought like I did, that something was off about the night you disappeared, that you might still be out there: He'd changed his mind. Sometime between when he'd wallowed with me in silence because we'd both been banned from your case and now, Officer Kelly had become convinced you were dead. I could read it in his eyes. The sympathy. The pity. The poverty of hope.

Fortunately I had plenty of practice hiding my own hope from all the adults in my life.

"Yeah," I said as if I meant it. "Okay."

In the car I said to Toby, "I think we're on our own."

He smirked. "That's okay. I think I have a plan."

To FERRET OUT YOUR cyberbully, we created a fake Instagram account, populated it with enough photos to suggest it belonged to someone on the Wahoos and then sent WhisperingWahoo a vague and enticing DM:

Want to capture something else scandalous? Teddy and Toby take a lunch break together at the Bottomrock dam every day at noon.

We thought about arranging the setup for after hours, but lunchtime seemed safer. Daylight. Plenty of people within shouting distance. Not that WhisperingWahoo was some sort of ax-murderer. Probably.

Still, there was an aura of danger as we lay together uphill of the dam, shielded by the woods and a rocky outcropping. The wind whistled. Water churned through the dam and plopped into the river. A lunch break passed with no sign of anyone. Another passed the same way. I started to think our mark was too clever for this setup. How had you figured out who WhisperingWahoo was?

We didn't talk as we waited, in case the troll should overhear us and turn back before we could lay eyes on them. We sat atop last fall's leaves, shoulder to shoulder, thigh to thigh, and my mind kept going back to Toby's hand skimming my body as he cinched the backboard straps. I was still trying to ignore the charge between us. Trying not to think about how his fingers, cracked from chlorine, had touched the tip of my chin and sent something sparking through my veins. How my head had slotted so neatly into place when he held me. Because as much as I liked Toby, he would always be the boy who'd watched you disappear.

But he was also the boy who'd devised a plan to catch your cyberbully when the police would not, who was willingly sacrificing his lunch break to lie in wait beside me for a possible murderer who might never show.

The fact that we had orchestrated a sting felt silly and scary, all at once. It couldn't possibly work. It had to work. Toby's fingers found mine in the brush as the woods groaned and kids laughed in the distance.

Leaves crinkled underfoot. Toby and I straightened.

Someone was coming up the path.

Long, dark blond hair and broad swimmer's shoulders.

Bryce stopped at the head of the dam and looked around.

I was on my feet fast, shouting as I trampled down the hill. "I can't *believe* you! You were her friend!"

Bryce paled. "Teddy?" he stammered. "What are you . . ."

Toby emerged from the woods behind me. He was shaken. Bryce was his friend, too. It took a beat before Toby managed the line we had scripted, before we'd known who might come calling.

"I saw you that night, you know." Toby did his best to drape the lie in an ominous aura. We knew there was a good chance WhisperingWahoo would lie about the midnight meeting, if that's who you'd really been scheduled to meet. This line was supposed to force the troll's hand. If he'd really been there the night you'd gone into the lake, he'd likely believe Toby and respond in kind. If he hadn't been there, his confusion would be genuine.

Bryce's eyes narrowed. "What night? What's going on?"

"You harassed my sister for months, pretending to be her friend, and now I want to know what happened the night she disappeared!"

Bryce stared back at us blankly. I watched him swallow his nerves, then puff his chest up. "I didn't harass her," he said finally, with no trace of irony on his voice.

"What would you call it, then?" Toby asked, a hardness to his voice I hadn't heard before as he stood up for you.

Bryce shrugged. "A little harmless ribbing? Izzy needed someone to deflate her ego every once in a while. What I want to know is why you two psychos were waiting in the woods playing junior detective."

Anger and desperation, two feelings I was growing too familiar with, rose in me. "I want to see the video."

Bryce stilled. "What video?"

"The one you threatened to post."

"Oh. That." He looked at the lake again. "It was a bluff."

"Then . . . why?"

Bryce sighed. "Why what?" How could he stand there staring at his nails like he was bored by us? How could he not feel guilty for the pain he'd brought you? How could anyone laugh with you and encourage you and be your friend, then say those awful things under the guise of anonymity? Desperate to have this lead amount to something, I felt a renewed strength to fight for you.

"Why keep saying all those horrible things? Did you ever think about how Izzy must have felt? And why start it back up again this summer with me and Toby? Why—"

"I think Teddy's trying to ask why you're an ass, which, in my opinion, is kind of a pointless question. Though if you do have an answer, I'm keen to hear it." As Toby crossed his arms, I smiled inwardly. He and you shared a blunt honesty and confidence, which I admired.

"Look, what do you want from me? An evil villain monologue? 'Cause clearly that's how you've cast me. Izzy thought she was this perfect athlete, Coach's favorite, deserving of anything and anyone she wanted and someone needed to take her down a peg, okay?"

"Anyone she . . ."

"Like him, even though he was with Taryn." Bryce flicked his wrist in Toby's direction. "Or . . . anyone. Can I go?"

"She messaged you that morning. One of the last messages she ever sent. You realized that, right?"

Bryce paused. "That's what this is about? Look, I met with her that day, okay? At lunchtime. We buried the hatchet." He reached into his pocket and dug out his phone. He showed me a selfie, time-stamped for a little after one in the afternoon on the day you'd disappeared, of you and him smiling, though your smile seemed fake to me. The background looked like the weight room at your pool in Cambridge.

And you were wearing one—and only one—blue-and-gold peacock earring.

"See? She got over it. You guys will, too." Bryce tucked the phone back into his pocket. "*Now* can I go?" He didn't wait for permission, but Toby called after him anyway. "You and me—we're done."

Bryce said nothing, just kept walking away.

My hand found the small of Toby's back as Bryce left. We may have lost a lead, but Toby had just lost a friend. "Forget it," Toby said, stepping back from me. "Bryce isn't worth another thought."

"I know." I nodded. My last realization had hollowed me out: You'd lost one of your peacock earrings before you'd gone to the lake that night. You could have lost it earlier that day, sometime before meeting Bryce. Or you could have lost it at the campsite across the lake days, weeks, months before your fateful swim, and continued to wear the unmatched earring anyway because it must have meant something to you. But to me, the lost earring wasn't proof of anything. It didn't mean what I'd hoped it meant.

She must have lost it some other night, the chief had said.

All my leads, every single one, were just dead ends.

As one of the final park improvement tasks before the big dedication, Quimby wanted us to refinish the floor in the guardhouse. But maybe I should say *finish*, as I'm not sure it had ever been properly done. It was largely cement, with flecks here and there that might have once been an actual floor, or might just be stray drops of paint.

We closed the park for a day and carried the contents of the guardhouse outside, littering the beach with Bottomrock history. Outdated electronics. Piles of orange life vests. Buckets of beach toys. First-aid supplies and sunscreen. Rescue tubes that ranged from shiny new crimson to peeling, faded peach. Backboards. Rescue boards. CPR dummies. An AED. Cleaning supplies, bathroom supplies. Tools that should have been in the shed. Things past guards had left behind, including a Wahoo's swim cap, which could have been left by Toby, or Derek, or even me.

It took longer than any of us would have guessed to completely clear out the guardhouse and clean the floor, readying it for the waterproof, do-it-yourself sealant Quimby dropped off that morning. Far longer to clear out the house than to apply the finish to the floor. When we were done, we all crammed onto the porch, the double doors fanning outward to air the room, and gazed upon our handiwork. The sealant had given the cement an opaque, speckled sheen. Tannish in color, it would hide the sand we tracked in.

Quimby had left money for pizza and soda, and we took an early dinner break to eat at a picnic table on the beach. I fluttered my toes in the sand, letting it weave between them. The empty can of sealant was on my end of the table. Nadia and Pat were flirting, and Derek was charting out the most efficient order for bringing everything back inside so we could get home as quickly as possible. I read out loud to Toby, who was sitting beside me, "For best results, do not disturb for twelve hours." We hadn't spoken much in the couple days since WhisperingWahoo—Bryce—had turned out to be just another person who had no idea what had happened to you.

"Twelve hours?"

I pointed at the can.

"So we can't bring this stuff back in tonight," Toby said.

I shook my head. Derek had risen from the table and was wiping his hands on a napkin. "All right, let's get back to work."

"Umm, Derek?"

"Yeah, Teddy?"

"We can't bring any of this stuff in until tomorrow morning."

"We can't just leave it out in the open all night." His voice hinted at panic.

"It says the floor needs twelve hours to set." I gestured to the can.

"Quimby will kill me if something gets stolen." Derek's brows and lips were both drawn in tight lines. I looked around at all the stuff we'd unearthed from the guardhouse—none of it, save maybe the AED, was worth stealing.

"Or even just shat on by birds." Pat laughed.

Derek's panic was mounting. "Seriously, guys, we can't just leave all this stuff out here."

"What if I stayed? To guard it?" Everyone looked at me in surprise. Nadia and Pat and Derek and Toby, especially Toby, they all knew, given how many times I'd dashed out of the park before the sun could set, that I never stayed after dark. I tried not to, since you.

But I had before you. And suddenly I felt like I needed to now. "I'd like to do it."

"I can stay, too," Toby said. "I mean, if you want some company."

"Yeah, okay." I smiled at him. "I'd like that."

"If you want to go home and get stuff—like a tent or whatever—Pat and I can stick around for a little bit," Nadia offered.

Derek began to calm. "Okay. New plan. Nadia and Pat will stay for a few hours, then Teddy and Toby will come back and stay overnight. We'll all come in early tomorrow, to bring everything back inside. Say, seven thirty?"

And so it was settled. I told Nadia I'd be back by nine, and since it made no sense for Toby to head home to Cambridge only to come back to Bottomrock, he was coming home with me.

I wondered how Mom and Dad would react to the idea that I'd volunteered to spend the night with Tobias Smith at Bottomrock Park.

TWENTY-TWO

In Which I Go to the Lake at Night

DAD, AT LEAST, TOOK IT SURPRISINGLY WELL. WE FOUND HIM IN HIS Adirondack chair in the backyard, aimed at the birdbath and the sunset. A pair of binoculars lay on the armrest.

"Your phone will be on the entire time?"

"Yes."

"And you'll check it regularly?"

"Yes."

"And you'll stay on the beach?" The question he was really asking: *You won't go for any midnight swims?*

"Yes, of course." I had no intention of going in the water.

"All right. Young man, I need your phone number."

"Of course." Toby took the phone that Dad handed him and added himself as a contact.

"There won't be any alcohol consumed during this 'assignment'?" Dad put finger quotes around the last word.

"No, Dad."

"Take two tents."

"Dad . . ." I flushed. Toby was staring at his feet, but under the shadow of his bangs, I thought I saw some red on his cheeks, too.

"Fine. Take two sleeping bags, at least," he teased. He picked up the binoculars. "Not the double-zip ones!"

I rolled my eyes. "Come on," I said to Toby. "I think we're cleared." As we turned to leave, Dad snagged my wrist. "Call your mother about this, okay?" he said gently.

I nodded.

Inside, Toby asked me what a double-zip sleeping bag was. I was leading him to the basement to gather camping stuff, and I was glad that the light on the stairway was dim enough that he wouldn't be able to see the blush that had returned in full force on my face. "We have these two sleeping bags that zip-together into one giant sleeping bag. It's my parents'." I pulled the chain light at the bottom of the steps, illuminating the half-finished basement. The brown carpet. The retro orange couch that sagged to the floor. The boxy TV that was too big for the end table it rested on. And the built-in shelves that housed your collection of swimming memorabilia. Fourteen years' worth of trophies and medals, ribbons and plaques. Someone had left the shelving lights turned on, and the whole display glowed.

I jogged past your shelves and began to root around the closet for supplies. Maybe you'd taken some of this stuff when you'd gone to Maine with K. Maybe I'd find some scrap of a granola bar wrapper and then I could look into where you'd bought it and spend another two weeks getting nowhere, solving nothing.

"Hey, Toby?" I popped out of the closet.

He gazed at the trophy shelves. "I wondered where these were," he murmured.

"She had too many to keep them all in her room."

Toby glanced over at me, and for just a moment it seemed that his face was full of sadness. Then he smiled, quick and slight. "She got more than me, that's for sure. What'd you ask me?"

I hesitated. If he wanted to spend some time looking at your awards, working through whatever it was he needed to work through, who was I to stop him. "Umm, could you dig out the tent and bags? I have to call my mother."

"Where's she?"

"A teacher retreat thing in the Berkshires."

"Ah." He shook his head, like he was waking up. "I'll get 'em. You go call."

I went upstairs for some privacy. Mom answered on the first ring.

"Teddy? Is something wrong?" The panic in her voice tugged at me. She and I had been avoiding each other since I'd come clean about Australia. And now I was calling her unexpectedly on her weekend away with colleagues. They were taking courses, I think. Workshops on the craft.

"Everything's fine," I said. "Dad wanted me to tell you something."

The line was quiet. Clearly Mom was going to wait for me to elaborate.

"We put this new sealant on the floor of the guardhouse and it has to dry and all of the stuff is out on the beach. So I said I'd guard it tonight."

"Guard it? From drowning?"

Was she making a joke? "From thieves."

"You're spending the night at the park?"

"For work," I reiterated.

"Alone?"

"No." I paused. "Toby's working, too."

This time, I waited for her to fill the silence. It took longer than

I would have liked. "Can't someone else do it?" I wasn't sure if she meant instead of Toby, or instead of me.

"Mom." I measured my words so they all carried equal weight. "I want to do this."

"Okay," she replied at last. "Call me in the morning."

"I will."

Toby had placed the tent and sleeping bags in a pile at the foot of the stairs. He was sitting on the sofa, so sunken into it that he could probably feel its frame. I sat in the opposite corner.

"Why did you say you'd do this with me?" Unlike me, Toby had been to the lake after dark. He told me he'd come back often, replaying the story of that night, trying to make it work.

"I didn't want you to be alone." His words lingered in the space between us. Then Toby scooted over. Getting comfortable? Or getting closer? "And besides." It wasn't a large sofa. Our sandals now touched at the toes. "You're not the only one here with ghosts."

We each stared at our laps for a little while, until I couldn't take another second of quiet. "What's your mom like?" I don't think he'd called to tell her he was working through the night. I don't think he ever asked for permission, for anything.

"Mom's a surgeon." Toby offered up info I already knew.

"That's really impressive."

Toby shrugged.

"And what was your dad like?"

Suddenly it felt very wrong that I had never asked Toby about his father. After all the time we'd spent talking about you, how could I not have granted him the same chance to talk about his dad?

"He was a doctor, too. Anesthesiologist. It's how they met."

I shifted closer. I didn't even realize I was doing it until it was done.

"After the accident, they, uh, brought him into the hospital where they both worked, and she was in surgery at the time."

"And they had to pull her out of it?"

"No, that's the thing. Her boss decided not to pull her out of it. So she was doing this long operation and her husband was dying and by the time she was free, he was gone." Toby ran his hands over his legs. "She was furious. Said he should have pulled her out of surgery, let her say good-bye. Someone else could have finished the operation. Anyway, that's why we moved here. She didn't want to work there anymore."

If someone had denied me the chance to say good-bye to you, I'd never want to see them again, either. Toby stared at the floor between his feet. He had a hand cupped over each knee, and I reached out to cover one. He hooked a thumb over my little finger as silence settled around us once more.

"Teddy," Toby started to say, and I knew from his face and his heavy tone that he wanted to talk about our investigation, and I wasn't ready to go there, so I said, "Want to hear more of the changing stall saga?"

Following my lead, he arched his brow and that smirk of his stretched out across his lips. "It's a saga now?"

"This will be, like, my third installment of telling, so yeah. Saga." I got up to flip off the lights. "For the ambience." I picked a flashlight off the pile of camping supplies and flicked it on. Putting the light faceup on the coffee table, I sat back down. "So Tony and Thea walked over to the edge of the lake. They looked out at the water, to see if there was something out there that might be making the gurgling sound. But the water was unrippled. There wasn't any wind, and the night was so eerily quiet that you couldn't hear the lake lapping the shore. Just their breaths, and this odd gurgling. But the gurgling, they realized, wasn't actually coming from the lake." I paused. "No commentary this time?" I asked.

"This time I'm riveted." The wide beam of the flashlight cut a line under his chin. I shifted to snatch the light off the table, bringing our bodies closer than I'd intended, my shoulder brushing his chest. Quickly I rose. "That's perfect. We can finish the rest later. Now"—I took a deep breath, readying myself as I pointed with the flashlight to the glowing face of his watch—"we have to go guard the lake."

As I DROVE DOWN the long gravel driveway for the park, I thought, for probably the millionth time, how strange it was that you'd ever come here with Toby. When I looked at him, it was hard to remember the boy who'd been your friend who I'd barely known. I saw only *my* Toby, who wore his hair gelled straight up like he was a character from one of his comic books and who liked my snark and who had been with me every step of our failed mission. Because it had failed, I realized. The deeper I dug, the less I seemed to know. Every lead we'd uncovered turned out to lead nowhere. And I couldn't keep doing this to myself.

Bottomrock had no parking lot lights, and under the canopy of the surrounding woods, I could barely make out the footpath. But the moon was bright enough to reflect on the white sand, and Nadia and Pat had left on the guardhouse's outdoor spotlights, lighting up the beach. We sat inside the car for a minute, listening to the frogs sing.

"We can probably guard the stuff from up here, if you'd rather. I mean, there's only one way to drive into the park. I'm sure it'll be fine."

"Derek was overreacting earlier. It'd be fine if we just went home."

"Is that what you want to do?"

"No." I was only taking a moment. "I'm just giving Nadia and Pat time to get dressed."

Toby laughed. We climbed out of the car.

The humidity enveloped me immediately. The frogs were louder without the car as a barrier, their croaks arousing the quiet of night. I clicked on the flashlight as we started down the path.

Once we cleared the forest, it was much brighter, so I turned off the light. Pat and Nadia waved, and Nadia pulled me aside once we'd reached the beach. "Are you going to be okay here, all night?"

"Yeah," I said, sounding less certain than I felt. "I have to be."

"You know I live, like, five minutes away and can come back anytime, all right?"

"It's fine. Go finish your date."

A big, stupid grin spread over her face. "Am I being dumb? This thing with Pat? 'Cause we're going to different schools in, like, three weeks?"

"No, I think you're being brave," I said, looking at Toby. He and Pat were unpacking the tent, snickering about something.

"So you and Toby?"

"We're not anything."

"Yeah. Okay. You've been not anything all summer, then." Nadia touched my wrist, then dashed toward the boys.

The four of us hung out for a while, playing rummy at the picnic table. The breeze knocked our cards into the sand a few times. Pat and Nadia left a little after ten.

When they were gone, I drifted to the edge of the water and gazed out on the lake. It's funny: For a year I'd been scared to come here after dark. Scared of the things it would make me feel and imagine. But now I was here, I'd been here for more than an hour, and it had felt just like normal. Bottomrock was just a place, and the lake looked particularly gorgeous in the moonlight.

"So . . ." Toby had his hands in his pockets and was looking out at the lake, as well. "K."

"Yeah." I toed the water.

"We're letting it go?"

"I can't . . . I'm afraid . . ." I stopped there.

"What are you afraid of?"

I don't know what it was—his gentleness, or maybe his directness, or maybe his unique blend of both—but Toby had a way of tugging out answers I was too scared to give. "That the answer isn't the one I want. That maybe Keith and Laura are right and Izzy—"

"Hey." Toby took my hands and held them both. "She didn't do that. I know she didn't do that."

"How can you know?"

He leaned toward me. For a moment I felt my throat close in panic because I thought he was going to kiss me, and I knew if he did, I would kiss him back and then where would we be? But he only pressed his forehead against mine. "Because I know." He said it with such confidence. I had to believe him.

"Okay."

"But we can be done looking."

I nodded. Our foreheads rubbed together. I stepped back so I could see his face and ignore the sparking that was in my veins again. I kicked up some sand and listened to the dusty pellets clink as they shotgunned into the water. "I used to come here at night sometimes. Over the winter, when the lake is solid and snowcapped. In the fall, with Petra, to tell ghost stories. And the guards like to stay late sometimes, as you know . . ."

"I know you never stay."

"Not anymore." The lake looked so peaceful in its stillness, a great blue abyss sitting under the stars. "I've always really liked it here, in general, but especially when no one else is here. When it's just a lake in the woods." I sat down in the sand. Toby did, too. "But I'd forgotten how beautiful it is in the dark."

"Teddy?" Toby hesitated. The way we were sitting, the tips of our knees touched. "Why did you say you'd stay?"

He threw something into the water. A stick, by the sound of it.

I said softly, "I'm tired of letting her take this place."

Across the lake, dark outlines of trees carved the skyline. It didn't look so far from this angle. One mile of sleek water, ghostly in its darkness.

"Can we . . ." I turned to Toby. "Go in the water?"

Panic flashed across his face.

"Not a race. Not even to the middle. Just to the dock. I just want . . . I don't know what I want. To take something back, maybe."

He softened. "We're not wearing bathing suits."

I smiled up at him. "So?"

I made him turn around while I stripped to my underwear. I waded into the water slowly, and I didn't think about how this was the very thing Mom and Dad did not want me to do, or how the mystery of what had happened to you here was unsolvable. I thought about my toes wiggling in the gritty lake bottom that felt just the same in the dark as it did in the day. When the water reached my waistline, I gave Toby permission to turn around.

He dove under the shallow rope and resurfaced on the other side with water clinging to his bare chest and dripping off the ends of his hair. We grinned at each other like goofballs and shivered just a little.

The dock was rough from the nonslip paint, but still pleasantly warm from the day's heat.

"You know," Toby said as we lay on our backs, not touching, but close enough that I could hear him breathing. "It was kind of silly to make me turn around when you were just going to show me your underwear anyway."

"Oh, whatever. Maybe I just didn't want you to watch me undress. And you don't have to look."

"I'm not. I'm looking at all these wonderful stars. Iris. Rhea. Castor. And oh, Cassandra!"

"You're just naming characters from mythology."

"Most stars are named after mythological characters, aren't they? Or else just boring numbers. So, those must be star names, and I must be looking at them, even if I can't point out which ones they are."

"Not necessarily. Maybe Rhea isn't bright enough tonight to see. Or maybe Iris went supernova."

"Where is your imagination, writer?"

"I'm using it to imagine Iris turning into a black hole and dooming the civilization of Kryptonians who live nearby."

"That's plagiarism."

"Not if these people are krypton-based life-forms. Then it's just creative adaptation."

"Krypton-based?" Toby laughed.

I rolled my head toward Toby's face. He really was staring up at the stars. His chest rose and fell as the dock swayed gently. Drops of water trickled down his temple. His lips curled, but he kept his gaze upward. "I can see you out of my peripheral, you know."

"So?"

"So it's rude to stare."

"Can I ask you something?"

"Not if it's about stars because I honestly don't know anything."

"It's about Izzy."

He closed his eyes. "You can always ask me about her."

"Why did she call you a jerk?"

He burst into laughter. "What?"

"The first time she ever mentioned you, she called you a jerk." I left out the part where you called him gorgeous.

"Oh." A smile stretched across his face. "Well, that'd probably be because my first day of Wahoo practice, I beat her in the two-hundred-meter butterfly. Though I can assure you it never happened again."

"Of course. She never would have let it. But that makes sense now." You hated to lose. "Can I ask you something else?"

"You know you don't have to preface every question with that?"

"Do you think she's dead?"

He stilled. Shuttered his eyes again, briefly, before he turned to his side, bringing our faces close together. There was enough moonlight for me to see flecks of green in his brown eyes. "Yes," he said finally. "I do."

"That's what everyone thinks." I returned to my back.

"Have you changed your mind?"

"I don't know. I think maybe I've decided I don't want to know."

Toby was quiet for a minute. I blinked some lake water away from my eyes.

"Like, ever?" he said finally.

"Yeah."

More silence.

"There's not much water in the outback." He said this not with judgment or indulgence, but with sincerity.

"Maybe she had enough of water."

"Maybe." He rolled onto his back, too. "Do you think you're going to find her out there?"

I paused. In the weeks and months post-you all I could think about were the stories of how you made your grand escape. Of your threat to do the walkabout alone. I'd taken that wilderness survival class, I'd researched tour companies, I'd made myself bulk up. But now? When I thought about it, really thought about it, I knew I wasn't going to magically stumble across you. "I'm going to Australia because I just . . . need to. It was something we were going to do, and now it's something I'm going to do."

This game we were playing—question and answer while facing the sky—made it a lot easier to speak true.

"So I have a question for you," Toby said.

"Shoot."

"Theodora. That's your full name, right? Theodora Ware."

"Yes."

"Teddy Ware."

"Whatever joke you're about to make has been made a thousand times already."

"I'm not about to make a joke. I just wondered why you're Teddy. And not Thea. Or Dora."

"If I tell you, you'll make a joke."

"Only if you want me to."

"Theodora and Isobel are my grandmothers' names. I'm named after my mother's mom. She's Thea. I was supposed to be Thea, too. But when I was three years old, I found out that Teddy was a nickname for Theodore, which was basically my name, and I thought it would be really, really cool if I had the same name as my teddy bear, who I had very creatively named Teddy. And then it just kind of stuck."

"I see."

"You think I should be Thea, don't you?"

"I don't, actually. I like Teddy. It suits you. Now I want the rest of the saga." He spun to face me again. The dock shook.

"Where was I?"

"The gurgling wasn't coming from the lake."

"Right. The gurgling wasn't coming from the lake. It was coming from the changing stalls. But as Tony and Thea walked to the stalls, the gurgling suddenly stopped. They waited a moment, staring at the stalls, to see if it would start again. When it didn't, they turned back to each other and they . . ." I rolled my head in his direction. My throat suddenly felt very dry. "They leaned toward each other." His deep brown eyes looked black in the starlight, glistening, almost, from the water that still clung to his lashes.

I kissed him.

I hadn't planned to. I just pushed forward until our noses were smashed together and our lips brushed.

He pulled away with a laugh.

I don't know about you, but I'd never had anybody laugh when I kissed them before.

"No, hey, it's—" He must have been able to read my embarrassment even through the shadows. "You knocked my forehead. Here." With his hand on my waist, he pulled me close, changing the angles of our bodies. "Can we try that again?"

This time he leaned in. Something heavy and tingling and good glimmered as his mouth fit with mine. I had never felt a kiss with my whole body before, either. Even though his hand stayed still on my side and his other had found purchase in the strands of my hair, he might as well have touched my every nerve, for all the energy that fizzed beneath my skin.

I pulled away, my breathing heavy and my pulse beating everywhere.

"I'm sorry. Was that—"

I cut him off with another kiss. The slightest press of our bodies or pull of our lips caused the dock to sway. All the reasons I'd had for not wanting to do this sank into the lake as I thought that maybe, this is what you would have wanted all along. To bring together your sister and your best friend. To see us happy.

Suddenly I became very aware that we were nearly naked and maybe I was inviting something I wasn't ready for. I rolled away, far enough that Toby had to let go. He smiled at me. "You're some storyteller."

I flushed. "We have a tent to set up."

"Did you pack the double-zip bag?"

"God." I shoved his shoulder playfully. "No."

"So you weren't planning on seducing me, then."

"I haven't seduced you at all."

"You suggested we go swimming in our underwear. And then that story . . ."

Goddamn his stupid, adorable smirk.

"Izzy was right. You are a gorgeous jerk."

"Gorgeous? You didn't mention that before."

"It wasn't relevant!" I laughed as I rolled into the water. The dock shuddered when he followed me in. With four strokes Toby caught up to me. His arms looped around my waist, holding me afloat while he treaded water. "I'm glad you kissed me."

"Oh yeah?"

"I didn't know if I was allowed to try."

Our toes tangled. "You're allowed." We kissed again, softly. His thumbs chased the notches of my spine.

"Teddy? I want to tell you something about that night."

His hands stirred a flutter that his words erased. Were they a tease or a promise? But I shook my head. "I'm done with that." I had to be. Dwelling on the night you'd gone was a rabbit hole that carried me away to a nightmarish wonderland of obsession and distress. In all our digging this summer, the only things Toby and I had managed to uncover were more questions without answers, and the only way I would ever stop—could stop—was if I drew a hard line.

"You're sure?"

"Does it change anything? Whatever it is you want to tell me?"

"No."

"Then, yeah, I'm sure."

I'm sorry, Iz. Maybe to you this seemed like giving up, but I had to let you go.

TWENTY-THREE

The Happiness Interlude

SUNLIGHT SIFTED THROUGH THE TENT FLAPS. TOBY SLEPT ON HIS side, hugging one corner of his sleeping bag. His hair looked crunchy from the dried lake water. In his sleep, he smiled.

I felt lighter that morning. For nearly a year I'd been living with the weight of your mystery as a second skin and now it was finally shed. I didn't want to wake Toby, but I also felt a bit creepy watching him sleep, so, phone in hand, I crawled to the flaps and began to slowly unzip. I would call Mom like I'd promised and watch morning rise over the water.

But when I emerged, Derek was sitting at the sign-in table bearing three take-out coffees on a cardboard platter. "I didn't want to wake you guys. How was it?"

I don't think Derek was angling to hear about the kisses Toby and I had shared on the dock, or again in the water, or again on the beach in between our attempts to pitch the tent in the dark. "Fine. Once we scared all the wolves away from the CPR dummies."

"Wolves?" Derek asked, and I thought maybe given my audience I should have picked something more obviously sarcastic, like monsters. It took him half a moment before he got it. "Oh, right, ha. Wolves."

"Are you early?" It was only ten after six.

"I think maybe a little. I thought you guys might want these." He handed me a coffee. "I tried tapping the flap, but you seemed pretty out."

"We were up late. Pat and Nadia stayed awhile, playing cards. And thanks." I took the coffee—which was too warm for this August morning—and sipped it anyway.

"No problem. So how come I didn't get an invite to cards?"

"It just sort of happened."

"Next time?"

"Sure." I smiled because he was being nice, and he had no idea what he'd interrupted. He didn't know that I'd been hoping Toby would wake soon and find me at the shore. I wanted to see if there was still something there in the light of day, now that we no longer had you to bring us together. Last night felt almost like a dream, a fleeting farewell to our shared, failed mission.

"Well, we'll have to make it happen again soon. I'm back to campus after this weekend."

"Already? It's barely August. Don't tell me that means—"

Derek laughed into his coffee. "Don't worry. I'm not leaving you with Quimby for the last third of summer. Pat will run things during the week."

"So why are you going back early?"

"I'm going to be an RA this year. We have to go back for training."

"Sounds fun."

He shrugged. "It was the easiest way to get into the good dorm.

And get a single. But I'm sure hours of leadership training and emergency preparedness drills will be a riot."

"You love those sorts of things. Being bossy. Following rules."

"I break rules on occasion."

I snickered. It was a stalling laugh. Derek was edging toward flirting, and with Toby possibly waking soon, I really didn't want him overhearing and drawing conclusions. I cradled my cup and rolled my toes under the sand. "So Pat's supervising during the week?"

Derek nodded. "I'm still around every weekend till we close."

"Oh."

"Ouch. Please, conserve your excitement."

So I gave him the biggest, stupidest, snarkiest grin I could muster.

"I thought I heard voices." Toby's voice brought back the hitch in my chest. He blinked bleary-eyed and ran both hands through his stiffened hair. I think he smiled at me, but I couldn't bring myself to look directly at him. I was afraid everything I was feeling would be telegraphed on my face, and it all felt just a bit too personal for Derek's eyes.

"Derek brought coffee." I flipped my hand at the remaining cup. Toby's hand grazed my back as he picked up the coffee, and I shifted away. Clearing my throat, I said to Derek, "Since you're here now, do you mind if we go home to shower and change? We'll come back in time to help bring all this stuff inside."

"Sure, go. See you in a few." He waved us off.

At the top of the path, Toby asked if he'd done something wrong.

"No. It's just—"

He nodded. "Last night was a mistake."

"It was?"

"I get it. It's okay. I'll get over it," he said, though his hang-dog face begged to differ.

"No." I shook my head. "It's . . ." And there was your voice, telling me to be brave. "Last night wasn't a mistake for me."

I stepped toward him, looping my arms around his neck. The thing between us was still there in the daylight, without you. "God, you look like a lost puppy."

Toby smirked. He knew—he must, surely, by now—that his doofus grin always got a rise out of me. "I might look like a lost puppy," Toby whispered, his words quivering at the edge of my ear. "But you smell like one."

I moved to whack him, but he halted my swing with a kiss. We were both laughing, and it took a moment for our play to turn. My arms slackened. I folded into him. Toby was the one who broke first, stepping around until the car was between us.

"I wanted to do that earlier." He had one hand on the passenger-side door. "It wasn't a mistake for me, either."

WE HAD OUR own secret now.

Well, we had technically had one before, but that was just us keeping your secrets even as we tried so hard to unearth them.

Now the secret was wholly ours.

I told myself that we weren't lying. We were choosing not to over-share. Mom and Dad knew Toby and I had started spending more time together, but they didn't ask for details, so we didn't give them. And our coworkers didn't need to know how we lingered behind at the end of the day to kiss at the car. Or that when things were slow at the park, we snuck off to the dam and dipped our feet in the water. Toby would draw and I'd write, only now I wasn't writing about you. I'd started a story for Toby's space soldier, Moira, the first new piece of fiction for me to work on in ages. I just had this science-fiction comedy epic in my head, and then I was putting it on the page as Toby and I sat side by side at the dam, drawing and writing together.

And we were together in a sense, but we weren't anything official. We didn't go mini-golfing or to the movies. Instead we stole kisses pressed against the trees. We applied sunscreen liberally, just to be able to touch each other. If anyone had asked me if Toby was my boyfriend, I would have said no. *Boyfriend* was both too simple and too significant. It implied at least a semi-permanence, and in less than a month, I was going halfway around the world and he was starting college. We couldn't be more than what we were, and what we were was two people, finally filling an ache left by your absence.

Sometimes I wondered if Toby and I fell into secrecy the same way you had. Not because we made a conscious choice to hide, but because we made many smaller choices to not mention something here, now. To keep this moment private. To wait for someone to ask.

I was waiting for Nadia, but if she noticed any change between Toby and me, she kept this observation to herself. It was Mom who said something first.

"You seem happier lately." She stood in the open doorway of the living room, a basket of clean laundry perched on her hip. I closed the comic Toby had let me borrow and put my phone down. We'd been texting. He wanted a play-by-play of my thoughts as I read through each issue of his favorite series, the one about the couple with the kid in the midst of an intergalactic war.

"I think I am."

"Because of Toby?"

I flushed.

"It's okay. I'm not upset." She sounded a bit upset, but I didn't object. Mom shifted the laundry basket.

"Can I help you fold?"

"Of course." She brought the basket into the room and placed it on the floor between us. We began divesting the bin of clothes. Folding and organizing piles on the coffee table.

"Are you . . ." Mom trailed off deliberately, leaving me only to guess where her thoughts had gone.

"Mom." I stretched out the word. She and I had the "use protection" conversation twice already. The first time had just been the two of us. You were at swim practice, and I was getting ready for my first "date," which was really just a group hang at a bowling alley, except I'd been asked to come hang out by someone I liked. In hindsight that conversation, which was brief and factual and which I told you all about, after the fact, was way less awkward than the one I'd been subjected to after hanging out a few times with Nadia's cousin Luis. Dad had been there for this second birds-and-bees talk, and the two of them had gone on for close to twenty minutes about how important it was that I feel safe and respected and not pressured and how it was okay for me to want pleasure, too, and . . . I know they were just trying to be good, progressive parents, but I knew everything they were saying already.

"Actually, I was going to ask if you were thinking about sticking around."

"Oh." The idea of leaving Toby behind for the complete unknown of Australia terrified me, but I was equally terrified of staying, which would entirely be for him. I grabbed one of my Bottomrock shirts to fold. My phone buzzed. "No. I'm still going."

Mom pursed her lips as she shook the wrinkles out of a hand towel. "Is he going with you?"

"Would you want him to go with me?"

"It would be better than you going alone."

"Mom . . ."

She took another hand towel and whipped it in the air.

"Mom."

She folded the towel into thirds, and then used her arm like a hanger to fold it once more, in half. I hated this. The stilted silences. Her refusal to just get into it with me. The concern she so clearly couldn't shed. If there was any way for me to alleviate her worries without sacrificing my own needs, I wanted to do it. "Mom, please look at me."

"Teddy, I'm trying to understand why you want to do this and I just . . ."

"Let me know when you figure it out." I laughed.

"Be serious, honey. If you're planning to risk your life having some adventure, at least know why."

"It's not really a risk."

"There's no reason for it."

"I have to."

"Because you're trying to prove something to Izzy?"

I shook my head. My phone screen was lit up: three new texts from Toby. "No. I think maybe I'm trying to prove something to myself."

Mom put the folded towel on a pile with the others and gave me a hug. We held on to each other for longer than we had in quite some time. When we pulled apart, she touched my cheek. "Now about the other thing . . ."

"Mom!"

"All I want to say is, I'm glad."

"You're glad?" I had a pair of underwear in my hand, which is not the best piece of laundry to be holding when a parent starts alluding to sex.

"If Toby makes you happy, then yes, I'm glad." She swiped the underwear out of my hand, folded it quickly, and added it to the pile. "Now go answer his texts before he thinks you've fallen through a crack in time."

BOTTOMROCK AFTER DARK had reacquired its magic. A moonbeam shot across the surface of the water. The rhythmic thrum of insects and frogs. A crisp chill in the summer air. And the lick of water along the beach, punctuating the night.

Sometimes Toby and I doubled back after closing. Like before, we would swim out to the dock and lie facing the stars. There was a game we played, in which one of us would point out an invented constellation, and together we would devise a mythology.

When we grew bored of the game we would lie still, cuddling or holding hands, while the water undulated the dock and the stars blinked. More than once I fell asleep that way, and woke an hour or so later, locked in the sensation of perpetual swaying.

"I could lie like this forever," Toby said on one of these nights. Our bodies aligned shoulder-to-shoulder, arm-to-arm, toe-to-toe.

"I think I'd get hungry first." Forever was a long time, and Mom's words, about how it would be nice if I had someone to go with me to Australia, were fresh on my mind.

"We'll bring sandwiches."

"A perpetual supply?"

"They're magic sandwiches."

We were having a bit of role reversal. Usually I was the one with the fanciful ideas and Toby was the one who either played along or spoke reason.

"I'm going to Australia in September."

Toby said simply, "I know."

"And you're going to art school."

"Am I? That's cool."

"Be serious please." I sat up. Toby did, too. We faced each other, cross-legged, like two kids in an elementary school show-and-tell group.

"What's up?"

"I want to stay in the Fortress."

"Umm . . ."

"With you. In the Fortress, where everything is calm and there's no past and no future, there's just *now*. But I can't stay in the Fortress because I'm going to Australia in September."

"Why is it a fortress?"

"Like the Fortress of Solitude. I thought you'd appreciate a metaphor from comics."

"I don't think I get the metaphor."

"I'm saying I can't stay here forever."

Toby took my hands. "Obviously." Moonlight played in the water droplets on his chest. His thumb traced the lines of my palm. "Do you not want to go to Australia anymore?"

"I do. I just wonder . . . What's the point?"

"Of?" Toby now moved his fingers in light swirls across my knuckles. It was hard to think with him touching me like that. Maybe that's why he was doing it. In answer to his question, I lifted our hands up.

"The point of this."

He kissed my fingertips.

"I asked you to be serious." I said as laughter escaped me, doing little to persuade him of my point.

"I *am* being serious." He pulled my other hand up to his lips and lightly pecked each finger at its bend. "So you're going to Australia in September. That's not now."

As Toby kissed me, I realized he was right. The two of us had spent so much time shut in the past. The point was to be happy in the present. And I was, for a time.

TWENTY-FOUR

Journey to the Center of the Lake

WE WERE FORCED OUT OF THE FORTRESS ON A SWELTERING SUNDAY
in mid-August with a jam-packed beach. We had a four-guard rotation going between the two beach chairs and the two docks. Even
Derek jumped in, to give the rest of us some much-needed relief. Our
lips hurt from the blare of whistles. Our eyes hurt from the glare of
the sun. The morning was brutal, midday worse, but by midafter-
noon, the flocks of patrons began to dwindle. We lowered the active
guard rotation to three, and then to two. On a break, I grabbed my
notebook, Toby his sketchpad, and we snuck into the woods, headed
for our spot at the dam. We followed the trail, teasing at hand-holding
because it was too hot to hold for any significant length of time. We
hadn't quite reached the dam when a whistle blast cut through the
woods, followed immediately by two more. My heart lurched.

One whistle was a warning. Two: a rescue.

Three blasts was the code for a missing child.

Surprisingly I did not panic. As I started to run, Toby fell into
place beside me.

Nadia had already started evacuating the water. More than two
dozen people stood dripping on the sand and listening to Derek as he

divided the adults and some of the older kids into volunteer teams. We needed to form a chain to do a shallow water sweep. And we needed people to head into the woods.

Pat popped up beside us carrying a bucketful of extra whistles, our entire supply of walkie-talkies dangling from lanyards around his neck. "Kid is six. Arden. Dark brown hair, kind of curly. Small for his age. Wearing a blue bathing suit with a crab on the right leg."

Arden Patterson. My heart clutched as I flashed to last summer, when he and his older brother, Aiden, used to follow Nadia and me around like loyal puppies. They hadn't been around as much this summer. And now little Arden was missing.

"Last seen?" Toby asked.

"Mom said he asked about using a paddleboat this morning, she said she'd take him and his brother when there wasn't a line. He went to the dock with a few other boys, including his brother. They say he swam back to shore. Mom didn't see him come out of the water, though."

"But he could have," I said.

We'd reached Derek. He lowered his megaphone and turned to us. "Nadia, deep water search at the docks. Pat, you're leading these people"—he pointed to the largest volunteer group—"in the shallow water search. Toby and Teddy, take a team of volunteers each"—he gestured toward the two smaller groups—"and search the woods. Start on opposite directions, make your way around the rim trail first. You remember your whistles?"

"Once if we've found him," Nadia said. "Twice if a rescue is required."

"Derek?" Pat had begun to unburden the walkies. The bundle moved around from person to person like handouts in a classroom, shrinking as it circulated. "I checked the boats like you asked. One of the paddleboats hasn't come in yet."

The lake was still and boatless.

Not a second passed before Derek said, "Change of plans. Toby, Teddy, you're our best swimmers. Take a rescue board each, go look for that boat. The rest of us . . ." He turned to the groups of volunteers. "We think Arden took one of the paddleboats. We're going to break up into groups and circle the lake, try and see if we can spot that boat. Take walkies and whistles. We'll find him." This last sentence directed at the petite woman who stood crying next to Derek. Ms. Patterson. At Derek's words—confident, soothing, sure—she inhaled sharply and nodded. Her hand tightened around her other son's.

Derek was breaking protocol in having us all search for the missing boat instead of diving under the docks, where Arden was last seen. But that was more than an hour ago. If he was there—well, us searching elsewhere for a while wouldn't make any difference.

The park had only two rescue boards, each stored in a rack on the backside of one of the lifeguard chairs. Toby and I each snagged one and marched to the shore, on opposites sides of the swimming area. We could have taken a canoe or one of the kayaks, but the board wasn't much slower and would make it easier for us to bring back an injured child.

Or a body.

I tossed the board into the water and launched myself on it as it glided away from the shore, momentum propelling the board forward like a perfectly skipped stone.

Back on the beach, the volunteer groups were starting off down the trails. Calls of "Arden" echoed across the water. Flat on my board, a walkie draped around my neck, I soared across the surface of the water. My arm churned in classic freestyle strokes while I kept my chest inclined so I could see what lay ahead. I skated over congregations of lily pads. The bottom of my board scraped the odd boulder hidden just beneath the lake's surface. Toby's board was little more than a red blur. His butterfly shoulders were built for this. He rounded the bend in the lake and was gone.

Bottomrock Lake is a backwards, flattened C, with the beach at the bottom hook. Most of the coastline is sloped rocks or muddy banks that drop off sharply. The center of the lake is deep enough that there's no plant life visible from the surface, but at the top of the C, the lake narrows. The water here is shallower and muckier and gets more so every year as the forest nibbles the lake away. There's a niche just around the bend with steep rock slopes at the foot of a gnarled oak. The oak's limbs overhang the water in thick swirls. There used to be a rope swing off the largest. Petra and I would head for this spot during those few summers when we were old enough to play at Bottomrock without constant parental supervision, but young enough to still want to play. We'd fling ourselves into the lake and come up spurting. The water was deeper—and less weedy—then.

You didn't join us because, of course, you were swimming. Or doing some other activity—weight training, running, stretching—meant to prepare you for serious sport. You probably wouldn't have come, anyway, as this was back when you held fast to any and all rules, and swimming outside a designated swimming area was definitely breaking a rule.

The rope swing was cut down three summers ago. And after Quimby found out someone had tied on another, the branch was sawed off, too. Kids still came to the niche sometimes—the rocks look like slides, and if it's rained recently, you can get a decent dip into the water. But their slope makes it hard to exit, and the more the forest has overtaken this corner of the lake, the less appealing swimming here has become.

As I made my way around the curve, a paddleboat came into view. Riderless and adrift, the paddleboat's rudder was clogged with weeds. Toby's rescue board was balanced on the rocky embankment. Where had he gone? Why hadn't Toby blown his whistle?

I stopped paddling and let momentum carry my board to the empty boat. A head surfaced. Wet hair clung to a wide, pale face. Toby took a deep breath before he resubmerged.

I slid into water that was barely above my waist. My feet sunk into muck. Battling suction with each step, slick, cool mud slipped between my toes. I could see now what Toby had spotted. Why he was diving and resurfacing like a starved duck. Why he hadn't blown his whistle. A bright orange life vest drifted alone several feet from the boat.

He hadn't yet found the boy it belonged to.

I ran—as much as one can run through weeded water and sediment—over to Toby, catching him by the shoulders as he came up for air. "Did you radio Derek?"

"No, I . . . I have to find him." He started to dive, but I held on. "Where have you searched?"

"Under the boat. Now behind it."

"I'll take the side away from the shore." I lifted the walkie that dangled around my neck. "Derek?"

Almost immediately: "Did you find him?"

"No. But we found the boat. It's where that old rope swing used to be."

"Just the boat?"

Toby was under again, combing.

"There's a life vest in the water. We'll need more people for the search."

Derek's pause here was longer than before. Then the click of an open transmission came. "I'm having Nadia call it in. We'll be there in five. Maybe less."

Call it in meant 911. It meant, *This is beyond us.* It meant volunteer rescue divers.

Not that we wouldn't dive and keep diving. This boy wouldn't disappear the way you had. The lake wouldn't swallow him up. I shook as I took off my lanyard and placed the walkie in the paddleboat. As I did what I had to do, what I'd been trained to do, finally using a skill I had never once thought, even given everything, I would actually have to put into practice.

Underwater, I opened my eyes and parted the weeds. I slunk along the bottom where the vegetation was jungle-thick and slippery with algae and I spread the weeds like Moses. I covered about fifteen feet before I came back up for air. Then I took a step to the right, to the slightly deeper water and repeated in the opposite direction.

Honestly, it amazes me that I managed to keep focus on one mantra: Find him. Maybe he went down not that long ago, I thought, just before Toby rounded the bend, maybe he's still got time. When I remember this search in my dreams, it's you I'm expecting to find. But in that moment, I wasn't thinking—consciously, anyway—about you. Only the little boy in the crab bathing suit. I kept expecting to see a pop of royal blue in the muck. With every parting of the weeds, I kept expecting to find him.

A touch on my shoulder startled me back to the surface. Derek had waded in. His T-shirt was wet to midchest and sweat crinkled the hood of his bangs. He steadied me with his hand. "Teddy. We found him." I couldn't place the tenor of his words. Happy? Somber? I imagined a little body floating offshore as my heart clenched and my eyes—bleary from being open underwater so long—refocused on the bright, dry world of the surface. Toby was standing waist-deep in the water on the other side of the paddleboat, Pat beside him. I didn't see anyone else. Definitely not a six-year-old boy in blue swim trunks.

"He's fine. He got the boat stuck in the weeds and climbed out. We found him on the trail, trying to head back to the beach. He missed Lake Trail somehow and was on Cross Trail. But he's fine. He's with his mom and the paramedics are checking him out, just in case. He's fine."

I realized then—on Derek's third *fine*—that he was holding me. Done in by exhaustion and fear, I'd collapsed into his arms.

Derek released me as I pulled away. "You two did good." He looked to Toby now. "Pat and I will bring the boat back around with the boards. You can walk back to the beach, if you'd like. Maybe get some water?"

We walked barefoot and silent down the path to the beach. I didn't realize I was trembling until Toby hugged me.

"I'm okay," I said, even as my body continued to shake.

"Okay," Toby said back. "But maybe I'm not." He was shaking, too. Pebbles digging into our feet, lake weeds drying on our shins, we pressed together until the shaking stopped.

By the time we made it back to the beach, Arden and his family, the paramedics, and all of the patrons were already gone. Nadia was sitting at the sign-in table, fingers threading together nervously.

"Are you okay?" She hopped to her feet as we came out of the woods.

"Yeah." The word came out steadier than I felt.

"Derek closed the park for the rest of the day. Arden was fine. A little sunburned, maybe, but he wasn't even scared when we found him. He didn't know he was lost."

I nodded. Something churned within me but hadn't yet come to the surface. My mind was stuck in the lake. I couldn't stop myself from writing a different story. A little boy climbs out of the caught boat. He tries to unclog the rudder, slips in the mud, hits his head. Or: He tries to go ashore, but the slope is too steep and slick and he slides, over and over again, into the water, until exhaustion overwhelms him. Or: He tries to swim back to the beach and simply can't.

We helped with the rest of the cleanup. The distraction untangled my thoughts, streamlined them with routine. As we restrung life vests, Toby's gaze met mine and lingered. Not in the flirtatious way of the past two weeks. In a way that said, *I know, I'm back there, too.* There, where he really had been and I really hadn't, but which I'd imagined and rewritten so many times.

Derek and Pat brought the boards back first, then walked to the niche to retrieve the stolen paddleboat. One of us fucked up: letting a small boy take a boat from under our noses. We would probably never know who.

After we finished the cleanup, Derek asked if any us wanted to stay to unwind. Pat said he wouldn't mind, but no one else expressed interest, and we left shrouded by the same fog that had dulled everything since Arden was found. The fog of adrenaline recalled.

I didn't go home, though. I went to Toby and asked if he would take me somewhere, anywhere, to forget.

TWENTY-FIVE

How I Stopped Waiting for You

TOBY BROUGHT ME TO THE ROOF OF HIS APARTMENT BUILDING IN Cambridge. From there, we could see the Charles and the lights of Boston sparkling across the river. There was a rooftop herb garden maintained by one of Toby's neighbors, and the scents of rosemary and thyme mingled with the salty breeze carried from the harbor. On the street, three stories below, car engines chugged and crosswalks beeped.

We spent a while on the roof, sitting in two lounge chairs, gazing at the city and listening to the traffic. Eventually Toby reached for my hand. He tipped his head back. "The stars aren't as good here."

I tilted, too. "They're just as good as anywhere. You just can't see them."

"True." His fingers threaded between mine. "Earlier today—"

"I don't want to talk about it."

"I know but—"

"I *can't* talk about it."

The cars in this moment were impossibly loud.

"Okay," Toby said at last.

Our fingers resumed their dance, twining, tracing, catching.

Whatever energy that had been percolating within me, I channeled into the charge between us as I climbed out of my lounge chair and into Toby's.

When I came up for air, Toby breathed my name. My hands drove under his shirt, trying to lift it. "Teddy," he repeated, this time stilling my arms with his hands. "You're shivering."

"It's okay." I moved to kiss him, but he held me in place.

"Let's go inside."

"Your mom—"

"Is working an overnight shift at the hospital."

Toby's room was cluttered with books and notebooks and pieces of scratch paper filled with writing and drawings. I thumbed through some of his character sketches while he cleared the bed. There were some duplications of his favorite existing characters: Superman and Captain America and a large Siamese cat with a golden collar that I recognized from the covers of the indie sci-fi comic he'd been reading all summer. Even in varying stages of completion, they were all quite good. But many of the drawings were characters of his own invention, all these people without stories, chief among them Moira, the space soldier, for whom I'd started writing an adventure. I traced the contours of her high-tech armored chest plate, the bow and arrow in her hand. I liked her aesthetic—the space warrior who carried the simple weapon of a fantasy world.

"I started writing a backstory for her," I said. "It doesn't have to be canon, obviously."

Toby laughed. He was sitting on the exposed sheets of his bed, a twin tucked in the corner opposite the window. "When did you start writing this?"

"I've been working on it for a couple weeks. At the dam." I continued flipping through his sketchbook, concentrating on the careful lines of shadow on his characters, my nerves fluttering.

"I'd like to read it."

"When it's done." At the end of the book, I came upon a new character, one I hadn't seen him sketching at work. With a backpack slung over one shoulder and a whistle twirling in her hand, she was less sci-fi than any of his other works. It took me a moment—because it was a cartoon rendering, not a portrait—but I recognized the confident arch of her shoulders, the peaked right corner of her lips in her barely there grin. "Izzy?" I said, wondering why he'd given you a whistle and a bag with a pen sticking out of its pocket.

Toby shook his head.

"Me?" I noticed now the way her nose sat on her face, slightly askew.

"A version of you." Toby blushed.

On the rooftop I hadn't been nervous at all. I'd been acting instinctively, unpremeditated. But by bringing us inside, Toby had slowed everything down. I'd had opportunities to have sex before, but I'd waited. I'd thought I didn't really have a reason, just vaguely wasn't ready, though it's possible my reason was you. I'd told you all about my first hand-holding, first date, first kiss. Telling you—sharing the afterglow, seeing your thrill for me, hearing your cheeky yet wise commentary—had been just as much a part of those moments as the moments themselves. Before you'd gone, I'd always assumed that when the time came to have sex, I'd have you to talk to. About the before and the after. And maybe I'd put sex off not because the people weren't right or I wasn't ready, but because somewhere inside I thought there was still a chance you'd come back and this, unlike graduation and birthdays, was one growing-up moment that I didn't have to have without you.

I closed the sketchbook and walked over to Toby.

"Did you like them?" he said.

"Yes." I fit myself between his legs. He placed his hands on my hips, touching the sliver of exposed skin at my waist. I bent over and kissed him. We kissed like that for a while.

After our clothing had been shed, we lay on the bed facing each other. Even though I'd seen him shirtless every day at work, even though we'd swum in our underwear, this was different, a thousand times more intimate. I laid my hand flat atop his swimming muscles. I twirled the stray hairs that sprouted here and there across his chest.

"Do you have a condom?" I whispered as he ran a fingertip along my collarbone and down the space between my breasts, causing me to tremble.

"In the drawer." His finger circled my belly button and trailed lower. "I'll get one."

I arched back, reaching for the drawer of the nightstand.

"I can get it," he said again quickly, propping himself up to reach across me. My hand was already on the knob.

"Why? Is that some sort of guy thing? You have to retrieve the condom?" I laughed as he tugged on me, thinking he was playing a game. My hand swam through the drawer. I saw gray condom wrappers and the wired spiral binding of a small sketchpad and the curling pages of a retro-covered *Hitchhiker's Guide to the Galaxy*, and underneath all that, a thin navy booklet with rounded corners. I sat up further and I slid it free. A US passport.

My heart stopped. Of course I told myself that it had to be his own passport. Why was I snooping? I looked over my shoulder, at Toby, who'd gone so suddenly still, and I knew as soon as I saw the panic on his face that I was wrong. I crawled out of his bed and opened the passport and saw myself, saw you, staring back at me. Isobel Ann Ware, born in Greening, Massachusetts, eighteen years ago.

I picked up my shorts and pulled them on, shaking, my throat swelling and my eyes blinking fast, trying to flick away oncoming tears.

"Teddy." He jumped up and rushed over to me. He tried to hold me but I twisted away, wrenching my shirt over my head and clutching your passport. "It's not what you think."

But for once I didn't have a story. I could think of no reasons for why he would have your passport, but I did know, immediately, what it meant for him to have it. It meant that you didn't have it. It meant that my slimmest hope that you were out there somewhere in the world was gone. It meant that you were on the bottom of Bottomrock Lake, reduced to algae-covered bones. It meant that you were dead.

I left Toby's room, left the building, just kept walking, twisting down random streets so he couldn't follow me. I didn't realize until I'd wandered a few blocks away from his apartment that I hadn't brought anything with me: my phone, my wallet, the keys to the car I'd left at the train station. I hadn't even brought my underwear. It was late, and I was alone in a city I hardly knew, and you were never coming back.

I WANDERED AIMLESSLY. After a time, I reached the river and a bridge. To the left I saw the giant glowing Citgo sign. I didn't know Boston well, but I thought the Citgo sign overlooked Kenmore Square, which was near Fenway. I remembered the handful of times we'd been to Fenway together as a family, before Mom and Dad had given up trying to convert us to their baseball fandom. Now I knew where I was, but that didn't really help me. I still had no phone and no money. I didn't care about that, though. I didn't want to go home. I had texted Mom and Dad when Toby and I had come down from the roof, telling them I'd gone to Nadia's after work and planned to sleep over. They wouldn't miss me until morning.

I crossed the bridge, pausing halfway to look out over the river. I was still holding your passport. For a second, I thought about throwing it. I bet with a good windup I could get it pretty far. Away from the city lights on both sides of the river, the middle of the bridge seemed unbearably dark. I wouldn't be able to see how far it flew, or where it landed. If I'd had any money I might have taken the T to the airport and used the passport to go somewhere, anywhere that was flying out that night, but I didn't have money and so I tucked the passport into the back pocket of my shorts and kept walking.

When I reached the other side of the bridge, I realized I had stumbled upon part of the Boston University campus. I'd been walking and crying for a while and my body felt spent. I thought of Derek, who'd confidently taken charge of the crisis at the park, who'd been so understanding when he'd pulled me from my search. Derek had moved back to campus already. Would he be in his dorm? I asked a random group of college-age kids where I could find the dorm Derek had mentioned was his, and they gave me directions. I ducked inside on the heels of someone else, and then I asked that person if she knew Derek Danvers. She shook her head. "Sorry."

It didn't matter. I was inside someplace that I felt was safe, where I could sit down and maybe even fall asleep. I looked for the common area. I imagined drunk college kids crashed on the sofas in there all the time.

I was right about that: When I found the lounge, there was already somebody else stretched out on the sofa, asleep. An unfinished card game was spread out on the table, along with a few empty cans of Sam Light. The clock on the wall said it was 1:37 a.m.

I curled up in a chair. I kept seeing Toby's face when I'd found the passport. How everything stilled. He looked more than just upset. He looked pained. And then I thought of you. I still didn't know exactly what had happened to you, but I knew with a certainty that I had never allowed myself to think before that you were dead. I think I'd known this for a while. I closed my eyes and drifted off to sleep.

"Teddy?" Derek stood in the hall, in nylon running shorts and BU tee, slick with sweat. The windows of the common room glowed with the pink light of dawn. "What are you doing here? How'd you get in?"

I started crying.

"Hey." He walked over to me and patted my shoulder. "Hey, it's okay. Come here, let's get you somewhere more private, huh?"

I took the hand that he offered and he led me to his dorm. His bed was lofted above a desk. A beanbag chair and some free weights filled one corner, a television on a dresser filled another. A couple of boxes sat unpacked in the middle of the floor. Wafts of dirty laundry and deodorant scented the room.

"It's pretty sweet, right? All RAs get singles. I have my own bathroom, too. See?" He nudged open a door to reveal a tiny bath-room with a shower, toilet, and pedestal sink. "Do you need to . . ."

I shook my head. I'd managed to stop crying but was still so tired, I could hardly keep my eyes open.

"All right, then. Let's get you to bed, okay? You climb up there." He steadied me as I climbed the ladder into his bed. I crawled under the blankets.

"I'm going to take a shower, okay?"

I didn't answer, because I was already halfway back to sleep.

When I next woke, there was a hand inside my shirt, lightly exploring my stomach and inching upward. At first I thought I was in Toby's room, that finding your passport and getting lost in Cambridge and wandering to Derek's dorm was all some bizarre and vivid nightmare. And then the hand rounded my breast and squeezed, and my eyes shot open to the view of Derek's room. A breeze came in through the open window and a phone was buzzing somewhere. We were alone.

At some point while I was sleeping Derek had joined me under the blankets. I could feel his wrestler's strength as he drew my body tight against his. His lips pressed against the back of my neck, and with his hand still pawing my breast, I imagined he could feel my heart hammering. I didn't know what I should do because I didn't know what he was trying to do. He was acting like we'd shortcut a relationship, jumping from friends straight to familiar lovers. I couldn't seem to make myself speak, and the way he had his arms wrapped around me, I couldn't easily move. His hand moved down my body and started to unsnap the top button of my shorts. I tried to twist away, but he held on, his finger flicking the button open as he flipped me to my back, now pinning my arm painfully with his shoulder and moving his mouth to my collarbone. His weight left me short of breath. I tried again to wiggle free. When he lifted himself as he used his knee to part my thighs, I wrenched away so fiercely that I fell out of the bed.

"Jesus, Teddy!" Derek shouted as I scrambled to my feet. I'd landed on my side, and my arm and hip hurt like hell, but I didn't think I had broken anything. As Derek climbed down the ladder, I backed away from him and nearly tripped over one of his boxes. "What'd you do that for?" he barked.

"What were you doing?" I shouted between gulps of air. Not ten seconds ago I'd been asleep—how was this happening? My heart was still pummeling. He was standing in front of the door. I wondered how thick the walls were. If I screamed, would anyone come?

"Saying good morning," he said, so simply, so innocently, that I became very confused. He looked so earnest, like a puppy who'd chewed up a pillow and didn't have a clue he'd done anything wrong. Suddenly he didn't seem that threatening anymore.

"Like *that*?"

"Isn't that what you came here for?"

"No!"

"Well, fuck, Teddy. You show up unannounced at my dorm, you've got no underwear or bra, you climb into my bed, I thought . . ." He trailed off. I thought maybe he was remembering how upset I'd been when he'd found me, but then he said, "You're just like her, you know."

I staggered backward. You. He meant you.

"You're both teases. You should just leave." He stepped aside, leaving the path to the door clear.

I ran.

TWENTY-SIX

Missing Person Found

YOU'RE JUST LIKE HER, HE SAID.

Toby said you'd been in a secret relationship.

And you had nicknamed Derek "Ken" because he looked so perfect, he was like a Ken doll.

It made so much sense that it hurt. You hadn't told me you'd
been seeing someone because you'd been seeing the person I had
a crush on. Derek had been a Wahoo in elementary school. I knew
he was still friends with Bryce. It fit with Toby's story, that you'd
met someone at a Wahoo party. It even provided a reason why your
midnight meeting was at Bottomrock. But what happened between
you and Derek? He'd called you a tease; maybe it was Derek who'd
gotten you so riled before trials. Something bad enough to send you
to Dr. Connors? If you and Derek had fought, you must have gotten
back together, for long enough to make it to Maine and write your
initials in that goddamn book. And then what? Another fight? Why
hadn't he come forward?

The campus wasn't awake when I stumbled out of Derek's dor-
mitory. I was limping from the fall, and I did not relish the idea of
walking all the way back to Toby's, but I needed to get my things. I

needed to ask him about your passport. I had a pretty good idea of how to get back to the bridge, which would lead me to Cambridge. Then I would navigate my way back to Toby's.

I got as far as Commonwealth Avenue before I collapsed on the first bench I saw. My hip throbbed with its own heartbeat.

If I couldn't manage to walk five minutes from campus, how could I manage several miles to Cambridge? I needed to revise my plan. I could borrow a phone, but I only had two numbers memorized, ones that had been drilled into my head since preschool: the landlines for our parents and Petra.

When a young woman jogged by, I asked if I could borrow her phone for an emergency.

Bracing for a sleepy Ms. Schaffer, grumbling about who would possibly call this early in the morning, I was surprised to hear a man's voice answer. "Hello. Schaffer residence."

"Umm. Can I please speak with Petra?"

"Teddy?" The voice on the other end sounded uncertain but hopeful. I must have been speaking to Ms. Schaffer's boyfriend. I confirmed who I was as tentatively as he'd asked. How could he possibly have been expecting me to call? "Oh, thank God! Everyone's been looking for you. Where are you? Are you all right?"

"Everyone's looking for me?" The jogger glared at me, like my emergency couldn't possibly be an emergency if it was taking me this long to get to the point.

"Your boyfriend said you ran into the city after the two of you had a big fight. He said you didn't take anything with you—"

Toby did what? "Sir, I'm borrowing someone's phone and I really, really just need to speak with Petra, please."

"Petra's in Boston. So is Claire. So is everyone. They're all looking for you. Where are you? I'll tell them where to pick you up."

"BU campus. On Commonwealth Avenue. Near the—" I looked
at the jogger for help. Still shooting daggers at me, she said, "BU
Central stop?" I repeated her answer. He said he'd call Petra right
away, and she or her mother would come get me.

I thanked the jogger for the use of her phone, then sat back down
on the bench to wait.

IN LESS THAN ten minutes, Ms. Schaffer's navy sedan double-parked
opposite my bench, and Petra flung on her hazards and bounded
out. "Oh my God, Teddy!" She wove between two parked cars
and crushed me in a hug as soon as I stood to greet her.

Cars honked at the illegal pullover, but Petra just kept hugging
me. Stunned by her excitement, I barely noticed the sting in my arm
as she squeezed. "We were so worried. What the hell happened
to you?"

"Nothing." I didn't know what questions to ask first.

"That's not nothing. The whole left side of you is like one big
bruise."

I looked down. Bruises blossomed all along the side of my arm
where I'd landed. In places the skin was raw, scratched open like
a rug burn. Gently, Petra took my uninjured hand. "Was it Toby?"
she said softly.

"What? Of course not." I came back to myself then, to the absur-
dity of her having spent all night out in the city, looking for me.
"What are you doing here?"

"Everybody's looking for you."

"Who's everybody?"

"Your friends. Your parents."

"My parents are looking for me? In Boston?" Guilt dropped like a weight. I hadn't meant to cause such a frenzy. But then again, I hadn't been very clearheaded when I stormed out of Toby's apartment and wandered my way to Derek's dorm.

She nodded. "They have been all night. The police would be looking for you, too, if there wasn't some stupid law about having to wait some bullshit period of time before you could report an adult missing. Your parents called them."

At a long blare of a horn, Petra said, "I need to move the car. Can you . . ."

"I can walk." I hobbled to her car and slid in. Petra pulled onto a side street. She was still illegally double-parked, but at least now she was out of the way of most of the traffic. She said Toby called me immediately after I'd left. When my phone rang right beside him, he'd run out after me, but I was already out of sight. So he'd called Nadia in a panic. Told her we'd had a fight, and I left without my phone or my wallet. She suggested he wait, I might come back. She said, give her half an hour. He had. When there was still no sign of me, they'd decided together to call in the cavalry. Pat and Petra and her mother and my parents were all informed of how I'd left Toby's, devastated, and disappeared into the night. They'd called Derek, too, but he hadn't answered.

"Teddy, we have to call your parents."

"Don't call. Text. I'll do it." I reached for her phone. She looked down at my open palm like I might toss her phone into oncoming traffic. "Please, Petra. I can't deal with their worrying right now."

She handed over her phone with a sigh. I texted that I was safe with Petra, and that I'd be home by dinner. I said they shouldn't worry, I was fine. I said I was sorry, and I loved them. Not five seconds after I'd sent the text, Petra's phone rang in my hand. The words TEDDY'S MOM and a stock photo of a cartoon panda appeared on the screen.

I clicked decline and handed the phone back to Petra. As soon as it was in her hands, it rang again.

"She'll want to hear your voice," Petra said, so rationally that I almost took the phone back.

But I shook my head. "I can't. Please. There's too much."

Despite my plea, Petra answered the phone. "Yes, she's with me. She's okay. Um, a little scraped up, but she's fine, really." Some hair had escaped her ponytail, and Petra curled a clump behind her ear as she listened to our mother. I couldn't make out her words, but her tenor carried through the speaker and over the rhythmic clicking of the car's hazard lights. Mom had been crying. "She, umm, doesn't want to talk to you." Petra angled her head at me as she said this. As close to a reproach as she was willing to come. Then she covered up the microphone with one hand. "Your mom wants to know why you won't talk to her."

"Because she'll make me come home, and I'm not ready to do that."

Petra relayed this message, followed by, "I know. I'm sorry, really. I'll call you later." She hung up. "You better have a good reason for why I just hung up on your mother."

"Thank you," I said. "Where's your mom?"

"Driving around Somerville."

"Why Somerville?"

"We didn't know which direction you walked. Thought you could have ended up there just as easily as downtown." She placed both hands on the wheel, like suddenly she needed the support to hold herself up. The rest of her body looked slack, her eyes bloodshot. "You really scared us, Teddy."

"I didn't mean to. I didn't think Toby would start a manhunt."

"What did you expect? The poor boy had to deal with another Ware twin disappearing on him."

"The poor boy? You hate Toby."

"Yeah, well, you didn't see how upset he was last night." Petra's hands slid off the wheel. "Speaking of which, am I allowed to text everyone else and tell them you've been found?" At my nod, she picked up her phone and started typing. When she finished and looked up, I was holding my left wrist, rotating it in small circles to test its motion, wincing as I did. It was starting to swell. "Jesus, Teddy, what happened?"

"I fell."

"You just fell? Like on the street? Were you drinking?"

"No. I fell out of Derek's loft."

Her face changed. Less incredulous, more reserved. "He didn't answer our calls."

Probably because he was too busy assaulting me, I thought. I couldn't say that to Petra, though. It was too fresh, and I was too confused, and the words would not form on my tongue. "I don't know why."

"So you just . . . *fell* . . . out of his loft?"

I didn't say anything else.

"So why didn't you borrow his phone?"

"He kicked me out."

"Okay." Petra inhaled sharply. Clearly she was getting annoyed by my stunted answers. "Why did he kick you out?"

"I wouldn't sleep with him."

Petra's eyes popped but she didn't comment. She knew there was more to the story, but I sensed she was done pulling details out of me. The wall, temporarily felled by my brief vanishing act, now rose once more between us. I didn't want it there any longer, so I took a sledgehammer to it. I told her everything. The investigation, K, finding your passport. Ending up at Derek's dorm. How I'd woken with him touching me. What he'd said about you. She stayed silent as I talked, only stopping me once to reply to the group chain, assuring my friends I was okay.

"Wow," she said when I finished. "That's, I can't even. Wow."

"So you see why I have to go back to Toby's and talk to him."

"Yeah. I do. So that's our next stop? You don't want to go back into Derek's dorm and ask him anything? Or, I don't know, punch him?"

"I could live with never seeing Derek again," I said, though I knew that was an impossibility. If nothing else, I would see him at work next weekend. Besides, Petra was right, I did need to talk to him and settle, once and for all, what he knew about you. But that could wait. My priority now was Toby.

Petra dropped me off at Toby's building and went in search of parking. I rang the doorbell. Went inside at the buzzer. But it wasn't Toby who met me on the stairs. It was his mother.

"You must be Teddy." She offered a small, sweet smile, so different from Toby's wide smirk. Her salt-and-pepper hair was pulled tight in a bun that sat high on the back of her head. "Toby's not back yet. He left me here to keep watch. I'm Amelia." She barely paused for my quiet "hi" before rushing to my side. "You're hurt." A statement, not a question. Dr. Smith began examining the bruises all down my arm, culminating in the swollen wrist.

"It's actually my hip that hurts the worst," I said.

"The wrist looks sprained. I'll wrap it and get you some ice. I can take a look at your hip, too, if you'd like. You'll come up." I wasn't sure whether her last sentence was a declaration or an inquiry.

Dr. Smith led me into the bathroom, where she began to pull various supplies out of the medicine cabinet. She didn't address how I'd run away from her son, though she clearly knew multiple people had spent the night looking for me.

"How far did you fall?"

Apparently, she could guess this, too. "Maybe like six feet?"

"You didn't catch yourself." Another ambiguous statement/question that she didn't give me time to answer. "Hold your arm out in front of you like this." She demonstrated. "Okay, good. Now roll your shoulders back. Good. Let me see you wiggle your fingers. Good." Dr. Smith continued to position my body and give slight commands. She did a full physical, testing reflexes, taking blood pressure, listening to my heart as I breathed in and out. After each test, she said "Hmm" or "Good" and did another.

"Your hip and wrist took the worst of it," she said at last.

"How bad?"

"Neither is broken. Just bruised. Apply ice and minimize movement, and they should be back to normal in seven to ten days."

"Normal like I can hike or swim or do strenuous activity?" I was thinking of Australia and my walkabout.

"In seven to ten days. You'll be able to tell because you won't feel any more pain." For most people, a statement like this would be laced with sarcasm, but Dr. Smith wasn't at all sarcastic. She pulled an Ace bandage out of the medicine cabinet and lifted it. "May I?"

When the doorbell rang, she left mid-wrap to buzz whoever it was in.

I was standing next to the shower, my arm looking like a partially unwrapped mummy's, when Dr. Smith returned with Toby in tow.

He looked like he'd spent the night having his blood leached slowly from his body, and I felt just the tiniest bit culpable. Dr. Smith said, "I should finish wrapping her wrist. Then I'll leave you two to talk."

"Actually, Mom, can I?" Toby gestured at the unfinished wrap.

She looked to me for the answer. I nodded.

Alone in the bathroom, Toby reached for my cheek. I leaned away. "I thought you were going to finish this."

He picked up the loose end of the bandage. Gingerly, he unwound it a few times before he started to rewind. "Will you tell me what happened?"

"I fell."

"You fell."

"From a height."

"Oh, okay. Thanks for painting me a picture."

"No. No, you don't get to do that."

"Do what?"

"Smirk like that. Make fun. I'm mad at you, in case you can't tell."

"I can tell." He stayed quiet then, just wrapped the bandage around my wrist, pausing every now and then to test the edges of the wrap and make sure my fingers had room to wiggle. His touch still lighted something inside, even when I was trying so hard to snuff it out.

"You need to tell me why you had my sister's passport."

"Okay." He said nothing further.

"Well?"

"You want me to tell you here? In the bathroom?"

"Yes."

"Teddy . . ."

"Are you finished?"

Toby had tucked the end of the Ace bandage in—with expert technique, damn him—but was still holding on to my now cushioned hand. "Yes, sorry." He let go. His eyes drifted to the bruises splotching my arm.

"I fell out of Derek's loft." I wanted to be mean. To see the hurt on Toby's face when he realized I'd gone to Derek last night, but it wasn't worth it. His hurt only made the weight in my gut sit heavier.

"Oh." He gazed at the tiles. "I had her passport because I found it."

My pulse quickened as my anger flared. "You found it. Like, on the beach? In the car? It's evidence. How could you just keep it in a drawer for a year—"

"I haven't had it for a year. I've had it only a few weeks. I found it that day we were searching her room." His words hit a wall. He couldn't have found your passport in your room. I'd scoured every nook and cranny, more than once. Toby went on. "In her suitcase. There's this special compartment. It's meant to be sort of hidden. For storing travel documents safely. Mine's the same brand."

Toby was right: We shouldn't have done this in the bathroom. I needed to pace, and I couldn't do that in this tiny room. My biggest, best clue, the thing that I'd clung to before all of this K business started, and according to Toby, the answer had been waiting in your room for an entire year. I'd driven myself crazy, all because I couldn't manage to thoroughly search a suitcase. I clung to my anger to keep myself from feeling anything else. "So you found it in the closet and said nothing? For weeks?"

"I should have said something, immediately, but I . . . I thought, with K, maybe the passport didn't matter anymore. We could focus on finding them and then maybe after, maybe then . . ."

"You weren't going to show me."

Toby wouldn't meet my eyes. "Probably not."

"Why?"

"Because." He reached over my head and shut the medicine cabinet door.

"Because isn't an answer."

"It's not like I said, 'Hey, look, Izzy's passport, I'll hide this from Teddy for all eternity.' I found it. I knew not having found it gave you hope and I . . . I didn't know what to do. So I didn't say anything. And then the longer I didn't say anything, the harder it was to say something, and then when I did start to tell you, you told me not to." My face must have been a tapestry of confusion and skepticism here, because Toby elaborated. "On the beach. The night we guarded all the stuff."

"You were going to tell me something about the night she disappeared."

"Yes."

"You just said you found the passport weeks ago."

"I *did*. But when you said you were done with it all . . . I thought that included the passport. Teddy? Are you sure we can't go some-where else? Somewhere you can sit?"

"I'm fine." I wasn't. My hip was screaming, but I planned to power through.

"Have a glass of water, at least." Toby plucked a little paper cup out of a dispenser and poured me a thimble's worth of water from the faucet. I wouldn't take it.

"Tell me now."

"Tell you what now?"

"Whatever it was you were going to tell me then. I want to know now."

Toby put the paper water cup down and ran his hand through his hair. "When I told everyone about the race Izzy wanted to have that night, I wasn't being completely truthful."

"You didn't run around the trail while Izzy swam across the lake?"

"No, I did. But it wasn't the race she wanted to have. Originally, I mean. She wanted me to race her in the water. A swimming race."

"A swimming race," I echoed. His words stuck in the slush of all the stories I had told myself about that night. Somehow, I'd never imagined such a simple difference. You had wanted to race Toby in swimming. The *if*s started to fall. If you had wanted someone to swim across the lake with you, then you hadn't walked out into its depths intending to sink. If you had wanted someone to swim with you, then you hadn't planned to sneak away into the woods. If someone *had* swum with you, you might still be alive. This last *if* sunk inside me like an anchor. I could barely get out my next word. "Why?"

"I don't know why she wanted—"

"No." I was firm. Why you wanted to race Toby was immaterial. I could think up a thousand reasons why you'd have challenged Toby to a midnight race, any number of which could work with the things we'd learned about that summer and that night. What mattered was why Toby said no. "Why didn't you just race her?"

Toby lowered his head. "I've been asking myself that same question all year." His voice held the quiet timbre of shame.

Two months ago, the two of us had taken a canoe ride across the lake and Toby had told me he was working at Bottomrock to face his fears. Then, I'd assumed his fear was of the lake. But that had only been part of it. His true fear, the one I could see now etched on his face under a halo of yellow overhead lights, was that his decision that night had cost you your life. Maybe that's why he'd latched on to my theory that you hadn't died. He had needed to believe it was true, just as much as me.

Was that why he'd been helping me? Was that why he'd taken the job at Bottomrock? Maybe, in befriending me, in embarking on the search for K, he'd been seeking absolution. In that moment I couldn't bring myself to give it to him. He was right to feel guilty. You'd drowned in Bottomrock Lake, and that wouldn't have happened if he'd been at your side.

"Derek was K," I said, filling the silence between us with this final accusation. Then I left the bathroom and texted Petra, asking her to take me home.

TWENTY-SEVEN

The Importance of Being Honest

Nadia and Pat were waiting on the sidewalk outside Toby's house, chatting the way people do when a crisis has passed, with tired eyes and the remnants of anxiety still clinging to their voices. The sun spotlighted the stoop and a breeze stirred salt and car exhaust in the air, and for the second time that morning, I was lost to a friend's embrace.

"You're such a jerk." Nadia pinned my arms and squeezed. I hadn't even made it all the way down the stairs. "I'm so glad you're okay," she said into my shoulder.

"Not *that* okay." Pat nodded at my bandaged wrist. Nadia traced her hands down my arms until our hands hooked together. She did a visual inspection, and per her usual expressiveness, asked a question without a word.

"I'm fine, really. I had no idea I'd caused . . . all this. You guys really didn't have to come looking for me."

Once more, Nadia's face sketched her reply.

After more rounds of hugging and a lot of exclamations of "Where were you?" and "I'm so glad you're okay," Nadia reminded

Pat that he had to open Bottomrock, and he left begrudgingly. Nadia wanted to ride back with Petra and me.

"So," Nadia began. She was in the backseat but leaned forward to put her head between us. "What really happened?"

I filled her in on everything, too, right up to Toby's revelation that you'd wanted him to swim across the lake with you. I expected my friends, who had always been chilly toward Toby and unclear on why I wanted to spend time with him, to join me in anger. He'd kept your passport and he'd lied about the night you'd died. But in the last seven hours Toby had won my friends over. All it took, apparently, was for me to go missing, too.

"He has enough to brood about already without you adding on more," said Nadia.

"And besides," Petra said, "you know how Izzy was. She did what she wanted to do. Even if he'd raced her, she would've peeled away and still been alone when whatever happened, happened."

"When she drowned."

The car got quiet. I had never said those three words before. You drowned. I knew it was true, and still the idea of you losing control in the water, of being unable to get yourself safely to shore, was a mist. I could see it, feel it, but even now that I believed it, I couldn't quite grasp it.

It was just after nine a.m. when Petra dropped me at home. I was skipping work. I owed Mom and Dad an explanation. Besides, I was too injured to lifeguard. Our parents were in the kitchen. Mom paced. Dad sat at the counter, his hand braced against the back of his neck as he stared into his mug of coffee. When the door opened, they rushed over. Mom reached me first, swaddling me with a hug.

They weren't mad. Not that I'd lied about where I was and who I was with. Not that I'd run away from Toby. Not that I hadn't checked in, or that once found, I hadn't wanted to speak with them. For the third time that morning I revealed everything. What I'd been doing all summer, why I'd run, how I'd never intended to be gone forever (which was, as it turned out, the main fear that had run through their minds in the seven hours I'd been missing) but had just needed to be alone.

Somewhere in there, the conversation changed from me to you. Not about the night you'd left us. About the seventeen years you'd been with us and the marks you'd left behind.

Australia loomed large. Mom thought my injury meant I wouldn't go, and I think she was actually glad of it, but I told her what Dr. Smith had said and that yes, I was still going. She asked how I thought I could manage a city in a strange country when I'd just spent the night lost in a city twelve miles from my home. But the thing is, I wasn't lost. Not really. Not geographically, at any rate. And despite their search for me, in the end, I was the one who had saved myself.

The only subject I danced around was Derek. Of my injuries, I only told them I'd spent the night in a friend's BU dorm and fallen out of his lofted bed. Your time with him was still an unknown quantity, one darkened considerably by what had happened to me. I didn't know what had distressed you before trials and driven you to seek counsel with Dr. Connors, nor did I know what you'd been upset about that night you'd asked Toby to meet you at Bottomrock. I knew Derek might have the answers—or be the answer—but I still had to get them from him before your story would be complete.

———

I RETURNED TO work the following day. Even though I couldn't guard with my wrist wrapped, I could apply first aid and sign people in, and Pat was perfectly cool with these being my main duties. Toby was there, too, and I don't know why, but seeing him standing in the guardhouse, casually depositing his bag into his cubby, surprised me. I'd run the gamut of emotions where he was concerned, from a boy I wanted so badly to hate to one I was trying not to love. The end result was a cool, neutral glance as I put my own bag into the cubby next to his. Pat and Nadia were on the beach, so we were alone.

"You're loose." Toby pointed at my bandaged wrist.

"Yeah, well, I took it off to shower, so I had to redo it. This is the best I could do, one-handed."

"I can fix it, if you want."

And maybe to prove to myself that Toby didn't matter anymore, I held out my arm. "Go right ahead."

Toby gestured to the bench. I sat. He unwound the wrap in its entirety. Slowly.

"It hardly hurts anymore." A lie. My wrist and hip both still smarted. "You don't have to be so gentle."

"I'm being professional. Have you been icing it?"

"Not while I slept."

My statement was practically dripping in snark, but Toby didn't rise to my bait. He got me a cold pack from the first-aid kit and snapped the pack to activate it. "It'll be cold by the time I'm finished." He placed it on the table beside us and began fitting the bandage around my wrist. I looked at speckles on the newly refinished floor as he wrapped. Sitting there, wanting to hate him while little shivers went up my spine each time his fingers wound around: That was almost torture. I bolted from the guardhouse as soon as he finished and begged Pat to assign me whatever was left on Quimby's park improvement list. The dedication was coming up on Saturday, marking the one-year anniversary of your death. But the list was no longer on the refrigerator door.

"Teddy, I don't think there's anything left," Pat said.

"We finished everything?"

"We're all set for Saturday, yeah."

"Fine. But . . . can you put Toby up to guard first?"

He flashed a mischievous grin. "That I can do."

I continued to ignore or avoid Toby for the rest of the day.

The week repeated itself: Each day I let Toby rewrap my wrist but kept my distance otherwise. We'd reached the summer doldrums: the time of year when school was starting up again soon, and the people who weren't already done with summer were bored of spending it at Bottomrock Park. Rarely was there more than a pair of toddlers wading in the water. I spent most of the week hopping between the guardhouse and the sign-in table: wherever Toby wasn't.

Friday morning, Toby unspooled the Ace bandage in his quiet, professional way. His fingers paused in the meat of my palm. "I have to say something."

I arched my eyebrows. "No one ever said you couldn't talk."

Nadia had just put her lunch in the refrigerator. The door snapped shut. "Should I leave? Yeah, I think I should." She made it one step before I said, "No. You can stay. I'm done with secrets." Out of the corner of my eye, I saw her lean back against the refrigerator.

Toby shifted on the bench. I could tell he'd have preferred not to have an audience. "Fine. Look, you can hate me. You can be with Derek. And after the summer ends you can go off to Australia and I'll go to college and we never have to see each other again." Toby paused here, and I wondered if he could sense the way everything inside me had clenched up at his words. For as hurt as I was by him, the idea of never seeing him again hurt worse. "But I meant it when I said I wanted to help you find out what was going on with Izzy that summer, and you've solved it without me, which, fine. I still deserve to know. So you have to tell me. About her and Derek and what she was so upset about. Once you do, I'll shut up and never speak to you again."

Nadia pursed her lips and folded her hands behind her back as she pressed into the fridge. She was definitely suppressing commentary. My gaze flicked back to Toby. His lowered lashes crafted half-moon shadows under his eyes, and he looked like one of his sketches of a soldier after battle. "I don't hate you." The words were hardly more than a whisper, but I knew by the way his mouth crested at one corner that he'd heard me. "I'm just not sure if I can separate you from the night I lost my sister."

"I get that. I do. But please, tell me what happened with Derek."

When I wouldn't meet his eyes, Toby placed the unraveled Ace bandage on the picnic table. "If you still need that, Nadia should be able to handle it." Then he left the guardhouse.

With the door still creaking, Nadia plopped down beside me. "I thought you said no more secrets?" She lifted the bandage. I shook my head. I didn't want it today. Nadia nodded and started to roll the cloth back up. "Probably didn't need it yesterday, either," she remarked.

"It was a close call."

"Riiight." She bundled more cloth, occasionally glancing up to study me. "You should go tell him."

"Tell him what?"

"That you're not 'with' Derek for one? That Derek is a class-A douchebag scum bucket who almost broke your wrist, assaulted you, and maybe assaulted your sister? Do you even know how you're going to deal with him tomorrow at the dedication?"

"No."

"Maybe Toby can help."

"God, what did he do while I was missing? Brainwash you all? *You* said he was damaged."

"And I was right. But also wrong. He's damaged like you are."

"Gee, thanks."

"Because he loved her. I didn't realize this until I saw how absolutely wrecked he was when you ran out on him. I think you guys have been good for each other."

"If it weren't for him, I would have left everything alone."

"You'd have kept burying everything. You wouldn't have closure."

"And I have it now?"

"Maybe. Some. Or at least acceptance."

I flapped my flip-flops against the bottoms of my feet. "You're awfully wise for eighteen."

"Well, I *was* a valedictorian." Nadia took my uninjured hand. "Toby's right about one thing, at least. He deserves to know."

I knew this. I'd known it before Toby had pointed it out. Whether I could forgive him or not, whether I could forget his part in your death or not, he deserved to know what had happened with Derek. He deserved a chance to help me complete your story.

I found Toby at the dam, bare feet dangling in the water, unopened sketchpad on his lap.

"I have something for you." I slid into place beside him and slipped him one of my notebooks.

He ran his fingers across the cover. "What's this?"

"Literally it's the story I wrote for Moira." I stirred the water with the tip of a toe before I looked at him. When I did, I tried to put on my cutest snarky face. "Figuratively it's a peace offering?"

My playfulness didn't elicit one of Toby's smirks. Not even a tease of a smile. He slowly shook his head. "Teddy, I don't get you."

"I'm a puzzle. One with, like, ten thousand pieces and only two colors."

"See, that's what I don't get. You can hardly be in the same room with me, you flinched when I put on the wrap—"

"I didn't flinch." *I shivered*, I thought, remembering the way it felt to lie beside him on only bedsheets. There was a barrier of air between us now as we sat side by side on the dam, barely more than an inch thick, and it felt somehow both tantalizing and insurmountable.

"And now you come over here joking like it's two weeks ago and nothing's changed. It's not very fair."

"I know. I'm sorry. That's what the notebook is for. Which I want back eventually, but you can read it. Tell me I got her all wrong if you want. Anyway, I'm trying to say you were right."

The water rippled at the spot where his toes were dipped under.

"You deserve to know what happened." I took a breath. The long, flat plane of the lake twinkled in the sun, reminding me of all those fake constellations Toby and I had told stories about. "For starters, Derek and I are *not* together."

"But you did fall out of his loft?"

"Yes. Because I was trying to get away. From him." I glanced at the bruises that were only now starting to fade from my arm.

Toby cupped my chin. Fire flickered in his eyes. "He did this to you?"

"Indirectly." I'd spent the week dwelling on what Derek might have done to you. But since confessing to Petra and Nadia, I'd hardly given a thought to what he'd almost done to me. I shrugged Toby's hand away and told him, too. Everything. "And so you see, I haven't solved it. Not yet. I know Derek was K, but I don't know why Izzy was so upset."

"I'm sure you can hazard a guess." His sarcasm was sharp enough to slice.

"Yeah." It was too easy to see Derek pushing you for more than you were ready to give. "But Izzy went to Maine with him. So whatever was going on between them, it's got to have been complicated. Like, how did they meet? When did they get together? Maybe he isn't why she went to see Dr. Connors. Maybe that was really just about messing up at trials, and she was supposed to meet him that night? Maybe she ended up meeting him earlier than midnight, before she texted you and said she was not okay and whatever happened *before* you got there is why she was so upset and why she . . ." I paused because Toby had taken out his phone and was scrolling through his contacts. "What are you doing?"

"I'm FaceTiming Jasmine. See if she can tell us if Derek ever came to a party last summer." Toby held out the phone so we could both get in view of the camera.

"Toby? And Teddy! What's up, guys?" The camera jiggled and we got a close-up view of Jasmine's ear as she walked. "Sorry about that. I'm running. Lemme sit." She lowered the phone, giving us a view of her black nylon pants as she settled in on a park bench. "Is this about tomorrow? Do you need me to bring something?"

"Just yourself. You're carpooling with a few other Wahoos, right?" Toby said.

"Yeah, Meiling and Lila. Kevin wanted to come, but he had to fly out west for school. Nico and Bryce are coming separately, I think."

"Bryce is coming?" I almost couldn't believe his nerve. Then again, people like him had nerves in place of empathy.

"Yeah, why wouldn't he?"

"I don't know," I said, not wanting to get into his secret identity as the cyberbullying WhisperingWahoo.

Toby took over talking. "So, remember back when Teddy and I asked you about who Izzy might have been dating?"

"Sure."

"It was Derek Danvers," I said.

"No." Jasmine shook her head. "She wouldn't."

"We're surprised about it, too," Toby said. "Does he still get invited to parties?"

Jasmine flicked her ponytail. "He and Bryce still hang out sometimes. Honestly, I think Bryce has a hopeless crush. I should probably tell him Derek's a putz and then he'll stop bringing him around. Sorry if you guys like him."

"We don't," Toby said flatly, just as I said, "Why don't you like Derek?"

"It's nothing. It's rumors, probably." Jasmine shook her head dismissively.

"What rumors?"

"He gets drunk. He gets aggressive. Stuff like that."

"What do you mean by 'aggressive'?" My throat had gone dry as I remembered Derek's hand in my shirt while I slept.

"I mean—and it's not like I can point to specifics, I don't even remember who told me this stuff—but he has a reputation for being kind of forceful with girls. I don't know. But if Izzy dated him, then he probably isn't actually like all that."

I swallowed. Words wouldn't come. "Did you guys need anything else?" Jasmine asked.

"No." I tried my best to smile through the tension unspooling inside me. "Enjoy your run. We'll see you tomorrow."

"We have to talk to Derek tomorrow," I said after Toby had hung up. What Jasmine told us about Derek synced with my new view of him, but it still didn't click with you and him being together. Then again, you might have fallen for his charm before uncovering the snake beneath. I had.

"At the dedication?"

"He'll be here, before it starts. He has to open up the park. We can do it then."

"You don't want to just let tomorrow be about Izzy?"

"This *is* about Izzy. And I don't think I can stand there while a tree is planted in her honor and Derek pretends everything's swell."

"Then we'll confront him tomorrow," Toby said.

I added, "Together."

TWENTY-EIGHT

Your Tree Grows in Bottomrock

MOM STOPPED ME AS I ROUNDED THE BANISTER AT THE FOOT OF the stairs.

"You're dressed early."

I shifted my backpack—grungy in comparison to the navy dress I wore—from one hand to the other. We were planting your tree at nine. The park opened at ten. And like every other Saturday that summer, I had work. The backpack contained a change of clothes and my lunch. Your phone weighted my pocket.

"I'm heading over early." My nerves were already entangled like the knotted chain of a dock weight. What if Derek wouldn't tell me anything? What if he did tell me, and the truth was worse than all the stories I'd imagined?

Mom's lips pursed. "I was thinking we would all have breakfast. Head over together."

My knots tightened. Mom and Dad and I hadn't talked much about this ceremony, marking the first anniversary of your death. The project was Petra's catharsis, and I'd assumed they felt about it as I did: something obligatory to get through. Was I wrong? Did a tree being planted in your honor at Bottomrock mean something to

298

them? Perhaps Toby was right—I shouldn't be dealing with Derek on a day that was supposed to be about you.

But when I thought of him standing with your family and your friends, knowing that he'd kept secrets for you, that he might be the reason you'd fucked up trials, the reason you'd sought counsel for trauma, why you'd gone to Bottomrock the night I lost you—I couldn't imagine getting through the planting, or the reading, or any of it with him there. It had to be now. Before your ceremony began.

"I'm sorry, Mom. I kind of need to go there alone." I pursed my lips, only realizing after I'd done so that I'd borrowed the gesture from her. I slid off my backpack and dug out a book. There was something I could do now to make Mom feel a little better about my leaving without her.

"I was going to give this to you later today." It was a brand-new copy of *A Hitchhiker's Guide to the Galaxy*. "I think it was my turn to pick, when we left off."

"And this is your choice?" As Mom looked up at me, the glow of the overhead light framed her face, highlighting the smile in her eyes.

I shifted my backpack back onto my shoulder. "I have to read something when I'm out there. So I'm bringing a copy of this, and also a copy of *Emma*, which I know was next on our Austen list, and I'm sorry that I'm sort of picking for both of us, but I kind of have to. And anyway, I thought I'd read them out there and you could read them here, and we'll FaceTime when I'm back in Brisbane."

"That sounds perfect." Mom twirled a lock of hair that had fallen loose from my messy bun. "We'll see you at nine."

Toby was waiting for me in the Bottomrock parking lot. His mother was in the car with him. He climbed out of the passenger seat as I pulled in. I recognized his navy suit and swimming tie, and even the bright blue handkerchief poking out of his breast pocket. Back then, I'd found the suit annoying—too fun and serious all at once—and I never would have guessed that its wearer would endear himself to me so much so that despite everything else going on with Derek and your ceremony, my heart quickened to see him.

"My mom's going to wait in the car until nine."

I flapped the tip of Toby's tie lightly against his chest. "Is this the only one you have?"

"One of two. Do you hate it?"

I looked at the whimsical cartoon people, swimming every which way all up and down the slender length of fabric. "No. I like it."

Derek's car was the only other one in the lot. As we'd expected, he'd arrived early to unlock the gate. We found him on the beach, weighting navy tablecloths to the picnic tables with small stones.

Petra was supposed to arrive soon with the tree. I wanted to be done by the time she did. She'd put so much into this event—I didn't want to taint it for her.

"Teddy." Derek didn't put his usual enthusiasm into my name. Instead, he spoke with hesitation. Almost a question.

"You and my sister were together." Not a question. Derek dropped the stone in his hand onto the table. The wind whipped the plastic against his shins.

"I wouldn't have said together. Is that what she told you?"

I stopped walking. Looked to Toby. He was just as surprised as I was. Derek didn't know you'd kept him a secret. Then why had he not said anything before?

"What happened between you?"

"Look, Teddy, I'm sorry about what I said last week. That was really shitty of me." Derek stepped closer, and I instinctively back-pedaled. But that was the wrong reaction. I didn't want to cower. I wanted to make my presence felt. I stepped forward.

"What did you do to her?"

Derek shook his head. "Nothing. We hooked up."

"Like how you tried to 'hook up' with me?"

"You really shouldn't crawl into a guy's bed if you're not inter-ested in a little something," he said with a sneer.

"And you really shouldn't put your hands where they haven't been invited," I snapped, and got the satisfaction of seeing Derek cringe. I got the feeling he wasn't used to being called out for his "aggressive" behavior. "Is that what you did to Izzy? Is that why you guys broke up?"

"Broke up?" His voice rose with his hands, which settled in the threads of his hair. "Teddy, whatever Izzy might have told you, it wasn't like that with her and me."

"Then tell me, what was it like?"

"She started talking to me at a party. We were drinking. We started hooking up. That's all."

"Bullshit."

"What d'you want me to say? *She* came up to *me*. And I stopped, okay? I swear I stopped when she started crying." Derek looked to Toby like he was looking for backup. Like maybe, as a guy, Toby would commend Derek on his stand up behavior. Derek stopped whatever he was doing to you when you started to cry. Like such admirable restraint was worthy of applause.

Off to the side, I could see Toby's fists tighten. But he didn't move. This was my show. And Derek's story didn't fit with what we knew of yours.

"What party was this?" I was trying to think: Was what Derek described something that could have happened after your anniversary trip? Was it the thing you were upset about the night you'd gone to Bottomrock? Then what had upset you before trials and driven you to Dr. Connors?

"It was a Wahoo party. We met there. I recognized her because of you. And she knew who I was. Look, it's not my fault if your sister changed her mind in the middle of things. But it wasn't a big deal. I stopped."

"If it wasn't a big deal, how come you look so nervous?" Toby's words came out cold and flat.

"I'm done talking about this." Derek tried to move around us, but we both sidestepped, blocking his path.

"No. You're not. Because in ten minutes a whole bunch of people are going to walk down here. And unless you want me to keep asking you all these questions in front of them, unless you want me to tell them who gave me these bruises—"

"You did that to yourself."

"Because you were assaulting me!"

Derek held up his hands. "I don't understand why you're only bringing this up now."

"You don't have to understand. When was this party?"

"Early summer. June? July? It was before Izzy tried out for the Olympics. I know because we talked about that."

"And then you guys started hanging out after?"

"What? No. Izzy freaked out so much, I didn't want to hang out again. It was only that night."

"You didn't go to Maine?"

"No." As Derek shook his head, looking genuinely baffled, my anger was replaced with confusion.

"And that night . . . You didn't meet her here?"

"The night she . . . Are you out of your mind? *He* was the one with her that night, not me." Derek flicked his hand in Toby's direction. "Everyone knows that."

"So you weren't together, like a couple?"

"No. I thought Izzy would have told you all this stuff? I guess if she didn't tell you, it really was nothing."

Cars were crunching gravel in the parking lot. People were arriving for your ceremony. And Derek needed to not be here any longer. "Go," I growled.

"What?"

"She said go." Toby looked like he might drag Derek bodily back to his car.

"I'm not leaving."

"Yes, you are," I said.

"Quimby—"

"Give him an excuse later. Just. Go."

When Derek didn't move, Toby stepped forward again. "When the identical twin of the deceased disinvites you to her sister's memorial, you leave."

Derek glanced between us, his face so flushed he looked ready to billow steam from his ears, before he stalked away.

I turned to Toby. If I had any doubts as to what Derek had done to you before, I didn't any longer. He'd met you before trials. He was the thing you'd been so shaken by that you'd alarmed your coach. He was the cause of the trauma that drove you to seek counsel from

Dr. Connors. But Derek wasn't K. He wasn't the person you'd been celebrating an anniversary with. The person who'd drawn giggles from a girl who didn't giggle. He was only the guy who'd assaulted you at a party a few days before the most important race of your life.

I HAD TO SHAKE Derek from my mind. Toby and I pulled ourselves together before our parents reached us. Dad and Dr. Smith were chatting about birds.

Among your guests there was Petra, of course, and a handful of other people from Greening High. Petra's mother. All of the Bottomrock guards were there, minus Derek, as well as Bill Quimby. Even Officer Kelly and the chief showed up. The rest of the young people I assumed were Wahoos. Many of the faces I recognized from Bryce's party. Jasmine, Meiling, and Nico, as well as a handful of others, including Bryce, who I had determined I would ignore throughout the day. I knew from Petra's planning emails that one of your Wahoo friends had volunteered to read a poem after we planted the tree, but the emails hadn't mentioned a name. I assumed Jasmine. She was the most extroverted of the bunch.

We gathered around a grassy knoll beside the beach. The young dogwood sat on the wide bundle of its own roots. Its fanning branches were covered in so many emerald leaves I couldn't see a spot of bark beyond the thin column of trunk. Petra spoke of you. She told the story of a hike our families had taken together in the Berkshires with Petra's old dog Maxie. A bad winter had strewn the trail with downed branches while runoff from melting snow had etched new paths in the forest. And when we came to a creek, the dog wanted to cross it, even though the trail curved and ran parallel to the stream. You were our leader, always, and you wanted to follow the dog, but we overruled you, taking the trail that wasn't really a trail for almost an hour before we admitted you'd been right. Instead of you turning us around, your ears perked. You charged farther into the forest and led us to a frozen cascade. Water paused mid-drop down a series of notches, a spiral staircase of stone and stream. We picnicked there, and when we finally made our way back to the true trail, you and Maxie led us across the creek, over the felled spruce, and to the summit.

Because that was who you were, Petra said. A leader, yes, but one able to find good in the bad.

I'd forgotten that story somehow. Buried it under other, more recent memories.

After Petra's speech, we dug. One shovelful each, we went down the line until a hole big enough for your tree had been carved in the earth. Then Toby, Dad, and Nico lifted the dogwood by its bundled roots and set it in the ground. Dirt was shoveled back in. People started milling. Picking at muffins and doughnuts. Talking. Of the blustery day. The Patriots' upcoming season. You were sprinkled in here and there, but mostly they talked about nothing.

When the tree was settled, the dirt replaced around it, we regathered for the reading. But it wasn't Jasmine who separated from the crowd, as I'd assumed she would, and walked to the base of your tree. A young woman with a magenta streak in her dark brown hair peeled away from the circle of swimmers and stood before us. The breeze flapped a piece of paper in her hand.

I'd seen her before. On the front porch, the night of Bryce's party, she'd lingered with me and the spilled beer after Taryn and her other friends stalked inside. In shy staccato spurts, she'd told me how she had been new to the team but that she'd known you, liked you, and that Taryn was full of shit for claiming that Toby had been your boyfriend. I recalled dimly, Toby's Who's-Who coaching resurfacing in my mind, that her name was Lila, but also that Lila was short for something.

"Hi." The girl stopped. Her cropped hair caught the sheen of the sun. She cleared her throat and started again. "Izzy was my 'ambassador' to Wahoo swimming that spring. I was new and . . . well, Petra asked if anyone wanted to read anything and I said I would." She straightened the paper and began to read a poem about grief. In a rhyming cadence, the ghost of someone who had passed counseled their loved ones not to mourn too deeply, for their essence could be found in the beauty of the world. And I know the poem was *meant* to evoke this, but I couldn't help but feel you would have echoed its sentiment. As if you would have picked just this poem, had it been possible to give you a choice. Maybe its reader just knew you that well.

A gust of wind crinkled her printout, and Lila had to straighten it once more. Her reading was stuttered. She would get a few lines out, then pause, her voice cracking, before she would start again. During one particularly long pause, she looked down at the paper in her hands. Not because the wind had bent it. She stared at the words, and I knew what she was doing. I'd done it myself, many times. She was hiding her face, buying time as she willed her tears away. When she looked back up, her eyes were red, but clear. She finished the last stanza of the poem in a confident burst. "Do not stand at my grave and cry; I am not there. I did not die."

Then Lila looked at the paper again and said, "Thanks."

I watched her stuff the paper into the pocket of her charcoal dress. Watched her duck into Jasmine's arms, burrowing her head against the shoulder of a friend. Her eyes were closed. Her breaths hitched.

I'd found your K after all.

TWENTY-NINE

Forty-Seven Seconds

I LEFT MOM AND DAD AS THEY CHATTED WITH MS. SCHAFFER AND walked over to Petra.

"That was beautiful." Your tree was small now, but in a few years, it'd be big enough for kids to play on and families to picnic under. Birds would nest in it. Maybe bees would build a hive on it. "I'm sorry I didn't help out more."

"Hey, none of that. You didn't have to help. Not if you weren't ready to, okay?" Petra hugged me. "And I'm sorry, too. I think . . . I could have tried harder to be there for you."

"I don't know. I'm pretty stubborn. I might not have let you."

Petra laughed. "I'm gonna miss you while you're in Australia."

"I'll be back before you know it."

"With a thousand and one stories, and I want to read every single one." We hugged again, and then someone else wanted to talk to your dedication's organizer, and I moved on to find K.

Nerves fluttered through me. She still might know something. She might have been there that night. Might have seen you after Toby had. You were dead, of that I was convinced, but maybe K knew why.

I started to look for her, but Officer Kelly caught up with me before I could find her. "I need to apologize," he said. He was in full uniform, as was the chief, who I could see talking with Mom and Dad at the foot of your tree. Officer Kelly turned his hat in his hands. "I shouldn't have been so dismissive that day at the tennis court."

"Yeah. You shouldn't have. Because Toby and I found out who WhisperingWahoo was, like, three days later, without a court order." I reined in my snippy tone. "But it didn't matter, like you said. Izzy met up with them earlier in the day, made amends." My gaze darted around, looking for K.

"I see. Well, I'm sorry nevertheless. For that day, and . . . for not finding her." He turned his hat again. "Look, I can see you've got to make the rounds, so I won't keep you. Take care of yourself, Teddy."

I finally found K at the table in the woods where I'd sequestered myself during your first memorial. I tried to reconcile the things Toby had told me about her with the things I'd gleaned today, and on the day we'd met. She was younger than us, a rising senior now, so she must have been about sixteen that summer. She had hung back from Taryn's posse of mean girls to say something nice, so I knew she had an independent streak as well as a kind heart. She was bold enough to read for you. Shy enough to have trouble with it. She was petite but strong, with the sturdy shoulders and muscled legs of a swimmer well practiced in butterfly. Her bangs slashed diagonally across her forehead in a stylish cut that looked more grown-up than her rounded face and fledgling eyes. I had a guess for why you hadn't told me about her. She wasn't your secret. You were hers.

"Thank you for reading."

K's gaze darted up to mine and then away. "You're welcome." She had recovered somewhat. Her eyes were clear. Her voice, though soft, was free of the weight that comes with suppressing tears.

And a pair of peacock feathers clasped to her ears, a perfect match for yours.

"I didn't catch your name."

"Kalila. Osman." She made each word into its own sentence. "Was it . . ." Her eyes shot away again. "Too much?"

"No." I shook my head and reined in all my questions. As eager as I was to get answers, Kalila didn't deserve to have me springing out of the woodwork to grill her. Not on this day. "It was perfect."

K toyed absently with one of her earrings, eyes on her feet. "Izzy had a pair just like those," I said softly. "She lost one of them in the woods."

She looked at me finally. A moment passed. "So you know." Her words hardly more than a whisper.

"I finally figured it out."

"I thought about telling you, at the party. But . . ." She dabbed at the corner of her eyes with a knuckle. "Do you, like, have questions?"

"Oh, tons."

K laughed, and the depth of it surprised me. "Fire away, I guess."

"Not here. Maybe I can meet you somewhere? For coffee or something in a few days?"

"I'd like that. Toby has my number. You can tell him," she added after a pause. "I know you guys have been looking for me."

I nodded. "I'll text you later, then. And thank you, again, for reading." Then I touched her hand, saying thanks of a different sort, and walked farther into Bottomrock woods.

I'd learned so much today.

That you'd been attacked.

That you'd been loved.

Petra had planted a tree for you and I'd been thinking that was just another thing I'd have to get through, but her speech was beautiful and K's poem was beautiful and the tree was beautiful and would be there forever, overlooking the water where you'd had your last swim.

Toby found me at the dam, my sandals discarded on the path and my toes dipped into the lake. My dress was hiked up so the sun could warm my knees, and I batted my heels slowly but steadily against the back of the dam. A rhythmic thud, like a beating heart. After removing his loafers and socks and rolling up his pants, he sat down beside me.

"Hey."

"Hey."

"You okay?"

"I will be."

"Good." Our heels rapped in unison with the lapping water.

"So I figured something out." I fiddled with your phone as I told him about Kalila. Your last secret—that thing you were going to tell me—had come from this phone. I'd probably never know exactly what it was, but I had some ideas. Maybe you'd been planning to warn me off Derek. I'm sure you would have done so eventually, especially if it ever seemed like I might do anything beyond fantasize about him. But I preferred to think you'd decided to tell me about K.

"That's hers, right? Can I see it?"

I handed your phone to him. I could look through it again for pictures of K, but I didn't think I'd find any. Like all things in your life, when you had decided to keep K's secret, you'd committed hard.

Toby was looking at the unlock screen. "K-A-L-I-L-A," he said softly.

I eyed him quizzically.

"The numbers to unlock it. They spell her name." His words were almost lost under everything else—wind rustling leaves, birds cheeping, people chatting on the beach, their voices carried across the open water. Toby placed your phone in my hands and I slipped it back into my dress pocket. My exchange with K. Her matching set of earrings. The passcode. It was all confirmation of something I'd known for sure since she'd stood before your tree with a poem in her hand. Kalila's grief was different from Meiling's, who'd coveted you. It was different from Keith's, who'd felt responsible for you. And it was different from Derek's, who didn't understand what he'd done to you. Hers was a wound in some active place—the palm of a hand, the bend of the knee—where use reopened the scab again and again and again.

We sat side by side, fingers threaded together, as the morning sun reflected off the lake and your second memorial wound down. The park would open for the day soon, though I wouldn't be working. When I heard the crunch of leaves behind me, I expected it to be my parents or Petra or maybe Nadia, come to find me. Bryce's looming silhouette was a jolt.

"Not today," Toby said, standing, but Bryce merely lifted his hands, palms out.

"So I got here a little early. I wanted to talk to you both. Umm, apologize?"

"Seems to be the day for that," I muttered.

"But then I overheard . . ." Bryce fiddled with his phone as he spoke.

"You're posting about a memorial? Do you have any dignity?" Toby tried to snatch the phone, but Byrce dodged, handing it instead to me.

"I didn't know. I swear to God, I didn't know."

On his screen was a video, forty-seven seconds long. A darkened bedroom. Two bodies pressed together. One lifted his head for a moment, flicking his blond hair out the way and exposing Derek's face—and yours—to the camera. I stopped the video. My mouth was suddenly very dry.

"I thought it was consensual," Bryce said as I stared. Derek had had one hand at the base of your throat.

Without saying anything, Toby took Bryce's phone and pressed a few keys. "I just texted that video to myself. You don't have to watch it," he said to me, "but maybe Derek can finally face some consequences." He tossed the phone back to Bryce.

"I'm sorry," he said. I think he meant it, though I can't say for sure. My mind was in that darkened room, writing versions of the forty seconds I hadn't had the stomach to watch.

THIRTY

The Story of You

I MET K AT YOUR FAVORITE BUBBLE TEA SHOP.

We sat at the table by the window that you liked. I'd been tempted to prepare a list of questions—how very *you* of me—but I didn't want to overwhelm Kalila. My nerves by this point had become so jumbled by anticipation that I felt jittery and heavy just looking at her. Across the table, she swirled her straw around, causing the pearls in her tea to rise. I sipped mine as silence settled around us like an icy blanket. We both looked up from our teas at the same moment, opened our mouths to speak, and then laughed. She was nervous, too, and that made everything easier.

"So . . . just to be clear because I've been wrong about this more than once this summer: You and Izzy were seeing each other? Romantically, I mean." Which sounded so formal but what should I have called it? I had no idea what *it* was.

"Yeah." Kalila cupped her lips over the straw and took a long sip. Her fingers played with the edge of a napkin.

"For how long?"

"Six months."

Half a year. You'd lied to me about having a girlfriend for half a year. I tried to not be hurt by that—clearly, you'd had your reasons, and they were probably good ones—but Kalila must have seen something on my face or in the way my grip tightened on my cup because she said, "She wanted to tell you."

Her eyes shifted to the window. "It seems so stupid now. The reason why I didn't let her tell anyone about us." K laughed to herself. "My parents . . . they really want me to focus on school? They both went to Harvard and they're like, obsessed, with me getting in. So I'm not supposed to date or even really go to parties, though sometimes I can pass those off as networking." She smiled. "That was Izzy's idea."

"That sounds like her," I laughed. "She could convince our parents to let her do just about *anything*."

"So you don't hate me?"

"Of course not." I understood you wanting to keep Kalila's secret. Her reasons for having it didn't matter. You'd loved her. Trusted her. If she had asked you not to tell anyone, of course you would have respected that.

I set my cup down without taking a sip. "How did you meet? I'd like to hear the story, if you don't mind."

The more we talked, the more comfortable K became. You'll be glad to hear that she told her parents about you, not long after you died. They weren't angry about the lies as much as they were concerned about their daughter's heartbreak, and they've relaxed their rules some in the last year, allowing K more of a social life so long as she keeps her grades high and completes her heavy load of extracurriculars.

K and I talked about you for a long time. I can't say if I'll ever see her again, but I walked away from the bubble tea shop with more answers than questions.

I can write your story now.

You made swimming seem seductive. The thrill of the race. The weightlessness of water. The wonderful drain of a body spent. And so your coach asked you to mentor a new recruit. You met Kalila Osman for the first time in Coach Connors's office by your pool, and she looked up from under dark bangs that cloaked half her face and gave you half a smile. The kind of smile that holds something back, not hesitant, but purposefully reserved. You thought, There's more here, to be earned.

You partnered with her in the weight room. Taught her the team's special drills. You discovered a girl who loved to laugh. Whose hands exploded in the air as she talked. Emboldened by the way she'd clasped your hand once at a swim meet, you lingered by her locker after practice one day until everyone else had gone and there you kissed her.

You spent a lot of time together, hiking, picnicking in the woods. The campsite at Bottomrock was a favorite meetup spot, but there had been others. You'd been content among the trees.

At an artisan market up the coast you'd picked up matching sets of peacock feather earrings, another secret connection. You'd lost one of yours—the one the police had found at the campsite, you and K had gone there to be alone often—but still stubbornly insisted on wearing the other from time to time. You must have been wearing it that night, and the second earring, like you, was lost to the lake.

There was a party. Kalila—Lila to her friends, K to you—wasn't allowed to go but she asked you to go anyway and enjoy it for you both. So you went and you messaged your girlfriend. You guys used Snapchat, so your messages were ephemeral. That night you'd been giving her a play-by-play of the party as you drank a little beer, played a little beer pong with Nico, when across the basement you spotted a familiar face. How many hours had we spent talking about how beautiful Derek was? How sweet he was with the kids at Bottomrock? How cool he seemed, challenging other guards to rescue board races and winning, every time.

OMG, you messaged K that night. *This guy Teddy's totally in love with is here. I'm gonna go convince him to ask her out.*

You're going to embarrass your sis, K had messaged back.

No. I'll be subtle. He won't even know I've tricked him into liking her.

That was the last message you sent that night.

And I will forever be pierced by the thought: You didn't have to do that for me.

I wish you hadn't.

This next part is supposition. It takes the bits and pieces I've gathered all summer, together with the things I know of you, of Derek, and pastes them together. You hadn't been drinking much. You were flying to Omaha soon to try out for the Olympics. Derek knew who you were, immediately, which you thought was a good sign. That meant he'd been paying attention to me. You tried to talk me up, but he tried to talk *you* up, flattering you with praise on your near-Olympian status. And you were too inexperienced to realize that with his smiles and flattery he was flirting, so you kept talking. He got you alone in some bedroom and you couldn't get away even though you tried, you were so strong and so fast, but only in the water. On land he had size and he had leverage, and when you realized you couldn't escape, you started to cry. He stopped.

And you buried it. When K saw you the next day, you were jittery and quiet and you flinched at her touch, so she asked what was wrong. You said nothing was. But no matter how many laps you swam, how many times you flipped your body underwater and torpedoed off the wall, you couldn't get Derek out of your head. He came with you to Omaha and shattered your dream.

K knew something had happened; she pressed you to tell her a few more times—when you'd shied away from her caress, when a far-off look skated across your eyes, after your abysmal performance at trials, but you always denied anything was amiss. Until one day she said, "Look, if this guy did something and you don't want to talk about it, fine. But your sister *likes* him, right? You should at least warn her." And you'd responded with a cadence far meeker than your usual tone, "I know. I will."

Derek had battered your confidence. Maybe you'd tried to rebuild it by taking risks. The walkabout you so suddenly pushed for. The cliff-jumping you'd done in Maine.

You hadn't let him break you. Not entirely. You sought help from Dr. Connors, and you kept falling in love with K. She said things seemed to be getting better. *You* seemed to be getting better. The missing camping supplies had been a gift for Kalila, to mark the anniversary and promise future adventures.

K *was* supposed to meet with you that night. But in the end she hadn't come, unable to sneak out of her house. She'd messaged you she wasn't coming, and you invited your good friend to the beach instead, challenging him to a midnight race. He said no. You went anyway. The reckless swim that had cost you everything.

This is when I lost you.

It's still just a story. And there are some shards I'm still missing. Why hadn't I been a part of your attempt to move on? Had you been waiting for me to notice your pain? Or had you been hiding it from me, hoping I'd never have to know? And that night: Had you really been so upset by a canceled date? Somehow I doubt it. Maybe you were growing tired of keeping someone else's secret. Maybe something had triggered memories of Derek. Or maybe it was your missed chance at the Olympics. The scary realization that swimming wasn't going to be your life.

It's still just a story, but I know enough now to thread your narrative into a story that feels true.

THIRTY-ONE

In Which Another Summer Ends

"SO YOU'RE REALLY GOING?" NADIA ASKED ME ON OUR LAST DAY AT
Bottomrock. Derek had quit, and Pat was—for the sole week remaining in the season after your tree dedication—officially head guard.
That Sunday afternoon we were all sitting at the picnic table behind
the guardhouse. Nadia was sprawled across Pat's lap, her bare feet in
the air and her chin perched in her hands. I sat on the opposite bench,
having long ago given up trying to read. Slouched in a beach chair, Toby
picked at the charcoal under his nails. He'd been sketching most of the
morning. The park was closing in two hours, but it was too chilly for
swimming and too overcast for sunbathing. There was no one there.

"I'm really going." I rotated my wrist. The swelling was down,
the bruises on my arm little more than faint shadows. My hip no
longer stung with each step. I snuck a glance at Toby, but he wasn't
looking in my direction.

"That's so awesome. I should have done something like that." A
beam of afternoon sunlight had edged out the clouds, and Pat leaned
his head into the warmth.

Nadia patted his chest. "You still could."

"Think about it. We'll be in Sociology 101 being lectured to death and she'll be on a beach—"

"In the desert," I said.

"Floating on crystal waters with two umbrella drinks—"

"Cooking packets of powdered potatoes—"

"Swimming with manta rays—"

"That I might actually do."

"See? Nadia, let's drop out of school and go to Australia with Teddy."

"Sure."

Pat suddenly sat up straight. "For real?" He looked terrified.

"Yeah, why not? Toby, you in?"

Toby looked to me.

"We'll need you to name the stars," I said after a moment, and watched, satisfied, as his mouth curled, one corner higher than the other, in that Toby smirk that had driven me mad all summer. "I've been thinking we need a Janus," he said.

"Okay." Nadia peeled herself off Pat's lap. "Now I think you're talking in code."

"It's just as well." Pat rose from the bench. "No one's here on the last day. I think it's time."

We gathered ourselves slowly, not wanting to surrender that last bit of summer laziness. But Pat was right. It was time to unhook the swimming area ropes, row the docks ashore, and close Bottomrock Park for the season.

Despite the chill of the early September day, the water was warmed from an entire summer of sun. We swam to the first dock. After hauling the anchors up in pairs, we rowed the dock aground. The four of us were standing on the second dock, one anchor already heaved aboard, when I spotted something large and bulbous floating by the dam. My mouth dried up and my heart just about stopped.

The bobbing thing looked like a body.

I gasped. Toby followed my gaze. "Teddy, don't," he said, but I had already dived in. I heard a splash as he did, too.

What were the chances you'd surface now? Would there even be anything left but bones? Toby was a much better swimmer than I. My head start was meaningless. He surfaced beside me. But then he kept pace. Saying nothing. Only swimming. Our heads up like we were performing a rescue. Nadia yelled something from the dock, but her words were muffled by the water sloshing around my ears with each stroke.

I slowed. We'd closed the distance, enough to see that the bobbing thing was indeed a body. But not yours. Not even human.

As we treaded, Toby's hand found mine underwater.

A large snapping turtle floated belly-up about twenty feet away, bloated and very clearly dead.

"Snappy," he breathed, relieved.

But Toby hadn't seen yet what I just did. A flicker of blue and gold wedged between the big turtle's front toes.

Your other peacock earring.

My throat constricted and panged. Lake weeds tickled my heels. And I finally, finally let myself cry. Toby knew enough not to try to say something consoling. He bicycled beside me as tears turned to sobs, and when my body started to shake, he wove his fingers between mine and offered his butterfly shoulder until I was hiccuping against him and all my grief and anger, all my guilt and lost hope had rolled off my chin into the lake. Our feet treading in sync to keep ourselves afloat felt like the most natural thing in the world. "We can't leave him there," I said, my head still on his shoulder.

"Let's fish him out from the dam with the pool net and bury him in the woods."

Nadia and Pat helped, once they realized what was going on. We marked Snappy's grave with a stone. Pat said a few words. "You were a good turtle, who gave the children of Bottomrock Park many years of fright and delight. If it was possible to bury you under the dock, we would have."

"Teddy? Did you want to—" Nadia asked.

I shook my head.

By now it was past the time the park should have closed. Dusk settled in the forest and sunk over the beach, glazing Bottomrock with shadows.

"Have a great trip," Nadia said as we all walked out of the woods. Pat stopped to put the shovel in the toolshed and lock it up. "Instagram everything." She hugged me. "And be safe, okay?" she added, whispering into my ear as her arms squeezed firm.

"Always."

"Teddy." Pat offered his hand and at the last moment swooped his arm around me, scooped me up in a bear hug, and lifted me off the sand. "Stay cool, kid."

"I'm a month older than you."

Pat laughed as he put me down.

That left Toby, lingering by the stoop to the guardhouse steps, hands in his pockets as he waited out all my good-byes.

"I'm not mad, anymore." I stepped toward him. He stepped toward me in turn.

"I know. But thanks for saying it." He riffled a hand through his hair. His summer highlights shimmered as they caught the last bits of light from the setting sun. "So I read your story. The one you wrote for Moira."

"Oh God." Flush flooded into my cheeks. "Was it awful? I was going for this kind of epic comedy and I don't know if the sand planet—"

"I thought it was pretty awesome."

"Really?"

"I kind of want to draw it. Would that be okay?"

"Of course! She's your character!"

"But you gave her a story." Toby smiled. "Anyway, this means I'll have to keep your notebook a little longer."

"It's okay. You'll get it back to me. And I was thinking I might write another, if you're game."

"Yeah? I might be down for that." Underneath his trademark smirk there was something more, working its way to the surface as he figured out what else he needed to say, and whether he would say it at all.

Finally he said, "I know what we were saying before about Australia was all just jokes, but . . . I would go. If you wanted me to."

My heart quickened. "What about art school?"

He shrugged. "It'll be there in a year."

I almost said yes. Threw my arms around his neck and told him to come. I had this fantasy of sharing a tent in the outback. Swimming alongside him as we cleaned up the reefs. Laughing as we got lost playing tourist in Sydney. But to ask Toby to join me would defeat the purpose of why I wanted so badly to go.

"It's not that I don't want you to come," I said, stopping there.

"But." Not a question. An acknowledgment. He tilted toward

me until our foreheads met. We balanced against each other as the light faded.

"I think I'm half in love with you," I said on a breath.

"I think I'm half in love with you, too."

There was a joke that popped into my head then, one that I didn't say. That together, we were whole.

Which was why I had to go, and why he couldn't come.

I stepped back first. When I turned around, I saw the lake, unadorned by ropes and buoys. Just a stretch of serenity against a backdrop of wild. I said once that it wasn't fair how you'd come here to disappear. That this place was mine. But it wasn't mine. Not any more than it was Toby's. Or Nadia's, or Pat's. Not any more than it was Bill Quimby's or the countless park-goers who swam here year after year, or the countless others who hiked the trails.

And besides, you may have disappeared into the lake, but that's not where I'll find you. You're at your training pool in Cambridge, trouncing Toby in butterfly. At a natatorium in Texas, qualifying for the Olympic trials. You're at the house where we grew up, backyard birdwatching with Dad and begrudgingly studying literature with Mom. You're in a cabin in the woods in Maine, toasting to a six-month anniversary with K.

You're halfway around the world in the desert with me, smiling as I figure out who I am without you.

Toby was waiting for me when I turned back around. Twilight had turned to night. The insects and frogs chimed as always, unaware that summer was ending. "I thought I'd walk you to your car," Toby said, rising.

"Nice thought." I took his hand.

"So, I never did get the rest of that story."

It took me a moment. I threaded our fingers as we walked up the path. "The changing stall saga?"

"Yup."

"Do you want it now?"

"When else?"

I stopped. We'd reached the top of the path. It was time to part ways. I smirked, though I don't know if he could see it in the starlight. "Next summer."

ACKNOWLEDGMENTS

PUBLISHING A NOVEL HAS BEEN A LIFELONG DREAM OF MINE, AND there are a lot of people who have supported me throughout the pursuit of that dream. I'd like to take a moment to thank some of them.

To my agent, Beth Miller: I couldn't have asked for a more perfect agent. You saw the spark in my manuscript when so many others hadn't, and you didn't stop advocating for Teddy's story—and for me—throughout this whole journey. Thank you.

To my editor at Hyperion, Kelsey Sullivan: As Beth said after you made your offer, "Finally, someone who gets it!" Thank you for loving my words and my characters. You pushed me to make this story stronger, even when that meant making it shorter!

To the people at Hyperion who turned my story into a real, live book, including Nicole Rifkin, who brought Bottomrock Lake to life with her chillingly atmospheric illustration, Phil Buchanan, who designed this book's beautiful cover and interior, as well as Guy Cunningham, Crystal McCoy, Holly Nagel, Christine Saunders, Matt Schweitzer, Marybeth Tregarthen and everyone else at Hyperion who has championed and will champion this book, thank you for, quite literally, making my dream come true.

To Alessandra Birch, Chad Buffington, and Cecilia de la Campa at Writer's House, who worked so tirelessly to get my book out into the world, thank you.

To my writing group, the members of whom have ebbed and flowed over the years, but especially to Claire, Adam, Bethany, Cassandra, Joe, and Graham: Thank you for giving up so many Sunday afternoons discouraging my worst writerly impulses and encouraging me to keep writing.

To the teachers I've had over the years who didn't bat an eye when I let it be known that I wanted to see my name on the spine of a book, especially Rosemary Ellis, Ms. Horton, Christina Askounis, and Rick Reiken: Thank you for your confidence in me, and above all else, for teaching me how to write well.

To my Topstone family: If any of you decided to read this book, I'm sure you recognized Topstone in its pages. Though my characters and my story are fiction, the setting is without a doubt inspired by the many, many summers I spent at Topstone Park, guarding the lake and playing roofball with you all. Thank you for helping to make my summer job so memorable.

To Diana and Nick, who collaborated on (and put up with) some super-elaborate play scenarios as we acted out stories with our dolls and action figures: You helped me learn to plot. Thank you.

To my mom (my earliest editor) and my dad (my earliest fan): Thank you for your unending support. You always believed in and encouraged me, and without you, I would not have had the time, space, and love necessary to grow up and become a writer. I finally did it! Now brag away please.

To my Nana, whose continued faith and *interest* in my writing has bolstered my confidence and steeled my drive: Thank you.

To my Dave: You probably should have gotten a mention in the writing group paragraph, since you're a part of that, too. But I had to save the big one for near the end. You were my best critic at our grad classes at Emerson long before you were my partner-in-life. Part of the reason we work so well together is undoubtedly because constructive criticism was our first major form of communication. *After You Vanished* would not exist without your love, support, and yes, your critiques, whether delivered in the margins of my very early drafts or over late-night, wine-hazed conversations. So thank you.

And lastly, to my Luke. I wrote most of this before you existed, and I finished it despite your existence, but nevertheless: Thank you for being the most adorable, smiley little guy. You can't read this book yet, but one day—I hope—you will. May you only be a *little* embarrassed by your mom when that day comes.